The Kirov Wolf

A Detective Pete Nazareth Novel

R.H. Johnson

Hampton, Westbrook Publishing
Princeton Junction, New Jersey

First Edition

Printed on acid-free paper.

He's mad that trusts in the tameness of a wolf. . .

William Shakespeare, *King Lear*, Act 3, Scene 6

Other books by R.H. Johnson

Widow-Taker

A Measure of Revenge

Hunting in the Zoo

of the jarring sounds and pungent odors that attended this sultry summer evening in Midtown. They were in love, and love blinded them to the risk of wandering recklessly in the night.

He checked his timepiece: 10:17 p.m. Later than usual for a midweek dinner. Why was that? Had they lingered over a bottle of excellent wine, gazing into each other's eyes? Had they spoken of love and dreams they shared? Had they perhaps talked about leaving New York for someplace safer? Surely they knew this could be a dangerous city.

Such things mattered enormously to Volkov. He believed you could not do your job well -- which for him meant flawlessly -- unless you could float into another person's head like a wisp of smoke and see the world through his or her eyes. Achieving this level of intimacy with the prey is what separated masters from pretenders.

The couple paused, as usual, just before reaching the door to their apartment building. They turned to each other, as usual, and smiled. They kissed long and hard, as usual, to the great amusement of those passing by.

He studied their movements, as usual. But tonight he watched through a $13,000 thermal imaging scope mounted on his CheyTac M300 Intervention sniper rifle. Adjust for the steep downward angle. Deep breath. Hold it. Squeeze. Volkov delivered the .408-caliber round precisely on target, and the man fell dead to the sidewalk.

Things would get much worse before they got better.

2.

Detectives Pete Nazareth and Tara Gimble were among the first NYPD officers to respond. They lived only a few blocks from the apartment building where the man had just been gunned down and were on their way home from a stakeout in the Bronx when the call came over the radio. By the time they reached the scene Officer Shayla Givens had already turned her attention to the victim's girlfriend because the guy on the sidewalk was beyond help.

Gimble immediately checked in with Officer Givens to learn what she could from the living while Nazareth knelt respectfully alongside the body and communed with the dead. Years of homicide experience had taught him that even those who can no longer speak often tell their own stories best. From the condition of the victim's head he already knew the killer had undoubtedly used a large-caliber weapon, almost certainly a rifle, and that death had been instantaneous. The pattern of blood on both the front wall of the apartment building and the sidewalk clearly indicated the shot had been fired from above and to the victim's right. He eyed the roof across the street and readily imagined a sniper leaning over the ledge and squeezing off the fatal round. Highly professional work. In less than 15 seconds Nazareth knew that he and his partner were going to have their hands full.

The two young detectives were bright stars in the NYPD universe, greatly admired not only for closing the toughest cases but also for putting themselves in harm's way again and again in order to get the job done right. Since becoming engaged eight months earlier they had also become famous as "the partner partners," a description coined by the host of a popular morning TV show. Nazareth and Gimble were no longer just detectives. They were A-list media darlings among the New York press, in part because their professional accomplishments were outshone only by their good looks and strong personalities.

Pete Nazareth, who had just turned 34, was the ugly duckling of the duo even though he was frequently mentioned as something of a Brad Pitt lookalike with his square jaw, boyish smile, and piercing gaze. At 5-10 and 165 pounds he still looked as though he could run a sub-4:00 mile, as he had in college, though his athletic claim to fame was now Taekwondo and a long string of major sparring championships.

As a young Marine captain in a Special Operations Battalion he had earned a silver star while leading troops on a high-risk mission among the caves of Eastern Afghanistan. In an area known by the Marines as the Valley of the Shadow, Nazareth had gone hand-to-hand with a group of Al Qaeda hostiles who were dragging off one of his injured team members. His action had resulted in a small scar on his chin and three very dead bad guys. So he had genuine star quality, no doubt about it, but his fiancée was the real showstopper.

Tara Gimble seemed not to know how beautiful she was, but those around her definitely noticed. The 32-year-old detective wore her gleaming blonde hair fairly straight until it flipped slightly inward at her neck. Her blue eyes, high cheekbones, and strong narrow chin needed no help from makeup, which explained why she used it only when on a date with Nazareth, and then sparingly. An All-American soccer player in college, Gimble held a judo black belt, carried 120 pounds of well-toned muscle on her 5-7 frame, and was generally more than a match for any perp who doubted her toughness. She was also known to be pretty good with a gun. A year earlier, in fact, she had won a gold medal at the national police pistol competition in St. Louis while up against 97 of the country's top police marksmen.

Over the past year Nazareth and Gimble had together taken down three of the worst serial killers in New York City history: one who murdered widows; one who targeted immigrants; and one who went after the country's top Republican presidential candidate. In these and a host of other cases they proved themselves smart, tough, and driven. And successful. Yes, so far always successful.

Yet even though they were widely acclaimed as the City's top team when it came to solving homicides, their time as NYPD partners was nearly over. Their boss, Deputy Chief Ed Crawford, had been comfortable keeping them together while they were merely engaged. But following their quiet civil wedding a few weeks earlier he announced he would soon find new partners for each of them. In the meantime, they eagerly threw themselves into whatever screwball case came along. Crazy seemed to be their specialty, and tonight's scenario felt all too familiar.

"Her name's Ludmilla Pervak," Gimble said as she joined Nazareth next to the vic's body. "They share an apartment in this building and were just coming back from dinner when her boyfriend was shot."

"Does she remember only one shot?"

"At this point I'm surprised she remembers her own name because she's pretty shaken up. But, yes, she thinks there was just one shot. Officer Givens has a few witnesses she's going to interview now that we've got back-up." The neighborhood was ablaze with the flashing lights of three police cruisers, two ambulances, and a heavy rescue truck from the Emergency Service Unit.

"Why the ESU truck?" Nazareth asked.

"Givens was afraid the shooter might be hunting for other victims so she called for SWAT support."

"Ah, good thinking. But I guarantee you this isn't the work of some lunatic who decided to spray a crowd with gunfire. One shot, perfectly placed, from 30 stories up, at night. This guy's really good, and he had only one target in mind. If the young woman had been on his list," he offered, "she'd be dead too."

"At first she thought she had been shot because she was covered with blood."

"His."

"Yep. They were kissing goodnight before entering the building. It was a tradition," she said. "It reminded them of their first date. Whenever they came back from dinner or a show they stopped outside for a kiss."

"The killer's a pro. He studied them, learned their routines, and struck when he was good and ready. Very patient."

"Patient, yes. Subtle, no."

"Yeah," he nodded, "this wasn't meant to be subtle. The weapon he used probably could have killed from a half mile away. From 1,000 yards you're dead; from 100 yards you're hamburger. Any ID on the vic?"

"Russian, like the girlfriend, but that's all I have right now. We'll need to speak at length with Ludmilla when she's up to it. Tomorrow most likely."

"Tomorrow it is."

* * *

By the time the two detectives met with Ludmilla Pervak at 1:00 the next afternoon the young woman's grief had given way to fear. She seemed safe enough in the lavish apartment her boyfriend had purchased here in one of Manhattan's finer neighborhoods, but she wore the meek wide-eyed look of a laboratory mouse about to be dissected in a high school biology class.

In a frail monotone she outlined the basics of Sergey Gerasimov's life: 47 years old, haunted by nightmares of his time in a Russian prison, and hopeful that one day he and Ludmilla could return to their homeland. The two had fallen in love before his imprisonment, and soon thereafter she had wisely left the country before the FSB, Russia's chief security agency, could invent a reason to lock her away too.

"Sergey thought those in charge were fools," she said softly, "but he refused to believe they were deadly. Not until he was thrown in prison and treated like a stray dog did he understand how badly our democracy had been undermined by the old guard. I begged him to stay quiet here in America. But he was convinced they could no longer touch him."

"Do you remember any specific threats he received while you and he lived here in New York City?" Gimble asked.

Pervak wore an ironic smile as she shook her head. "That is not how they operate, detective," she explained. "They don't send warnings. They expect you to know your place and to keep your mouth shut. Back in Russia he was thrown in prison for saying too much. From that day forward he was supposed to remember his life belonged to them."

"But he refused to accept that?" Gimble asked.

"He *could not* accept that and still feel like a man. They had broken him in many ways, so for him the only means of escaping the prison of his mind was to help destroy the current regime. That was to be his life's work."

"Is there anyone at all in Manhattan you suspect of having wanted him gone?"

"No one I could name," she said. "When we were together with other Russians in New York City I sometimes saw looks."

"From people who seemed suspicious?" Nazareth asked.

"Suspicious, envious, too interested? I can't tell what I saw. But when we attended large gatherings I always noticed people who frightened me in some way. On the other hand," she added, "you must understand that paranoia is a way of life for Russians. But tell me, have you learned anything yet about Sergey's murder?"

"The investigation has barely begun," Nazareth said, "but we believe he was killed by a .408-caliber bullet. This is a very large round and almost definitely would have been fired from a sniper rifle."

"You mean by a professional killer?"

"Probably, yes. This is not the sort of rifle most people would ever think of buying unless they were going to war."

"And that, of course, is precisely where we are. We are at war, and they will be looking to kill me next."

"I really don't think so," Gimble assured her. "You were right there next to Mr. Gerasimov and could easily have been shot if that's what the killer had wanted."

Pervak closed her eyes and raised her face as if in prayer. "They are not always efficient," she whispered, "but they are always brutally thorough. Someone will soon decide that I should be killed as well."

"We'll make sure that doesn't happen," Nazareth told her.

Pervak smiled sadly.

3.

Sergey Gerasimov's fate had been sealed two months before his skull was blown apart in Midtown, when his assassin received a rare direct message from his handler that subtlety wouldn't work for this particular mission. Volkov usually operated off the grid and without specific guidance from the homeland. For decades, in fact, he had unobtrusively and skillfully eliminated some of Russia's most troublesome critics in the United States. But Sergey Gerasimov had crossed the line, so for him a bit of cyanide or a fatal hit-and-run accident wouldn't be enough. No, in this instance Volkov was told to send Gerasimov's admirers a blunt and bloody message: threatening the Kremlin was suicidal.

Thus the long arm of old-school Russian justice had reached across an ocean and snuffed out Gerasimov's life one August night as he walked home from a romantic dinner with Ludmilla Pervak, the brilliant young painter he had lived with for the past six months. It was a messy end indeed for a man who had once held much promise.

Sergey Gerasimov had become a billionaire several times over following the Soviet Union's monumental collapse. His wildly successful business ventures, most of them related to mining and natural gas, had emboldened him to change from a moderately outspoken critic of the new Russian order to a fierce opponent of newly elected President Ruslan Kotov. For this indiscretion he had spent two years in The Madhouse, a former mansion that over the space of several decades had variously served as an insane asylum, a Soviet reeducation facility, and most recently a prison where prominent enemies of the state were sent to rot for the remainder of their lives. Although the formal charge was embezzlement, everyone with a functioning brain knew Gerasimov's only crime had been not taming his criticism of the president, a man with a poorly disguised desire to reassemble the Soviet Union and serve as its supreme ruler.

Living conditions at The Madhouse had grown somewhat less ghastly by the time Gerasimov took up residence. Whereas in the facility's earliest days prisoners survived mostly on whatever rodents they could catch and eat, now the rats and the inmates had an equal shot at the bowl of gruel and slice of stale black bread that were placed at the cell doors twice each day. But if starvation was no longer a threat, insanity certainly was.

Gerasimov had been torn from his $100-million home in Moscow's opulent Rublyovka suburb and tossed into a damp cinderblock cell whose flaking paint and thick mold closed in like a spreading infection for 23 hours out of every 24. A lice-infested cot, leaky sink, and foul toilet were the room's only adornments. No radio, no TV, and certainly no conversation. Early each morning he was led to a field where for one hour he dug trenches in the rocky soil. After the first few weeks his hands stopped bleeding, and after six months he stopped caring that the trenches he dug served no purpose other than to break his will. The regime was winning.

Before Gerasimov's mind and body had succumbed totally to the depraved treatment, however, Amnesty International took up his cause and through a skillfully orchestrated public-relations assault on the Russian leadership managed to secure his release. But President Kotov imposed an important condition: permanent exile. Gerasimov would leave Russia forever and would forfeit every scrap of personal property the government could grab. By the time he established himself in New York City his fortune had been reduced to $1.2 billion -- money he had wisely hidden in offshore bank accounts prior to his incarceration -- while his hatred of the Russian president had grown exponentially. At every opportunity he spoke out against Kotov and in short order became a shining symbol of hope for Russian exiles everywhere, most especially in Manhattan.

The beginning of his untimely end was the interview he granted a *New York Times* reporter two months before his murder. "Ruslan Kotov is a thug as well as a madman," he had said of the Russian president. "His goal is to eliminate all traces of democracy in Russia and declare himself czar. But he will fail, and soon. Trust me on this. Kotov will either step down voluntarily or be dragged from his billion-dollar mansion on the Black Sea and hanged by the people whose rights he has trampled."

Gerasimov's inflammatory words proved fatal.

Three days after his murder Ludmilla Pervak scattered her lover's ashes in Central Park, according to his wishes, then fled to Ecuador under an assumed name. As far as she was concerned, staying alive meant disappearing forever.

4.

Vladimir Krupin, 67-year-old director of the SVR -- Russia's foreign intelligence service -- felt the blood drain from his face as he read the electronic report of Sergey Gerasimov's assassination in New York City. He correctly assumed that within minutes he would be summoned to the office of his boss, President Ruslan Kotov, a man who combined paranoia and bloodlust in one extremely dangerous package. Krupin and Kotov would most likely have received the shocking report simultaneously from the counterintelligence division, and both would have been stunned by its contents. Only Krupin, however, would fear he might pay for the news with his life.

Fifteen seconds later his phone rang. Kotov was not a screamer, and he softly uttered only one word: "Immediately." Nevertheless, Krupin vomited in his private bathroom before he was able to call his driver and begin the 30-minute trip to the president's Kremlin office.

Ruslan Kotov's massive oak desk stood before a rich paneled wall that gleamed in the morning sunlight. Directly in front of the desk was a small table and a pair of ornate upholstered chairs, a cozy workspace where two men could sit face to face while discussing matters of state. But there would be nothing cozy about this morning's meeting. Kotov remained seated behind the desk while Krupin stood uncomfortably at attention. The president wasted no breath on small talk.

"Tell me who killed Sergey Gerasimov in New York City."

"Mr. President, I learned of his death only moments before you called me," Krupin replied, his voice cracking slightly. "This was certainly not an executive action I authorized."

The innocuous phrase *executive action* was one Kotov and Krupin both knew well from their early careers as fellow KGB officers. Back then the 13th Department of the KGB's Intelligence

Directorate did a brisk business in abductions, assassinations, and "accidents" involving Russian dissidents living abroad. In this way the Soviet leadership had demonstrated its willingness to go anywhere and do anything necessary to eliminate threats, both real and imagined. Although the KGB no longer existed, executive action remained a popular method of silencing troublesome voices. But anyone who valued his life knew it was a tool to be used only with the president's blessing.

"If I thought you had authorized it," Kotov said grimly, "I would already have given you a choice between being hanged and being shot." He offered Krupin a faint smile more reptilian than human. "But obviously someone on your staff is responsible."

"If that is true, Mr. President, I will find him."

"You say *if* that is true?" Kotov challenged. "I just *told* you it is true. Please understand that I am not unhappy to see Gerasimov dead. But mine alone was the privilege of deciding when, where, and how he would die. I will not tolerate rogue operations."

"I will get to the bottom of this, I assure you." A drop of sweat fell from Krupin's forehead onto his upper lip, and his heart began beating irregularly. When he got back to his office in the Yasenevo District he would immediately swallow two of those pills the doctor had given him. With luck he would avert a heart attack or stroke.

Kotov's voice barely rose above a whisper. "Find the problem, Krupin, and put a bullet in his head."

He dismissed his security chief with a casual wave of the hand.

At 2:27 a.m. Ilya Petrenko nearly fell off the bed while grabbing the red phone on the night table. The secure line hardly ever rang at his home, and the sound was never welcome. He knew that he would not be falling back asleep tonight.

Petrenko juggled two roles that conspired to keep him on the ragged edge of sanity. He was best known as head of security for the Russian consulate in New York City, reporting to the consul general. But he also secretly served the SVR, reporting to the head of the directorate responsible for foreign counterintelligence. In this capacity his chief assignment was to keep tabs on both Russian citizens and exiles in Manhattan and, if necessary, to assist with any message-sending that might become necessary.

"Petrenko." The bedroom was dark, and he was alone.

"Krupin here." Petrenko struggled to control his bladder. A call from his immediate supervisor in the middle of the night would have been enough to rattle him, but a call from his boss's boss -- the man at the top of the entire Russian SVR enterprise -- roiled his innards. Nothing good could come of this.

"Of course, sir. How may I be of service?"

"By telling me who killed Sergey Gerasimov."

Petrenko walked quickly toward the bathroom as he spoke. "Sir, I heard about Gerasimov's death only yesterday and assumed it was authorized from abroad."

"Would I be calling you if it had been authorized from here?"

"No, sir, but surely this is not something I would have undertaken without orders." Petrenko knew with great certainty that acting without orders in virtually any capacity, let alone an executive action, would get him killed. Besides, he had never viewed Gerasimov as particularly threatening. Yes, the guy had been outspoken to a fault, but he had also seemed to love his money and his girlfriend more than he enjoyed meddling in Russian internal affairs.

"Perhaps we should discuss this at the Kremlin with President Kotov," Krupin offered. Petrenko didn't reach the toilet on time. He stood in a puddle of warm urine as he contemplated an audience with the two powerful bureaucrats. They would savage him with questions he couldn't possibly answer. He would mumble incoherently while being tortured. And then they would have him dumped from the weapons bay of a Tupolev Tu-95 strategic bomber 40,000 feet above the Arctic Circle.

Ilya Petrenko was a moderately efficient functionary who had so far managed to keep himself out of harm's way. He was an unimposing man at 5-9 and 186 pounds, and he was still unmarried at 53 though happily involved with several women who occasionally visited his lovely home in Riverdale. That place had been paid for in large part by a variety of carefully orchestrated schemes -- kickbacks from several consulate suppliers among them -- and in almost every way Petrenko had a very good thing going in America. Surely he would not have risked his lifestyle or his life for the sake of an annoying gnat like Sergey Gerasimov.

"Sir, I pledge to you on my life that I had nothing to do with this. I was with the consul general, Grigori Vasilyev, for two days in the American city of Miami at the time Gerasimov was killed. Besides this, I had no reason to want the man dead."

"He had a dangerous mouth," Krupin snarled. "You knew this. Your own reports frequently said as much."

"This is true, sir, but I never believed his words had risen to the level of a serious threat. Perhaps they would have at some point," he added hastily, "but I did not think that time had come."

"Listen to me well. Someone on your side of the ocean arranged for Gerasimov to die. I want his name, and I want it soon. Do you understand me?"

"Yes, sir, I understand completely. I will find him for you. This I promise." Even as the words slipped out of his mouth Petrenko wondered how he could possibly deliver on a promise he was sure Krupin would not forget.

Krupin sat quietly at his desk after ending the phone call and concluded he did not have the luxury of waiting for Petrenko to identify the killer in New York City. Time was not on his side. When President Kotov asked for blood he expected it to be delivered quickly, and failing to comply with the man's wishes was unwise for someone who hoped to experience the modest rewards of old age.

After much deliberation Krupin ordered the immediate arrest of one of his most senior staffers, Maxim Shchukin, who three years earlier had become head of Directorate S, responsible for illegal intelligence operations abroad. Shchukin was a reasonably competent though not universally admired 58-year-old official who in Krupin's estimation could easily be replaced. Two hours later Shchukin found himself naked and strapped to a gurney in a private room at Butyrka prison with electrodes attached to a variety of sensitive body parts. He eagerly admitted his crime within eight minutes, not caring at all what crime he had supposedly committed. As soon as he signed the confession he took a bullet to the forehead.

Vladimir Krupin thought it best to follow the president's orders to the letter.

5.

"Here's a surprise," said Deputy Chief Ed Crawford. "Our esteemed mayor doesn't think billionaires should be murdered in Manhattan, so he wants us to find Sergey Gerasimov's killer yesterday." Crawford shook his head in disgust as he poured another cup of the rancid coffee he brewed in a grimy pot behind his desk at One Police Plaza. He had never been a fan of Mayor Elliott Dortmund, a man whose political aspirations outweighed all other considerations, including common sense. And he was angry that his two top detectives, Pete Nazareth and Tara Gimble, would once again be nitpicked to death by City Hall while doing their jobs.

"Has he called about the three homeless people who've been murdered in the past month?" Gimble asked.

"Let's see," Crawford replied, "can homeless people write big checks to his reelection campaign? No, I didn't think so. But apparently Gerasimov had donated quite a lot, so this case is now your one and only priority. Where are we so far?"

"Where we usually are after only 48 hours," Nazareth shrugged. "Basically nowhere. Gerasimov's girlfriend is convinced it was the Russians, and certainly the guy had been rattling the Russian president's cage pretty hard. But why would they splash someone all over the sidewalk with a high-powered rifle and generate so much press? Of course, maybe that was the point. Maybe they decided the louder the message the better."

"That could be it," Gimble added, "but it's also possible we just have another garden-variety screwball with a gun. Right now we think the shooter studied Gerasimov and learned his schedule, but that doesn't mean it was a politically motivated killing. This could simply be someone who wants to stalk random victims and play sniper."

"Another goddamn sniper," Crawford grumbled. He thought back on a recent case involving sniper killings on Staten Island and the international press they had generated. "Please don't tell me we have another sniper on our hands."

"Too soon to say, chief. All I can tell you right now," said Nazareth, "is that whoever took the shot that killed Gerasimov is well armed and seriously good at what he does. My gut tells me he's a pro, and that causes me to lean in the direction of a Russian operative."

"Well, as usual you two have a blank check. Whatever you need, you've got it. Just let me know."

"Since you mentioned it," Nazareth said, "we could use some research support. A couple of sharp college interns would really help."

"Done. In the meantime, I'll assure Mr. Mayor we'll try to make sure no more billionaires are murdered."

"Anything to help Dortmund's campaign," Gimble offered sarcastically. "He's our man."

Over the next two days a team of three college students tackled the project Nazareth had laid out for them. Using every research tool at their disposal -- Internet, newspaper archives, libraries, and NYPD case files among them -- they were to identify all Russian citizens or immigrants who had died in New York City over the past 15 years. It was a monumental undertaking whose outcome was impossible to predict. But since Nazareth firmly believed the likeliest motive in the Gerasimov case was political, he hoped something in the data would steer the investigation in a promising direction. He understood at the outset that this was the sort of boring, time-consuming exercise that produced nothing of value 98 percent of the time. It was the other two percent that made the effort essential.

The detectives analyzed and organized the data as each of the interns fed tidbits of information into the system, and by 11:20 p.m. on the second night the message was plain to anyone who disliked coincidences. The death rate among Russians in New York City was normal unless you focused exclusively on those who had been labeled *dissidents* for one reason or another. Within that population the numbers were shockingly out of line.

"Over the past 15 years," Nazareth began as he and Gimble presented their findings to Chief Crawford the next morning, "at least 13 people identified as Russian dissidents have died in New York City."

"Which represents a death rate roughly 10 times higher than that of Russians who were not identified as dissidents," Gimble added.

"And yet these deaths never hit the radar screen because they each seemed quite normal at the time. Look at the causes: five heart attacks, three car accidents, two boating accidents, two house fires, and one drowning. This is all spread over 15 years. So you don't notice the pattern until you list all the deaths and causes on one page."

"And when you do that," Crawford observed, "it's pretty obvious someone has been very quietly getting rid of Russians who had bad things to say about the old country."

"I don't think there's any doubt about it," Nazareth said. "We looked only at the past 15 years. For all we know the same thing has been happening for the past 30 or 40. Either way, there's been a long, extremely patient campaign to eliminate Soviet or Russian dissidents who managed to get themselves noticed. But this raises an interesting question for us, doesn't it?"

"Yes, it does," Crawford nodded. "Why the sudden switch to heavy artillery?"

"Exactly. Either the Russians have drastically changed the rules," Nazareth reasoned, "or in this particular case they felt they needed to send an especially loud message."

"Which could make sense," Gimble added. "The other dissidents never really amounted to much of a threat, whereas Sergey Gerasimov had the money and connections to make things happen. Arrange an ugly end for him, and you might also scare off his supporters."

"And, for the record," Nazareth added, "his girlfriend has already disappeared. We have no idea where she is and probably never will. I'm sure he provided for her financially, and she's now most likely hiding someplace where she hopes they can't find her."

"Son of a bitch," Crawford growled. "What about all the freedom and democracy the Russians have talked about? All bullshit?"

"For the average Russian? No. They still cling to hope. But for President Ruslan Kotov," Gimble answered, "absolutely. Democracy is the last thing he wants."

"So he's killing people in our goddamn city?"

"Seems like it," Nazareth nodded.

"Then shut this thing down," Crawford told them. "Do whatever you have to do."

Nazareth smiled. "We'll absolutely do that, chief."

The detectives spent the remainder of the day running down the names of prominent Russian dissidents who lived in New York City and might soon find themselves in a sniper's crosshairs. Were they truly at risk? Nazareth and Gimble had no proof at all that someone had, in fact, been killing Russian dissidents in Manhattan. Maybe all they had was a highly interesting set of coincidences. In addition, all of those earlier deaths had taken place over the space of 15 years. How likely was it that another dissident would be killed in the near future? That certainly wouldn't fit the pattern. On the other hand, the brutality of Sergey Gerasimov's murder also didn't fit the pattern, and maybe that meant the new Russian regime was stepping up the pace of assassinations, if that's truly what they were.

In any event the investigation would have to wait until the next morning. On this particular evening Nazareth was having dinner at a Midtown restaurant with one of his former partners while Gimble stayed home and hit the weights. One of their apartment's two bedrooms had been transformed into a first-class gym where the two serious athletes could maintain their elite fitness levels, and Gimble was looking forward to a couple of hours of heavy sweating.

Nazareth dropped his wife off in front of their apartment building on East 24th Street, then headed over to Spice Symphony, his favorite Indian restaurant on Lexington Avenue near 32nd Street. As Gimble entered the lobby she noticed the burly man standing at the front desk alongside the concierge, Aurelio Rios. The man wore a tight black T-shirt with the image of a large silver skull on the front, and his muscular upper arms strained against the fabric. His left hand rested on the counter next to a vase filled with yellow and lavender Gerbera daisies. His right hand was out of view but seemed to be down near his waist. The guy stood about 6-3 and looked well over 200 pounds.

"Good evening, Mrs. Anderson," Rios said pleasantly. "Very good to see you." He forced a smile. The man alongside him looked away as Gimble returned the greeting.

"Thank you, Aurelio. You have a nice night." She paused before walking to the elevator, thought for a moment, then turned back toward the front desk. "You know, I think I'm finally going to start my new routine. For weeks I've been saying I'll take the stairs more often, so why not tonight?"

"That's a very good idea, Mrs. Anderson. Four flights will give you good exercise."

"Goodnight, then," she smiled.

"Yes, goodnight."

Gimble opened the door to the stairwell and began climbing. The hard heels on her new flats made a hollow metallic sound with each step, and she had nearly reached the first landing when the stairwell door automatically slammed shut below her. As soon as she heard it she quietly slipped out of her shoes and removed the Smith & Wesson 5946 from under her pale blue summer blazer. She kept her eyes on the door as she walked gently down the stairs.

Aurelio Rios, a slender man in his late thirties, had been the building's concierge for the past five years and knew every tenant by face, name, and apartment number. He also knew the names of children, nannies, cats, dogs, and parakeets. And he knew for a fact that Gimble wasn't "Mrs. Anderson" and that she didn't live on the fourth floor. Message delivered and received.

When she reached the lobby level she peered through the small window in the stairwell door and saw that Rios and the guy in the black T-shirt had disappeared. There were only two ways they could have gone: out the building's main entrance to the sidewalk or around the corner from the front desk toward the elevator. She gently opened the steel door and in her stockinged feet crossed silently over to Rios's station, where she heard the muffled sounds of someone screaming in pain. When she peeked around the corner she saw that the building's lone elevator was still at the lobby level. Gimble seriously doubted someone was being beaten behind the closed elevator door, which meant the sounds she heard were coming from the small manager's office at the end of the alcove.

She ran to the office door and gently turned the knob. Unlocked. This was good. What was not good was having no idea whether she was about to confront just one bad guy or several, and she didn't have time to call for backup. She correctly assumed the guy in the black T-shirt could easily kill a man Rios's size without much effort.

Gimble drove her shoulder into the door and swept into the small room with her gun drawn. No more than 10 feet away from her young Rios, his face bloody and broken, was being held against the wall by the thug she had seen at the front desk. But before she could raise her weapon she was blindsided by a second punk who had been standing alongside the door when she barged in. He planted a huge right fist on the left side of the her jaw, and she went down hard, dropping her revolver as she fell.

She was mildly dizzy as her attacker reached for her throat, but while lying on her side she managed to drive a powerful left kick into his ribcage. The blow would have stopped a smaller man, but this guy was roughly the same size as his partner and outweighed Gimble by at least 80 pounds. He stumbled backward slightly, then came at her again. She had barely gotten to her feet when the guy slammed into her like a linebacker, both powerful arms braced in front of him. The force of his charge drove her against the wall, but she successfully sidestepped a lunging punch that might have put her down for good. A kick toward his left knee flew off target and glanced off his thigh without effect.

Before Gimble could launch another attack a vicious punch to the back of her head left her barely conscious. The guy in the black T-shirt had joined his partner in taking Gimble down, and now he yanked both her arms back with his massive bloodied hands.

"Cut this bitch!" he screamed to his partner.

Gimble saw the blade coming toward her but couldn't make her arms or legs move. In that final instant of consciousness her brain sent a brief flickering message: "So, Tara, this is how you die."

She passed out before the guy with the knife had his brain splattered over a three-foot section of the office wall. The guy in the black T-shirt immediately let go of Gimble's arms and frantically dove for her gun on the floor. Before he could raise it toward the office door he took one bullet to the face and another to the top of his chest.

Rios was slumped on the floor with a badly swollen left eye, a shattered nose, and three missing front teeth. Yet he managed a painful smile as he said, "Thank God for you, Detective Nazareth."

An hour later Gimble looked up from her hospital bed and smiled at her husband. The concussion had rendered her unconscious for nearly two minutes, and she now had a fierce headache along with some lingering confusion.

"Rios," she whispered.

"He was patched up in the ER and sent home," Nazareth told her. "You saved his life, Tara. Well done."

She placed her hand behind her head to adjust an ice pack the nurse had placed on the pillow. "Cold but feels good," she nodded gently. "Who were those two men?"

"Ex-inmates of Dannemora," he said, referring to the notorious maximum security prison near New York State's northern border. "Apparently they were going after a woman in our building who had testified against them, and they wanted the master key. Rios refused to give it to them. If you hadn't jumped in when you did," he added, "they would have killed Rios, no question."

"Where are they?"

"At the morgue I suppose."

She looked puzzled. "How? I don't remember."

"That's because you were unconscious at the time," he smiled. "I stopped by to help you finish the job."

"What about dinner with Todd?" she asked

"I had gone only half a block when he called to cancel, so I drove back home. When I got to the lobby I heard what I thought might be World War III in the manager's office."

"Never saw the first punch coming," she murmured. "He was really big. I tried."

"If it's any consolation," he grinned, "you broke a few of his ribs. But he was so high on speed he didn't care much about pain."

"I can't remember."

"That's okay, Tara. Aurelio Rios will never forget."

6.

Anatoly Bukarin wistfully recalled the Soviet Union's golden age, an exciting time when he wielded more power than most kings. Heading a unit known rather benignly as the Special Directorate, he had reported directly to Nikita Khrushchev, controlled a budget larger than that of many small nations, and lived with his wife, son, and daughter in an imposing six-bedroom apartment within walking distance of his Kremlin office. Precisely what Bukarin and his team did was known only to Khrushchev himself. Others within the Soviet hierarchy generally supposed that the Special Directorate assisted with such boring but necessary matters as economic forecasting, agricultural production, or educational reform. But in fact Bukarin was in what he politely termed the *reconstruction business*.

One of the Special Directorate's primary missions in those days was to discredit any Soviet leaders, both great and small, who had not been sufficiently supportive of Khrushchev or his policies. Hundreds of innocent but troublesome men found themselves swinging pickaxes 16 hours a day in Siberian labor camps after Bukarin's elite operatives had planted evidence of treason, embezzlement, or gross immorality. The system was highly effective, naturally, since those arrested for crimes against the state were presumed guilty until proven innocent. It was a matter of great pride to Bukarin that no one who had been discredited by the Special Directorate had ever successfully produced sufficient evidence to save his skin.

The team also played a key role in destabilizing no fewer than eight governments outside the Soviet camp in an effort to help Khrushchev expand his regime's influence. In some cases all it took was a meaningful financial incentive. A hundred million here and a hundred million there bought some important friends in foreign countries. But often the unit's involvement was even more direct. Thousands of men and women whose loyalty could not be bought either died unexpectedly or simply vanished from the face of the Earth.

Finally, the Special Directorate quietly took the lead in silencing dissidents who had managed to escape the Soviet Union and unwisely continued to criticize state policies. In order to insulate the man at the top from all responsibility for these activities, Bukarin had made sure Khrushchev knew absolutely nothing of the assassination unit's existence. Bukarin alone chose the operatives. He alone knew who they were and where they were stationed. He alone gave the men their marching orders. And he alone controlled the operation's purse strings through a fund identified only as "President, Special" buried deep within the Kremlin's impenetrable budget. No one had ever known or cared what the annual expenses covered, and even after the Soviet Union's collapse the mysterious budget line remained untouched. After all, what bureaucrat would ever be foolish enough to challenge anything with the word *president* attached to it?

Alas, that budget line was all that remained of Anatoly Bukarin's former glory. By the time the Soviet Union had fallen and Russia had begun its exceedingly brief love affair with democracy, Bukarin was past his prime. Worse, he didn't dare tell the new leaders what he actually did for a living since he feared that revealing the true nature of his secret organization would get him fired or worse. Instead, he disguised his rabidly pro-Soviet, iron-fist beliefs in the presence of Boris Yeltsin, who had won the country's first-ever presidential election in 1991. Within a few months of that election he found himself in a cramped office reporting to the assistant of the assistant of the assistant of an obscure directorate. Those above him cared only about lining their pockets in the many illegal money making schemes that flourished during the period, and no one paid any attention to the plump, graying bureaucrat who gathered dust at his tiny metal desk.

For years afterward he shuffled papers and did his best to appear busy whenever someone of consequence passed by his door. The only real work left on his plate was a lone assassin, and there he had a serious problem. On the one hand, he didn't dare tell anyone -- not even this young new president, Ruslan Kotov, who seemed to embrace the old way of doing things -- that the state had never once in all those years actually abandoned its brutal version of justice. On the other hand, he feared what could happen if he officially shut the operation down.

Bukarin was certain that Volkov, his man in New York City, would forever carry out his assigned duties in perfect secrecy. Prison, torture, or the threat of death would never compel him to talk. But what might happen if the operation ended? Would Volkov want to return to Russia to live out the rest of his life? If so, would dangerous questions follow? How could they not! A man who renounces his U.S. citizenship often makes news in Russia, and TASS, the Russian news agency, would undoubtedly pounce on the opportunity. It was certainly possible that an enterprising reporter could succeed in peeling back the hidden layers of Volkov's story and thereby trigger highly unpleasant, perhaps even deadly, consequences.

Better to let the operation continue, Bukarin decided, than to risk allowing Volkov to come home after all these years. Besides, the program would eventually die a natural death since Volkov was the sole survivor of the men originally sent abroad for the purpose of thinning the herd of dissenters. Each man in Bukarin's "ghost detachment" had been assigned to a country, given ample funding, and told to blend in, live long, and get the job done. One of the men was killed within two months of reaching Tel Aviv, poisoned by an Israeli double agent. Two died of natural causes -- one in Germany, one in England. And another, the one who handled post-Soviet Hungary, lost his life when the Ilyushin aircraft on which he traveled had crashed and burned 48 seconds after taking off from Budapest. Others had met similar fates in a dozen countries.

So Bukarin, bitter and dispirited, endured one long, unsatisfying year after another, impersonating a busy man while actually doing only one bit of work at noon Moscow time on the last Thursday of every month. That's when he placed a phone call to Volkov's private number in New York City and hung up after four rings. Volkov, in turn, never took the call but merely listened dutifully every month for his handler's unspoken message. Four rings indicated that Bukarin was still at the controls and still watching.

Only twice in all those years had Bukarin allowed the phone to ring longer than four times so that he could speak briefly to Volkov. The first of those calls had come in February of 1981, when a Soviet Army defector living in Brooklyn began speaking out against the USSR's involvement in Afghanistan. The disastrous war was bad enough, Bukarin had reasoned, without the traitorous rants of Senior Lieutenant Oleg Dubov stoking the flames of international protest. Forty-five hours after that phone call Dubov fell in front of an R train at the Bay Ridge Avenue station and was declared dead at the scene.

The second of Bukarin's long-distance conversations with Volkov had come much more recently, when he had ordered the elimination of billionaire Sergey Gerasimov. Perhaps Volkov would have targeted Gerasimov on his own at some point, but Bukarin had decided that sooner was better than later since the loud-mouthed dissident was taking direct potshots at the Russian president. Just as one small section of rot can bring down an entire house if it's allowed to spread, Sergey Gerasimov's threats might have infected millions of otherwise docile Russians. Now the infection had been eradicated.

Two weeks after Gerasimov's murder Anatoly Bukarin sat at the wooden table in his tiny kitchen stirring a second spoonful of sugar into a mug of strong black tea. His lavish Moscow apartment had been taken away from him decades ago at about the time he suffered the first of four deep cuts in his salary. Now he lived year-round in what had once been his dacha, or summer vacation home, far outside the city limits. He hated all 700 square feet of the damp, moldering house, and he hated living alone now that wife Natalya had passed on. But he had long since swallowed his last ounce of pride and knew things could be much worse. Things would, in fact, get much worse in a hurry if he lost his current position and had to live on the pension provided for inconsequential bureaucrats like him. And if by chance he was booted from his lowly state-owned home he would be forced to live with one of his children or taste the barrel of his prized Baikal shotgun.

Bukarin carelessly sipped the hot tea and winced as he burned his lips and tongue. Yet he smiled through the pain when he noticed his beloved wife Natalya, young and radiant, standing at the back door. She wore a pale pink dress, the one she had bought on the first day of their honeymoon. She softly brushed her windblown hair from her cheek. She held a wicker basket filled with brightly colored tulips from the garden. He fell in love all over again.

Then he fell to the kitchen floor.

Bukarin was comatose in a cramped, yellowing hospital room for the next three days. His son and daughter came as often as they could and whispered comforting words to their father, but they sensed this would end badly. The attending physician had said that death would, in fact, be a blessing since the old man would most likely be severely brain damaged if he somehow managed to survive.

So everyone waited. Bukarin's children waited for death while the hospital waited for an empty bed. There were never enough empty beds anymore.

On the third day, shortly after 11:00 a.m., Bukarin opened his eyes. They were the eyes of a lamb being torn apart by a bear. His son Pavel, who sat alongside the bed, dropped the magazine he was reading when his father awoke and began moving his cracked lips.

"Wolf," he wheezed. "Kirov. America."

"What is it, father?" Pavel pleaded. "What do you wish to tell me?"

"Volkov," the old man said softly as his strength faded. "Wolf." Then Bukarin took his last breath.

Pavel dutifully phoned his sister to let her know their father had died. He mentioned the old man's frightened muttering at the end but chalked it up to failing brain cells.

"Just an old nightmare," Pavel told her. "Nothing more. And now the nightmare is over."

He had no way of knowing that the Kirov Wolf nightmare had only just begun.

7.

Professor Alina Yesikova lived by herself in a modest studio apartment only a three-minute walk from Washington Square Park. A widow since 1998, the slender white-haired woman had recently turned 70 and found it increasingly difficult to carry her groceries up two flights of stairs, especially in winter when burdened with a heavy woolen coat and snow boots. Yet she dreaded the thought of ever having to leave the place. The building was a beautifully maintained 19th-century gem in one of Manhattan's most exciting neighborhoods, and her office at the university was less than four blocks away.

She maintained a frantic schedule, teaching three extremely popular Russian history courses while working on her fourth book. Her current writing focused on the role of mass media, in particular the Internet, on U.S.-Russian relations, and her publisher was pushing hard for a November draft. So she could easily have justified turning away the two young NYPD detectives who arrived unannounced at her university office one Thursday afternoon. Instead, she invited them in and closed the door.

Nazareth and Gimble had found several prominent references to Prof. Yesikova while researching the deaths of Russian dissidents. She and husband Kirill had fled the Soviet Union in 1985 to begin their lives anew in Manhattan, both as university professors. But in late 1997 her husband returned to Russia believing he could play a useful role in strengthening the country's democratic institutions. She had begged him not to go, and for a few weeks thereafter he seemed content not to disrupt the fine life they had in America. In the end, however, his outrage over reports of government corruption drove him back to his homeland, where four months later he drowned in the Moscow River while walking back to his apartment late one night after dinner. Precisely how he had managed to tumble over the high concrete guard wall was, of course, a matter of great speculation.

Given this unfortunate history, the detectives were virtually certain Yesikova could help them separate fact from fiction in their current investigation. They decided not to tell her about the 13 deaths they had recently documented, but they didn't need to.

"Sergey Gerasimov's is the latest voice to be silenced," she told them, "not the first. Many others died before him, my husband included. But you must already know this, or you wouldn't be here."

"It's possible we might have found you simply because you teach Russian history," Nazareth answered honestly, "but, yes, it was the news article about your husband's death that caught our attention."

She smiled despite the lingering pain. "He and I could have lived out the rest of our time in peace, you know. Of this I am absolutely certain. Kirill and I had not drawn attention to ourselves after leaving Russia, so we were quite safe."

"But that changed when he went back in 1997, correct?" Gimble asked.

"Oh, yes. If you really want to get along well with the Russian masters," she sneered, "you should be two things: stupid and quiet. To be intelligent and outspoken, as my husband most definitely was, is something best done only if they cannot possibly find you. My late friend Sergey Gerasimov learned this the hard way."

"We have no evidence that his was a politically motivated killing," Nazareth said, "although it's certainly a strong possibility. What makes you so sure?"

"I was born and raised in Russia," she said flatly. "My country was part of the Soviet Union when I was a little girl, and it was still part of that foul monstrosity when Kirill and I escaped in 1985. I knew what it was to live in fear. A wrong word to the wrong person was all it took. I remember them pounding on our door late one night and taking my father away in a black sedan.

They executed him without a trial. This was perfectly normal, detectives. Routine, in fact. And as for democracy after 1991, what a horrible joke that was."

"A different form of democracy from what we see here in America, I take it," Nazareth said.

"In the absence of honest elections, a free press, and free speech it's difficult to make a case for the existence of anything even resembling democracy in Russia. When you add state-sponsored murder to the mix, of course, what you have is totalitarianism. And this latest president, Ruslan Kotov, is the worst kind of thug," she nodded. "Make no mistake about that. If he could resurrect the Soviet Union tomorrow, he would do it. If he could have himself named czar for life, he would do it. If he could make all of his enemies disappear at this very moment, he would do it."

"If Gerasimov was killed by a Russian operative," Gimble asked, "would that order most likely have come straight from the top?"

She laughed. "If you want to blow your nose in Russia today, it is safe to do so only if Ruslan Kotov grants permission. Without that, well, perhaps you are not so safe. As for assassinating someone without his permission, you would do that only if you no longer wished to live. Kotov is a man who believes in both the efficiency and the legitimacy of state terrorism, but I doubt he delegates much authority in this realm. He is most assuredly the person who would have ordered Gerasimov's murder."

"Do you have any idea what sort of agent would undertake a mission like this one?" Nazareth asked. "Would someone travel to New York City just to kill Gerasimov, or is it more likely we're dealing with someone who was already in place?"

"Prior to the Soviet Union's collapse in 1991 the 13th Department of the KGB took the lead in assassinating the state's enemies abroad," she explained. "If they targeted Soviet emigrés in America -- someone like Gerasimov -- they may have coordinated their actions with other agencies, but for the most part it was up to the KGB. And the KGB's agents, I can tell you, were stationed throughout the world, especially in major cities like New York."

"But the KGB no longer exists," Gimble noted.

"That name no longer exists," Yesikova replied, "but the apparatus remains. In all likelihood Gerasimov's killer has been living here in Manhattan for some time, quite possibly as a member of the consulate staff."

"A diplomat," Gimble said.

"On paper, yes. As a practical matter he or she is here for the sole purpose of undermining anyone or anything that could remotely threaten the current Russian leadership. Sergey Gerasimov was a powerful man, and surely Kotov viewed him as a threat. He had fabulous wealth and a strong voice. Too strong a voice, obviously," she added, shaking her head. "I feared months ago that he was, as the saying goes, a dead man walking."

"Did you ever tell him that?" Gimble wondered.

"Until he tired of hearing it, yes. But, as I have said, he was a strong man. I do think he planned to attack Kotov in some way. It's now clear that Kotov thought so as well."

"Are there any other Russian dissidents you've warned about having too high a profile?" Gimble asked.

"I lie awake most nights worrying about all Russians living in New York City, but now that Sergey has been killed I am most concerned about Feodor Sidorenko. He is a writer, perhaps the most fearless writer on our planet," she told them. "In his novels and essays he has brutalized Ruslan Kotov's regime, and because of this I view him as a marked man. Millions of people treasure his words, but no one will be able to protect him if or when his name rises to the top of the kill list. Would you like to meet with him?"

"Very much," Gimble said. "If you think he's at risk, we should see him right away. But it would be out of character for another dissident to be attacked so soon, wouldn't it?"

"Yes, it would. On the other hand, it was out of character for someone to be gunned down on the streets of Manhattan. That wasn't normal, detectives. But with Kotov," she added, "the word *normal* can change meaning in a heartbeat. If you deal with him or his people, it is always best to assume the worst. I'll gladly arrange for you to meet with Feodor Sidorenko."

Nazareth and Gimble left Yesikova's office no closer to solving the crime, and they were hesitant to accept completely her view that a Russian assassin was behind Gerasimov's murder.

"I'm not sure she's capable of being objective about this," Gimble said as they drove toward One Police Plaza. "Everything she sees is colored by the awful memories of her childhood and her husband's death."

Nazareth nodded. "No doubt about it. I'm having trouble believing a Russian hit man operating successfully in New York City for so long would suddenly change his tactics so radically. If we're correct in believing the same person killed 13 dissidents over the past 15 years, then we're dealing with someone who likes flying under the radar."

"And Gerasimov's killing was just the opposite."

"For sure. I think we need to get another professional opinion on this before we buy everything the professor told us."

"Do you know anyone who can help?"

"Yeah, I do. If I can find him." He paused. "And if he's still alive."

8.

Every year trophy hunters from around the world trek through Russia's remote and heavily forested Kirov region, some 600 miles northeast of Moscow, where for a steep fee they amuse themselves by killing European brown bears, moose, elk, and assorted other wild creatures. But things didn't always work quite this way in Kirov. There was a time, in fact, when the animals hunted the humans.

In the middle of the 20th century, from the mid-1940s to the late 1950s, a number of villages in the Kirov region were ravaged by man-eating wolves. More than 200 wolf packs inhabited the area's forests during this period, their numbers having expanded rapidly after most of Kirov's hunters were drafted for service in World War II. The result was something from a bad horror movie. An untold number of children, most under the age of 13, were attacked while walking to school, playing in their yards, or hanging wash. Nearly two dozen of them were dragged into the woods and devoured. Others, the lucky ones, escaped with only savage wounds. The carnage didn't end until long after the war, when the region's hunters returned home and succeeded in killing thousands of animals.

What only a handful of people had ever known was that not all of the children who disappeared were victims of wolf attacks. On the contrary, many children who vanished without a trace during that period had been abducted by the state and raised exclusively for service to the Soviet Union. The top-secret effort was masterminded by Moscow's most powerful Communist Party officials and operated by an elite team of psychiatrists, physiologists, and geneticists whose goal was to create a small army of gifted and highly motivated patriots who could change the world. One sturdy and extremely intelligent child whose tutors eventually nicknamed *the Kirov Wolf* was destined to become the program's shining star.

Borya Volkov was only seven when his athleticism and high spirits got him noticed by a man named Khalturin, a sharp-eyed "talent scout" for what was known only behind closed doors as the Motherland Project. The boy was taller and heavier than most children a year older than him, and, remarkably, could run faster than almost all the 10-year-olds in his village. What truly set him apart, however, was his fearlessness. Khalturin watched from a distance one afternoon as two 11-year-old boys from a neighboring village attempted to steal Volkov's tin toy soldier and were in return beaten bloody with an oak branch.

Something else that made Volkov a choice candidate for the Motherland Project was his parentage. The boy's father was a surly drunk who worked at a sawmill when sober enough, and his mother was a sharp-tongued school teacher who frequently raised eyebrows with her highly unpopular opinions on the state of the educational system. While Soviet Russia was in great need of capable servants like young Volkov, it had no need whatsoever for weak links like his parents.

Late one May afternoon in 1955, four days after a 13-year-old girl from the village had been mauled by a large wolf, Khalturin stopped his black Moskvitch 400 sedan alongside Volkov as the boy walked alone on his way home from school. He flashed a badge, ordered the boy into the back seat, and told him not to move. Then he got out and from a large glass bottle poured a half liter of pig's blood along the road leading into the woods. Two hours later, by which time Khalturin had driven 68 miles southwest toward Moscow, Volkov's mother found the bloody evidence of what she assumed was her only son's death.

The village mourned along with the boy's mother and father for nearly a month, at which point the couple mysteriously vanished one night while their neighbors slept. They had packed some clothing, left half-empty glasses of local vodka on the kitchen table, and shut the unlocked front door behind them.

Their surprised friends assumed grief was behind the stealthy departure, though no one bothered to pursue the matter. A few locals considered a more sinister possibility but never learned the truth: young Volkov's parents had, in fact, been sent off to separate Siberian work camps. The husband lasted two months, the wife five. Both were executed when they could no longer swing a pickaxe or push a wheelbarrow.

This pattern had become quite common beginning in the mid-1930s, when millions of Soviet citizens were thrown in prison after being labeled enemies of the state. Precisely how many of them died of natural or unnatural causes while behind bars remains anyone's guess, but the number was high enough to produce an unlimited supply of orphaned children for whom life was generally grim. They were dumped in loveless, often foodless warehouses for the unwanted and were fortunate to get out with only psychological damage. But for those children judged capable of providing "elite state service" things could not have been better. They ate well, received expert fitness training, and enjoyed the best formal education the Soviet Union could provide.

The Motherland Project was modeled to some extent after Germany's state-mandated Hitler Youth program, which aimed to mold the country's children into what *der Führer* believed would be a generation of perfect citizens. But the Soviet program took the process to a frightening new level by abducting selected children and carefully grooming them to become loyal pawns of the bureaucracy, each according to his or her natural talents. In Volkov's case the most impressive talent was shooting.

For the first two days after his kidnapping the boy cried at night for his parents. This ended abruptly when on the third day he was given only a cup of water and a slice of stale bread for breakfast and informed he would eat nothing else if he ever cried again. He was also told in harshest terms that his parents were traitors to the Soviet Union and that merely thinking of them was a crime. Volkov never cried again, and after a month at the training camp he successfully put his parents out of his mind.

The boy's handlers quickly learned that in addition to remarkable eye-hand coordination he possessed a measure of patience that few adults could match. This combination of talents helped transform him within six months into the camp's finest marksmen under the age of 15. He felt an almost other-worldly connection to his small bolt-action rifle, and he refused to squeeze the trigger until every shot was perfectly lined up. By the end of his first year he was an exceptionally capable hunter whose kills included limitless numbers of long-tailed ground squirrels, common pheasants, mallards, and red foxes. Two months after his ninth birthday Volkov shot a Ural field mouse from nearly 50 yards, a feat his shooting instructor would not have believed had he not seen it with his own eyes.

There was something else about Volkov that made him special. Unlike most of the younger children, he never became emotionally involved with his prey. Some children hesitated, trembled, or whimpered before taking aim at a furry animal. Not Volkov. For him the hunt was all about process -- feeling the weapon in his hands, loading the round, lining up the perfect shot, and putting a bullet in the assigned target. The sequence of movements seemed to him utterly disconnected from the result. So shooting a lost kitten meant no more to him than shooting a rabid badger. He didn't crave killing, but he stepped up to whatever challenge was set before him. In time, and with sufficient practice, he would learn to kill people with the same professional objectivity.

The boy also proved to be an excellent student in the classroom and was especially adept at learning languages. By age 11 he spoke reasonably good English and adequate German. Two years later he could speak English better than many American children his age, and his command of German was well above average. His favorite subject, however, was art, particularly photography. For a number of worthwhile reasons his instructors strongly encouraged him in this regard, and in short order he enjoyed shooting with a camera almost as much as he enjoyed shooting with a rifle. It was all about process, focus, and impeccable results.

His academic success, though impressive, was nothing compared to his athletic achievements. He was known as a driven, often brutal competitor who demanded perfection of himself. By the time he turned 15 the other boys, including the 17-year-olds, had dropped his first name altogether and had begun referring to him respectfully only as Volkov, a Russian derivative of the word *volk,* or *wolf.* As a runner he knew no peer at any distance, short or long. He could lift more weight than any of the other boys. On the wrestling mat he was a serious danger to his opponents, three of whom suffered broken bones while testing themselves against the Wolf. But it was *systema*, a native Russian martial art, that most attracted him. It was a blend of striking, blocking, and throwing techniques that combined elegance and deadly force in one efficient package, and the other boys in Volkov's group suffered for his passion. He easily overpowered every opponent, sent four to the hospital, and eventually was allowed to train only with Colonel Viktor Ryzhkin, a 200-pound brute who wore heavy padding and headgear whenever he worked with Volkov.

In sum, he was the finest product the Motherland Project had ever created. He was a natural leader with an immense array of talents, and at the same time he was grateful to his core for the remarkable care the Soviet Union had provided for him throughout his childhood. Indeed, Volkov felt he owed more than he could ever repay, and on his 18th birthday, when he officially left the Motherland Project, he vowed to devote his life to state service.

He had no doubt that greatness awaited both him and Russia.

9.

"Okay, so you *think* you know his name, you *think* you know who he works for, but you're *sure* he can help us," Gimble said as she and Nazareth sipped their coffee in Amtrak's business-class car. Both of them hoped the day's trip to and from D.C. would shed some light on the deaths of Russian dissidents in New York City, but Gimble was still a bit fuzzy on the details.

"Well, precisely who he is and who he works for are sort of irrelevant," her husband smiled.

"Meaning you really have no clue?"

"Tell you what. I'll give you everything I've got on him," he offered, "and then you can judge whether he'll be able to take an educated guess on who might have murdered Sergey Gerasimov. Fair enough?"

"Perfectly fair. I like solving puzzles."

"Then you'll love this one."

The story began 15 years earlier in Mandali, Iraq, roughly five miles from the country's eastern border with Iran, at a military airstrip that officially didn't exist. This didn't matter since young Captain Nazareth and his Marine buddies also officially didn't exist. Neither did the quiet guy who went by the name Dalton Stark.

The mission for Nazareth and his team was to deliver Stark safely to a spot in the sky just outside Qom, Iran, some 450 miles away. If all went as planned, the Marines on board the stealth-modified OV-10 Bronco aircraft would never touch the ground or fire a shot. They would simply watch as Stark parachuted into the night to tackle a covert mission with potentially huge geopolitical implications. If, on the other hand, things went wildly wrong, Nazareth and his men were to protect Stark with their lives and somehow extract him from Iranian territory.

Nazareth and Stark had gotten to know each other reasonably well over the space of three days as they waited in the Iraqi desert for clear skies over Qom, Iran. The guy was a civilian employee of the U.S. government with a GS-15 pay grade, meaning he was the equivalent of a full colonel. But precisely what branch of the government he served was something he never revealed. Although he had been ferried to the airstrip by an Air Force jet, he made it clear to Nazareth he wasn't "one of them."

"Who do you think he worked for?" Gimble asked.

"No telling. The U.S. spends more than $50 billion every year on black-budget programs, most of which are designed to eliminate threats. But here's the thing," he added. "Only a handful of people in D.C. actually know what those threats are since they're all top secret. And the programs targeting those threats are beyond top secret. Furthermore, the people who run those programs are way, way off the radar. They basically don't exist."

"So Dalton Stark was a phantom?"

"Pretty much. Nice guy, careful about what he said, and clearly very capable. By that I mean he was smart as hell and was also fit beyond belief. For example, I knew a lot of guys who could do 100 chin-ups in an hour, but Stark could do 100 in a row and then immediately bang out 100 push-ups. He did this outdoors when the temperature was 115."

"But never hinted about his background?"

"Nope. At the time he worked out of Bolling Air Force Base, which is where the Defense Intelligence Agency was headquartered, but he never mentioned the name of his organization."

"And you didn't ask?"

Nazareth laughed. "Junior captains don't interrogate full colonels. Besides, I knew this entire operation was above my pay grade. He did offer me a little background on how he got involved in government service, but beyond that all I got was a phone number in D.C. in case I ever needed to reach him."

"And you called him to set up today's meeting?"

"Well, I called the number. The woman who answered just took my name and gave me a day, time, and place."

"That's it?"

"That's it."

"So where are we meeting him?"

"An apartment near the corner of 15th Street NW and F Street NW."

Gimble did a quick double-take. "That's right across the street . . ."

"From the White House, yes." He shrugged. "That's all I know. The woman didn't mention Stark's name, and she didn't ask why I wanted to see him. All I said was I needed to speak with him, and she set this up."

"Spooky."

"As in *spook,* right."

"You said he gave you some background on how he got involved with the government."

"Yeah, I think it was sort of a cautionary tale," Nazareth nodded. "He knew I was wondering what I'd do when I left the Marines, and he was letting me know to choose my career wisely."

"You think he wasn't happy with what he was doing?" she asked.

"No, I actually think he loved whatever it was he was doing. But he seemed to be letting me know that the path he took was a bit complicated in some ways."

"For instance?"

"For instance, he told me he was recruited mid-way through his senior year of college," he explained, "and within a week was given a list of people he could no longer associate with. One of them happened to be the girl he was dating."

"You can't be serious. Why would the government care about who he was dating, for God's sake?"

"Because she had been identified as a security risk. Her parents had been born in Ireland and were considered Irish Republican Army sympathizers. That was enough. He could either drop the girl," he said, "or drop the career."

"So he chose the career."

"He chose fighting the Soviet Union. Remember," he added, "at the time he signed on a lot of people thought World War III was just around the corner. In that context saying goodbye to a girlfriend was an acceptable decision."

"I'm not sure I like your friend Dalton Stark," Gimble replied, shaking her head.

"Like him or not, it's guys like Dalton Stark who make the world safe for the rest of us."

Gimble seemed skeptical. "Care to tell me how he makes the world safe for us?"

Nazareth paused, weighing his words carefully. "I can't give you all the details, Tara, but I can give you a few."

"Okay."

"Back to our mission in the Middle East. Dalton parachuted into Iran a few miles east of the rural mountain village of Fordow, which is maybe 25 or 30 miles south of Qom. Fordow, coincidentally, is where Iran was at the time operating a top-secret underground uranium enrichment plant. By some estimates," he added, "that plant would have been able to produce a ton of weapons-grade nuclear material within three years."

"I've read about Fordow, but what I heard about came years later."

"In 2009, to be exact. The episode I'm talking about came earlier and was hardly noticed," he said, "because it was mentioned only briefly by the Iranian news agency. Two days after Dalton Stark jumped out of our aircraft a man by the name of Ahn Chol-Su died after throwing himself off the roof of a building in Fordow."

"Ahn Chol-Su doesn't sound too Iranian."

"Correct. He was a North Korean nuclear scientist who had been living in Fordow and lending his expertise to the Iranian effort."

"Got it."

"But here's the really interesting part. This detail was filed a few days later by a BBC reporter who was briefly jailed and then expelled from Iran for his efforts. The North Korean scientist had somehow managed to strangle himself with a nylon cord before leaping from the roof."

"**DEAD MAN CLIMBS TO ROOF AND JUMPS**," Gimble laughed. "Now that's a headline you don't see every day."

"Almost never," he grinned.

"Mr. Dalton Stark at work?"

"Your words, not mine."

The apartment Nazareth and Gimble entered in Washington later that morning was a first-class space with a world-class view. Dalton Stark had answered the doorbell himself and motioned them toward a living room whose floor-to-ceiling windows looked out to the White House grounds. Stark was a picture of calm, as dangerous people often are. Dark brown hair, alert green eyes, and a healthy tan on his rugged face. He stood 6-3 and weighed just under 200 pounds, all of it muscle. This was not your typical 60-year-old.

"It's great to see you again, Pete," he said warmly, "and very nice to meet you, Tara. Congratulations on your recent marriage." Neither detective was surprised to find that Stark knew more about them than they knew about him.

"Are you always this well informed, Mr. Stark?" she smiled.

"Dalton," he replied. "And, yes, I stay as well informed as I can. I'm a huge fan of you and Pete. You've done some great work together, and I fully expect you to solve this latest thing with Sergey Gerasimov."

"The woman I spoke with the other day never asked why we were coming," Nazareth said, plainly surprised by the mention of Gerasimov, "and I never mentioned the case we're working on."

"You didn't come here for a White House tour, did you?" he chuckled.

"Right again," Nazareth said.

"Well, that's why we're meeting here at my home instead of at the office," Stark explained. Anything we discuss over there is on the record, and today's conversation can't be on the record. Agreed?"

"Absolutely," Nazareth nodded.

"Good. Okay, you're wondering whether Sergey Gerasimov's assassin is a Russian operative. Am I correct?"

Nazareth and Gimble tried, but failed, not to look stunned. "Yes, but how in the hell could you possibly know that?" Nazareth answered.

"Because you and I think somewhat alike, Pete, as I learned years ago. You don't look for the easiest answer, which explains why you're able to solve so many complex cases. And in this instance," he added, "the easiest answer is that Gerasimov was a random victim of some gun-toting New York City lunatic. But that's the wrong answer."

"You think it's likelier he was killed for political reasons," Gimble asked.

"Absolutely. As far as I'm concerned the only question is who exactly would the Russians allow to pull the trigger? And that," he said, "is why you're here." It was a statement of fact, not a question. "Let's have some coffee and move out to the balcony. It's a beautiful day."

"It's also much more difficult for someone to eavesdrop when we're outdoors, correct?" Nazareth grinned.

"Direct hit."

Nazareth and his host grabbed mugs of strong black coffee while Gimble opted for ice water with a slice of lemon. As they strolled onto the large shaded balcony Stark answered a question that was on his guests' minds.

"I'm a little jealous of folks like you who are still getting it done in the field," he offered. "Now they pay me more to do less."

"I take it you've moved on to senior management," Nazareth said.

"You need to be wary of the word *management* in my business because it implies a measure of control that doesn't actually exist. I can manage things like training and operational priorities for my team," he explained, "but once the actual missions go live all I can do is sit back and hope they turn out well."

"And you miss being the guy who makes sure they go well," Gimble said.

"Most definitely. I can still do 98% of what I once did in the field," he told them somewhat wistfully, "but the operational standard is 100%. Anything less is unacceptable, and the reality is I've gotten older."

"Also wiser," Nazareth laughed.

"Oh, yeah. You don't cheat death as often as I have and not get wiser, Pete. And I'm certainly wise enough to know I've got a good deal here in Washington. What I do is still important. The enemies change, but the mission remains the same."

"Can I ask if you're married, Dalton?" Gimble said.

"Thirty-seven years in October. Beth's in Tokyo for a couple of months right now, and she won't be happy she missed you two."

"I take it you've told her something about us," Nazareth said.

"I told her about a young Marine captain who saved my butt in the Middle East, and she took it from there. She says that following you two in the press is like reading a series of great crime novels."

"The news articles miss a lot of the gory details," Gimble told him.

"Yeah, but Beth has a wonderful imagination. She knows how things work between good guys and bad guys. Speaking of which, let me lay out what I'm thinking about Sergey Gerasimov's killer."

"That would be great," said Nazareth.

"Okay, here we go. He was killed by a .408 round, almost definitely from a CheyTac rifle."

"That was never made public," Gimble said, amused by Stark's candor.

"Correct," he nodded. "He used an American-made gun because he's too smart to keep his favorite Russian rifle in his home. The rifle he used to kill Gerasimov would have cost $25,000 or more when fully equipped for night work, and that price tag essentially rules out your run-of-the-mill street thug. So does the accuracy of the takedown. From that angle and distance only a pro could have scored a direct hit with a single shot."

"We all agree so far," Nazareth nodded.

"The next part requires a leap of faith. Would Russia send someone over here just to separate Sergey Gerasimov from his head? Answer: no. There are fewer than 10 agents in Russia who could do what this guy did, and I know who they are. I also know where they are at all times, and the Russians know I know. So scratch that idea."

"Consider it scratched," said Gimble.

"Would they have used a U.S. hit man for something like this? Absolutely not. First, they would never breach their security protocol by using a non-Russian shooter for something this sensitive. Way too risky. They can't afford to have the assassination of a man like Gerasimov traced back to President Ruslan Kotov. Second, the American shooters who might be willing to accept this sort of assignment aren't nearly as good as whoever killed Gerasimov. The best of them would have been damn lucky to score a torso shot under those conditions, and that particular guy was in Phoenix at the time."

"Okay, so where does that leave us?" Nazareth asked.

"In the worst possible situation, unfortunately. My educated guess is that you're looking for a Russian agent who's been in the U.S. for a long time, possibly longer than you two have been alive and probably longer than I've been on this job. He's completely invisible and most likely doesn't look, sound, or act Russian. His job is to blend in and strike when given the order."

"A sleeper?" Gimble asked.

"Technically no. A sleeper is someone who lives quietly in place and is then activated at some point for one specific mission. The guy you're looking for," Stark said, "has probably been active for quite some time. The Gerasimov hit was just his latest work."

Gimble showed Stark the list of 13 Russian dissidents whose deaths they had recently documented. "We've come up with a list of names and dates we think is revealing."

Stark quickly scanned the list and nodded. "I recognize all the names," he said, "and it's no coincidence they're all dead. Nine of them were outspoken dissidents who hated the Soviet Union, Russia, or both. Four of them were Soviet agents who had begun working for the U.S. We spent a little time trying to find the person who killed the four agents, but we had to move on. Our plates are always too full, unfortunately."

"Does it seem reasonable to you that the same person would operate quietly and discreetly for all those years and then suddenly blow someone away with a high-powered rifle on a New York City street?" Gimble asked.

"Doesn't surprise me. This guy knows we don't have a clue about his identity, so he's free to work however he wants. And in this case he was sending a strong message to Gerasimov's friends here in the U.S. I would expect him to go back to subtlety now that the high-priority target has been eliminated."

"Any reason to think he may target someone else soon?" Gimble wondered. "If this is the same guy who killed the 13 others, he generally lies low for a long time between victims."

"Hard to say, Tara. There's a lot of infighting going on at the top in Russia right now," he offered, "and Kotov is particularly dangerous with his back to the wall. This could mean he's especially intolerant of criticism at the moment. If that's the case, Gerasimov's death could simply be the first in a cluster of assassinations. You won't know until they either happen or they don't."

"Lucky us," Nazareth groaned. "Should we assume he's getting his orders directly from Moscow?"

"You won't like my answer much, but I think it's the correct one," Stark told him. "I'd say there's a reasonable chance this guy is operating all alone. This would be standard procedure with a deep-cover agent because it seriously reduces the risk of discovery. As I said before, you could very well be dealing with someone who's been in the U.S. for years, even decades, and managing his own program. We all do it this way, Pete, and it works really well."

"So we just follow the trail of bodies?" Nazareth said, clearly exasperated.

"That's one way," Stark replied. "The other is to keep a close eye on all other prominent dissidents in New York City and hope you notice some small detail that seems out of place, since you're certainly not going to see anything terribly obvious. I can virtually guarantee you the killer is well outside New York City's Russian community and passes for American extremely well. But he's human, therefore makes mistakes."

"We need some luck, Dalton," Nazareth said.

"Hard work trumps luck, Pete. You and Tara will make this guy go away."

"I love your confidence," Gimble smiled.

"You've both earned it," Stark said seriously. "If you two ever get bored in Manhattan, I can liven things up for you."

They could tell Stark wasn't kidding.

10.

Resnick crept warily out of the mangrove forest, an impossibly complex tangle of roots rising from the tidal mud of Sanibel's northern shoreline along Pine Island Sound. His heavy gear complicated the passage, and one wrong step could easily produce a broken leg or worse. He knew that no one would hear a drowning man out here.

Yet he was elated by the fruit of his morning's effort. He had set up in the dark at 5:40 a.m., savored the spectacular crimson and burnt-orange Florida sunrise at 7:09, and then spent an hour and a half shooting all the birds on his list: great blue heron, black-bellied plover, roseate spoonbill, and even a magnificent swooping osprey that had been about to sink her talons into a seven-pound redfish. *Think before you shoot* was his mantra, and on this morning he clearly had thought extremely well. Nearly every shot had been flawless.

Alex Resnick was very good at what he did.

As he stepped softly into the tall grasses near the water's edge he stayed alert for alligators. They grew big here in the J.N. "Ding" Darling National Wildlife Refuge, as much as 12 feet long and 800 pounds, and were most definitely at the top of the food chain. A solitary man, on the other hand, was somewhere near the bottom.

A tall, wiry sort with craggy features and silver hair, Resnick rarely worried about threats of any kind. Behind the icy gray eyes was a brain that worked faster and far more efficiently than most, allowing him to maintain control even when confronting what he liked to call *unbalanced* situations. By anticipating trouble he remained virtually immune to it. In this present instance, for example, he knew that the best defense against an alligator is seeing the creature before it sees you. And this is what he planned to do. If that failed, his next option would be running.

An alligator's top speed is generally no more than 11 miles per hour, and then only for a short burst. Even though Resnick had recently turned 65 he could still run 100 meters in 13 second flat, or roughly 17 miles per hour. So he was confident he could outrun any gator he might encounter.

The third and best option, of course, was a gun powerful enough to stop an alligator.

"Hey, there, Mr. Resnick. How'd you make out today?" Mary Sue Landers was already climbing from the Jeep to meet him. Her long brunette hair flowed casually over the shoulders of her light tan uniform top, and her welcoming smile seemed a bit out of place on someone who looked perfectly comfortable wearing a large handgun on her belt. But the 27-year-old federal wildlife officer genuinely liked Resnick, whom she had met a week earlier when he arrived at the refuge for his initial briefing. He had all the necessary permits, understood the rules, and went about his business quietly and professionally. She had been pleased to make sure he wasn't pestered by tourists during his working hours.

"Just fine, Mary Sue. Perfect morning in every way," he replied. "In fact, I think I'm finished here. I've gotten every bird on the list as well as some spectacular sunrises. I can't imagine the editor not being pleased."

"Well, if you're pleased," she smiled, "I have no doubt the editor will be. The whole staff here has been excited about having you with us, and we can't wait to see how this all turns out."

Resnick had been hired by *Vanishing Wilderness*, one of the world's most prestigious conservation magazines, to document the natural riches of Sanibel, in particular the J.N. "Ding" Darling refuge that occupies 6,400 acres of the small barrier island on Florida's Gulf Coast. Of those 6,400 acres roughly 2,800 have been designated by the U.S. Congress as a federal wilderness area, meaning they are to be preserved forever in their natural state. The magazine planned to devote at least 10 pages of an upcoming issue to Sanibel's pristine beauty, so hiring one of the most highly regarded photographers in America was a no-brainer.

Resnick had already made a name for himself as a young, highly adventurous nature photographer by the time he convinced the great Ansel Adams to take him on as an apprentice. That was in early 1979, when Adams was 77 and firmly established as America's greatest landscape photographer. Although they had worked together for only six months, Resnick came away from the experience with the kind of knowledge no book or classroom could ever have provided. He was forever after in awe of the master, and he was deeply honored to be in the audience when President Jimmy Carter presented Ansel Adams with the Presidential Medal of Freedom in June, 1980.

"I have something for you, as a matter of fact," Resnick said as he set down the black waterproof box containing a small fortune in equipment, including a $45,000 Hasselblad digital camera equipped with a $5,000 telephoto lens. "I think you're going to like this, Mary Sue." He pulled a large cardboard-reinforced envelope from the case and handed it to her.

"What's this for, Mr. Resnick?" she asked.

"For helping make my visit here so pleasant. I will not forget your kindness, and I hope you'll remember our time working together."

"You don't need to worry about that," she laughed sweetly. "We've all been honored to have you here." The photo she pulled from the envelope rendered her speechless for perhaps the first time in her life. Resnick had captured a great blue heron standing alongside its nest, her elegant long neck arched regally above the five fledglings and her magnificent wings dramatically outstretched toward the golden morning sky. The image was signed *A. Resnick* at the lower right.

"Oh, my God," she said breathlessly. "Is this the heron . . .?"

"Yes, this is the one we saw fly overhead the first day you showed me around the refuge. I had a feeling she might be heading toward a nest over by the mangroves, and I was right. I took this picture two days later."

"But this is too much, Mr. Resnick."

"Not at all. You helped make this an extremely productive trip, and I want you to share in the results."

She leaned forward and hugged him. "Thank you so much, Mr. Resnick. This will have a place of honor in my home forever."

"And I will forever remember Sanibel and you," he nodded.

This had, in fact, been one of the most enjoyable assignments of his long and illustrious career. Getting paid handsomely to do something he loved was a gift in itself, and Resnick's daily fee of $5,000 plus expenses made his lifelong passion for nature photography extremely satisfying. In addition, the work generally required him to visit some of America's most breathtaking locations, hardly a challenge for a man as curious and observant as he was. The Grand Canyon, Muir Woods, Glacier National Park, Hawaii's Na Pali Coast, and countless similar places had come before the Sanibel assignment, and he had enjoyed them all.

But he was truly taken by this small Florida island, where an astonishing 68% of the acreage remained protected as conservation land. A lifelong romantic, he believed in preserving not just nature but also things like old values: respect for authority, loyalty to one's roots, and selflessness among them. Much about the modern world troubled him greatly, so a place like Sanibel, where wilderness matters more than the next new housing development, appealed to his sense of priorities. If he had a choice, this was the sort of place where he could live happily ever after in fairy tale fashion.

Fairy tales, however, played no role in Resnick's life. One assignment was almost over, and others awaited him. This afternoon at his expansive rented home on West Gulf Drive he would select the best of the week's photographs and email them to the editor of *Vanishing Wilderness.* Then in the evening he would retreat to the raised deck overlooking the dunes and toast the glorious sunset with a glass of his beloved Jewel of Russia vodka.

Tomorrow would arrive soon enough. An early flight should have him back at his apartment before noon. And if the weather cooperated he might sit on his balcony with a light lunch and watch the Hudson River make its way relentlessly to the sea.

11.

The day began badly for Grigori Vasilyev. Just after sunrise he took a call from Ruslan Kotov himself, and the Russian president was incensed.

"No one in Moscow can tell me who killed Sergey Gerasimov," Kotov began, not wasting time on a polite greeting. "Perhaps I should have asked you first."

Serving as Russia's consul general in New York City was on most days a highly enjoyable job with excellent perks. Dealing with President Kotov wasn't one of them. The tyrant was as appealing as a wild boar and far more dangerous, and Vasilyev expected no good to come of this conversation.

"Mr. President, I am sure no one here at the consulate had anything to do with Gerasimov's death." In fact, he was not at all sure, since he distrusted his staff as much as his staff distrusted him. He had an especially bad feeling about Ilya Petrenko, the consulate's security chief, but he had no evidence the man was a traitor, an SVR agent, an assassin, or anything other than what he appeared to be. "No one on my staff admired the man, but neither did anyone have a reason to kill him."

"The fact that he was an outspoken traitor was not reason enough?" Kotov demanded.

"What I meant, Mr. President, is that no one had the proper authority."

"And yet Gerasimov is dead."

Vasilyev was shaking so badly he could barely hold the telephone to his ear. He could easily imagine armed thugs dragging him from his desk and beating a confession out of him. And of course he would confess. Everyone confesses, especially the innocent. They always break first, in fact. But despite his confession he would still be killed, an example to all others who might presume to challenge the president's authority.

Over the past several months Russian dissidents in America had begun referring to Kotov as the Dark Lord, and Vasilyev suddenly understood why. The man had an almost supernatural ability to fill even his loyal supporters with dread. If this is what hell might be like, the aging diplomat wanted no part of it.

Vasilyev had already occupied the New York consular post for three years, more than enough time to amass a small fortune from his frequent sideline dealings with local politicians, contractors, and real-estate moguls. As consul general he possessed the unique ability to open doors for those who hungered after "Russian connections," and for the right price he stood ready to play doorman for discrete opportunists. He had wisely spread his fortune among a handful of healthy banks in Panama, Bermuda, and the Cayman Islands, planning for a day when he might need to disappear in a hurry. Costa Rica was at the top of his list, but he had also heard good things about Uruguay and the bikini-clad women at Punta del Este.

"He is indeed dead, Mr. President. And I will do whatever I can to identify his killer if that is what you want."

"Of course that's what I want," Kotov hissed. It was a serpent's voice dripping with venom. Vasilyev's breakfast rose to the back of his throat, and he swallowed hard to keep it down.

"Mr. President, I will begin working on this today."

"That's not as good as yesterday, Vasilyev, but I suppose it will have to do." With that Kotov hung up, leaving his man in New York to wonder precisely how he could find a Russian assassin when someone with Kotov's immense and far-reaching power had been unable to do so. Costa Rica was looking better.

Vasilyev had barely composed himself when his secretary knocked on the ornate oak door to say that two NYPD detectives were in the lobby asking to speak with him about Sergey Gerasimov's murder.

"They cannot force their way in here!" he snapped at the young woman.

"Yes, sir. They know that," she said meekly. "Security said they were very polite and simply hope they might have a few minutes of your time."

"Why do they think I can help them with this? Did they tell anyone that?"

"I don't know, sir. But I will ask." She turned to walk away.

"No, Ekaterina, don't do that." He gave the matter some thought as he looked out the window far into the distance. "Who cares, right? I have nothing to hide."

"Of course not, sir."

"Fine, then. Have Petrenko bring them to the sitting room after he puts their weapons in the safe. Then get us some tea."

"Yes, sir. Of course."

By the time security chief Ilya Petrenko escorted the two detectives upstairs Vasilyev had regained control of himself. In fact, it now occurred to him that their presence might be a fortunate accident of fate. President Kotov wanted the name of Gerasimov's killer, and perhaps the Americans could provide it. Vasilyev was not eager to abandon his comfortable Manhattan lifestyle just yet and would gladly do whatever he could to help the NYPD track down a rogue assassin.

Nazareth and Gimble entered an enormous panelled room adorned with extravagant gold trim, and everywhere they looked they found reminders of Russia's early czarist grandeur. The consulate building at 9 East 91st Street was a gleaming Renaissance-style limestone structure originally built as a palatial home in 1903 by one of Manhattan's most prominent families. Purchased by the U.S.S.R. in 1975, the building then sadly stood vacant between 1979 and 1992 because of political turmoil and therefore required extensive renovation before it could be used.

Press accounts suggested that 16 of Russia's finest craftsmen lived in the future consulate for two years while restoring every square centimeter of the place to its former glory. More rigorous assessments by three different U.S. national-security agencies indicated that only 12 of the Russians were skilled laborers while the others were actually top-level spies. Furthermore, those same agencies agreed that during the restoration period the Russians had succeeded in creating an elaborate underground tunnel system stretching nearly 300 yards toward the eastern shore of the Central Park Reservoir. Precisely why they had done so would never be known. No matter. The tunnel had been discovered, and both sides chose to act as though the incident had never occurred.

"Thank you for seeing us, Mr. Vasilyev," Nazareth said as he introduced himself and Gimble. "We know you're extremely busy, and we appreciate having some time with you."

"It is my great pleasure, detectives. I'm sure you know that Sergey Gerasimov was an extremely important member of the Russian community, and it is tragic that one so young and talented was murdered on the streets of this great city." He turned to his security chief. "Thank you for bringing them, Ilya."

"My pleasure, sir," Petrenko said as he turned and walked away.

"Our investigation continues, of course," Nazareth began, "but we have not yet turned up any meaningful clues to the killer's identity. One thing we're fairly certain of, though, is that this was not a random act. We believe a lot of planning went into the crime and that Mr. Gerasimov was the specific target."

"Do you have any theories on why someone would want him dead?"

"Unlimited theories," Nazareth nodded, "but nothing that stands out from the rest. Someone might have been jealous of his success, or angry over a bad business deal, or unhappy with his recent comments about the Russian president."

"Ah, yes, of course," Vasilyev chuckled. "You think perhaps a Russian spy killed him?"

"That's just one of countless theories, sir," Gimble smiled. "At this point we can't rule out anything."

"Well, I can assure you there are no evil Russians from a James Bond movie running around New York killing innocent people, detectives," he laughed. "My country is a democracy, same as yours, and freedom of speech is sacred to us. Sergey Gerasimov was critical of President Kotov, as we all know, but that would absolutely never have produced this sort of tragedy. This is not how Russia works."

"Can you think of any reason someone within New York's Russian community might have wanted him dead?" Nazareth asked.

"I am as uncertain as you are, detective, but I have been told that Gerasimov had a passion for gambling. There's nothing wrong with that, especially for someone who had as much money as he did," Vasilyev noted, "but it has occurred to me that perhaps his gambling led to some bad blood between him and the wrong people."

"Do you think his gambling may have involved criminals somehow?" Gimble wanted to know.

"This is only a theory, of course, but I strongly doubt that everyone who wants to gamble drives to a casino in Atlantic City all the time. I'm sure many people in this city place their bets through illegal operations of some sort. If Gerasimov did so, then yes, he may have run afoul of criminals."

"There are countless gambling rings in New York City," Nazareth noted, "including several in Brighton Beach."

"Sadly, yes, detective. It's no secret that certain Russian immigrants in Brooklyn do things that don't endear them to those of us who serve our great country. I must emphasize that I have no specific information on whether such thugs had something to do with Gerasimov's death, but it would not surprise me in the least."

"That's a helpful thought," Nazareth told him, "and we'll check on that possibility. May I ask whether you or members of your staff ever had dealings with Mr. Gerasimov?"

"No official meetings, if that's what you mean," Vasilyev answered. "I'm sure he and I must have crossed paths a number of times at parties here in Manhattan since we had many of the same acquaintances. As I said before, he was an important man within the Russian community. But he and I never would have stopped to chat with each other."

"Understood," Nazareth nodded. "Can you tell me whether the consulate maintains files on prominent Russians in New York? Things like news articles, letters, or maybe some photographs from the parties you mentioned? It would be extremely helpful to identify people who were closest to him."

"No, detective. In our computers we have many thousands of visa files, but nothing of the sort you're after. The consulate serves a narrow function. We don't keep track of people in the way you've suggested."

After 20 minutes the detectives were finished with their strong tea and Vasilyev's weak answers. The consul general seemed willing to help but hadn't offered much other than the notion of a gambling-related motive for Gerasimov's death. They would, in fact, ask their colleagues in Brooklyn to find out what they could inside the Brighton Beach gambling rings. But nothing Nazareth and Gimble had heard drew them away from the idea of a politically motivated assassination. They retrieved their weapons at the security desk and headed out into the September sunshine.

"Did you realize that freedom of speech is sacred in Russia?" Gimble joked.

"Well, I always thought that was the case, Tara," he answered sarcastically, "but it was heartening to hear the consul general confirm that for us."

"And I was delighted to hear they don't keep files on Russians in New York."

"Oh, yeah, I heard that."

"Pure crap, Pete. I'm willing to bet my last dime they have extensive files on every Russian in the city, especially the dissidents."

He shook his head. "I won't take that bet. We both know they have a big fat file on Gerasimov."

"I'd love to take a peek inside the consulate's computer."

"Now there's an idea," he grinned.

12.

On the day Volkov turned 18 in 1969 he left the Motherland Project's relatively genteel surroundings and boarded a military turboprop bound for Vorkuta, a Russian coal-mining town just north of the Arctic Circle and one of the most inhospitable spots on the planet. The first phase of his adult training would take place at a primitive gray compound surrounded by barbed wire in a program known simply as прочность, or *strength*. For three months, January through March, he would be called upon to prove his devotion to the Soviet Union by enduring a course of instruction so harsh that during the years of its operation nearly a third of all participants left either maimed or in body bags.

Each day began at 4:30 a.m. with calisthenics, running, and unarmed-combat drills. After that the candidates hit the classroom for intensive instruction in foreign languages, politics, and spycraft. Finally, by 3:30 p.m. the group was ready for outdoor military training on rugged terrain and in unimaginably severe weather.

The record low temperature during Volkov's visit came in mid-February, when the thermometer registered minus 54 degrees Fahrenheit. This happened to coincide with a field exercise that required each of the 10 trainees to hike five miles through knee-deep snow, build a shelter in the forest, and live off the land for two full days. Each trainee was on his own, equipped only with a rifle, a combat knife, 5 wooden matches, and the winter clothing he wore.

Six men turned back within four hours and spent the next seven days on limited rations because of their cowardice. Three others froze to death by noon the next day and had small achievement medals tacked to their pine boxes before they were buried. Volkov alone completed the mission. He returned to camp on the third day with a pair of roasted rabbits hanging from his belt and the pelts of two gray wolves wrapped around his upper body for extra warmth. He had found the solitude refreshing, he told the camp commandant, and swore he could have lived comfortably through the remainder of that winter.

His next assignment brought him to Leningrad, today's Saint Petersburg, less than 100 miles south of the Finnish border. Here he spent two years perfecting his English and German, mastering unarmed combat skills, and participating in dozens of successful KGB-led operations designed to undermine the government of Finland. In every conceivable way Volkov proved to be cool under fire and ruthlessly efficient in carrying out orders to the letter. He prided himself on being a doer, not a planner, and thus became an ideal candidate for some of the Soviet Union's most high-profile assignments.

Over the next four years he moved frequently both within and outside of Soviet-bloc countries, sometimes posing as a tourist and sometimes serving temporarily as a junior bureaucrat in a variety of Russian businesses or government offices. Regardless of the cover story he invariably had one mission only: executive action. Under the auspices of the KGB's 13th department of the intelligence directorate, Volkov was a trained killer who eliminated no fewer than 25 individuals who had been identified as grave threats to the Soviet Union. He was a unique asset in two respects: he never presumed to ask whether a particular target deserved to die, and his success rate was one hundred percent.

At first he applied his skills in places like Ukraine, Poland, Romania, Czechoslovakia, and Hungary, demonstrating an admirable willingness to work in any setting and with any method. Although he favored long guns, especially the powerful Dragunov SVD sniper rifle, he proved to be equally adept with pistols, knives, explosives, poisons, or his own two strong hands. After mastering his technique he moved on to higher-risk operations in Greece, Germany, France, and England, serving with distinction and ultimately earning for himself one of the most prized positions of all.

Volkov became one of five men sent to the United States as part of a global program to eliminate threats to the Soviet Union by whatever means necessary. In the words of his KGB handler, he would become a *resident disrupter* who operated totally alone and almost always on his own initiative. For security reasons he would essentially cease to exist. In fact, the only person in Russia who would know his identity and location was senior KGB officer Anatoly Bukarin.

The top-secret program was astonishing in that it placed virtually all responsibility in the hands of highly trusted agents who were almost completely off the grid. Each man in the program was given control of a well-funded Swiss bank account from which he could withdraw an amount equal to $35,000 in the first year, increasing thereafter by 5% annually. In Volkov's case this meant he now had access to more than $250,000 per year in addition to whatever he earned on his own.

Each man was given a simple set of operating rules. First, blend in and live as an American. Second, do what you know is best for the Soviet Union based upon your extensive training. Three, do not operate outside your assigned territory. Four, always be available for the prearranged contact with your handler. And five, if ever you cease to hear from your handler, continue the operation.

"For how long?" one of the men asked before departing for America.

His handler smiled. "Until the day you die, of course."

At 24 Volkov traveled to the United States on a forged German passport, quickly became a U.S. citizen, and began blending in nicely. Before long he was the sole remaining member of the original five "ghosts" who had come to America. One had died of a massive stroke after a short and miserable life in Chicago. The man in Miami had gotten his throat slit in an alley by a Cuban double agent and his body dumped deep within the

Everglades. Another had jumped from the top of 1100 Wilshire, a 37-story residential tower in Los Angeles, rather than be captured by a team of FBI agents. And the fourth was killed instantly by a Chevy pickup truck that had been carried half a mile by an EF5 tornado outside Dallas and dropped on his head.

In every way possible Volkov, the last man standing, was a successful American citizen except on those few occasions when he took a call from his handler, Anatoly Bukarin.

On the day he died Bukarin alone would know the Kirov Wolf prowled the streets of New York City. Everyone else would learn the hard way.

13.

Alex Resnick had grown accustomed to critical acclaim for his photography, yet he was unprepared for the lavish praise heaped upon him by Sandra Hodge-Cummings, the editor of *Vanishing Wilderness* magazine. She called late one morning from a lofty corner office on East 86th Street where she had gorgeous views of the Metropolitan Museum of Art to her left and the Central Park reservoir to her right.

"This is the most beautiful work I've seen in my 27 years as editor," said the woman who was widely known for her high expectations, sharp eye, and sometimes sharper tongue. "Your Sanibel photos will set a new standard for the magazine. I'm not easily impressed, Alex, but I must say I'm stunned."

"That's extremely kind, Sandra. May I assume the champagne's on you?" he joked.

"It's absolutely on me. In fact, that's why I'm calling."

He was a bit puzzled. "Really?"

"Yes. Earlier this morning I spoke with friends of mine at both the American Museum of Natural History and the Metropolitan Museum of Art about mounting a December exhibition of your Sanibel work," she told him breathlessly, "and they're ecstatic over the idea. This could be one of the most elegant fundraising events in recent memory."

The plan she laid out seemed like a winner for everyone concerned. Resnick's magnificent photos of Sanibel's abundant wildlife and rich natural habitats would be presented large, meaning at least three feet by five feet, at the two world-renowned museums that stood almost directly across from each other on the fringes of Central Park. Well-heeled guests would begin their Saturday evening with a 7:00 p.m. champagne reception at the Museum of Natural History and the first half of the Resnick show. They would then be conveyed by horse-drawn carriages across the park to the Metropolitan Museum of Art for the second half of the show in the Great Hall. This would be followed by a lavish sit-down dinner at the exotic Temple of Dendur exhibit, a reconstructed Egyptian monument dating back to 15 BC. The finale would be a live auction of five signed Resnick photos.

"Sounds like a highly ambitious event," Resnick said.

"Highly ambitious and highly worthwhile," she assured him. "If we publicize this properly and invite the right guests, we'll raise a half million for each museum and for the magazine. This could be a huge night for all three non-profit organizations just before the end of the year, when our wealthiest supporters are looking for tax deductions."

"Well, I'm certainly on board, if that's what you want to know. I'll gladly donate a few signed prints if that will help prime the pump."

"Oh, yes," she laughed, "that would definitely help prime the pump. But it will also be critical to have you in attendance, Alex. This doesn't work without you."

"I have some very important year-end shoots coming up, Sandra."

"Everything you shoot is important, Alex. We would work the date around your schedule, of course."

"Then that sounds fine. Just give me the dates that look best for you, and I'll do whatever I can to help you ring the cash register."

After the phone call Resnick scrolled through the calendar on his laptop to see exactly what December held in store. The main event would be a 10-day visit to Puerto Rico at the end of the month during which he would prepare a photo essay with the working title *Winter on the Island*. This one would be a labor of love, not only because he could enjoy 80-degree temperatures while everyone in Manhattan froze but because he was donating his time to help boost the island's tourism industry.

Also scheduled for December was his fourth visit to New York's Adirondack Forest Preserve, where he had recently begun working on a major *Seasons of the Adirondacks* project destined to become a stunning coffee table book by the following summer. After covering his costs, Resnick would be directing the book's sales proceeds to The Nature Conservancy to help preserve the wilderness area that gave him his start all those years ago.

Finally, he'd be shooting people. Although his primary artistic calling had been and always would be nature photography, he had been persuaded by the mayor himself to create a portfolio of cityscapes featuring the faces of men, women, and children who live, work, and play in Manhattan. The idea was to showcase the island as a home, not just a frantic treadmill for harried commuters. Precisely how much work he could get done on this project would depend on the weather, since he wanted some snow scenes in the mix. But regardless of the weather he would certainly do some shooting.

He had reached a point in his career at which he could afford to choose his paid assignments as he saw fit while also doing some pro bono work each year. He lived modestly but quite comfortably in an 800-square-foot one-bedroom condo near the corner of West and Bank Streets in Lower Manhattan. He had bought the place for less than $200,000 slightly more than 20 years ago, and he could now sell it for at least $1.5 million if he wanted. But he didn't. His large living room window offered a stunning panorama of the Hudson River, and he was no more than a five-minute walk to some of his favorite restaurants. Beyond this, of course, he would never need to sell the place in order to raise cash because he had more income than he could reasonably spend.

In celebration of the editor's kind words and the sunny September morning Resnick decided to take a long, vigorous walk along the Hudson River Greenway, the 11-mile-long paved path that sweeps along the river from the Battery to the George Washington Bridge. The air wasn't the best for exercising, but he had long since adjusted to life in Manhattan. He would enjoy the river views, the faces of people he passed along the way, and the opportunity to keep himself fit. For a man halfway between 60 and 70 he was in remarkably fine shape and did all he could to keep it that way. He ate and drank in moderation, kept decent hours unless working on a particularly challenging assignment, and managed to get a healthy dose of training every day.

He left his condo wearing a lightweight silver jogging suit and a pair of high-end New Balance running shoes, just in case his walk turned into something faster. A brisk breeze from across the river greeted him as he began heading north among the walkers, joggers, and bikers who shared both the morning and the pavement. The Jacob Javits Convention Center on West 34th Street seemed like a reasonable goal for this morning's jaunt. From there he could walk over to Jenny's Marketplace on 37th for a sandwich and coffee before turning back toward home. On second thought, he might just hoof it all the way up to Central Park. The day was still young, and it was all his.

For a man with an artist's eye every moment of a Manhattan day offers an abundance of riches. Sunlight gleaming on the water. Feathery clouds floating gently on the wind. A slender young woman with a $20,000 Luca Salvadori violin playing Vivaldi's *Autumn,* a bright red vase filled with $5 bills at her feet. Resnick drank it all in while maintaining a strong pace. His long, purposeful strides kept him moving considerably faster than other walkers and even a touch faster than some lumbering joggers.

He had food on his mind -- maybe pastrami on rye -- as he approached 23rd Street near the Chelsea Waterside Park and barely noticed the movement in a deserted area to his left. Something about the fleeting shape and its erratic motion struck a nerve, though later he would not be able to remember why. Instinct kicked in, and he ran toward whatever it was that had caught his attention.

Behind a broad pine tree with low, full branches two men in their early twenties had flung a young woman to the ground. One of them waved a knife toward her face while the other covered her mouth with his left hand and tore at her jogging shorts with his right. As Resnick drew nearer he saw terror in the woman's wide eyes and heard her muffled plea for help.

The punk with the knife was the smaller of the two at six feet and 180 pounds. He spotted Resnick and warned him off.

"Get lost asshole, or I'll cut your heart out."

His friend, a 6-3 bruiser built like an NFL linebacker, glanced disdainfully at Resnick and continued pawing at his victim. "Cut him, Mo," he commanded. "We ain't done here."

Mo sprang at Resnick and swung the 6-inch steel blade toward his throat, but the aging photographer showed no emotion as he calmly blocked the thrust with his right hand. He immediately stepped behind his attacker, locked his left arm under the guy's chin, and slammed his right forearm into the side of his head. The fierce blow was sufficient to knock Mo unconscious.

As the first would-be rapist fell to the turf his partner pushed away from the woman and began to rise toward Resnick. Rather than back off from his much larger opponent, Resnick lunged forward and locked a hand on each of the guy's ears while driving a powerful knee into his face. Unable to withstand the force generated by a muscular thigh moving at top speed, both ears separated swiftly and cleanly from the sides of his head, and he hit the ground screaming.

By the time the police arrived the young woman, a tourist from Italy, had calmed down enough to report what had happened. More to the point, she explained what had not happened thanks to Alex Resnick. She couldn't say for sure that other people had witnessed the attack and looked away, although she believed this had been the case. All she knew for sure was that she hadn't been raped, and possibly murdered, because her rescuer had been in the right place at the right time.

While officers were busy interviewing the victim and watching over her assailants, Resnick placed an urgent call to the mayor's office. Less than four minutes later Sergeant Charles Dudley's phone rang, and for the first time in his long career he found himself speaking to Chief of Department Matthew O'Bannon, the NYPD's top dog.

"Are you in charge of the crime scene, sergeant?" O'Bannon asked.

"Yes, sir. I'm the ranking officer here right now," Dudley answered.

"Good, then listen carefully. Mr. Resnick's name is not, I repeat, NOT to be shown in your report. Are we clear?"

"Yes, sir. But what name should I put down?"

"John Doe, Jim Smith, unidentified good samaritan," the chief huffed, "or anything else you want. Mr. Resnick doesn't want any publicity, and his very good friend the mayor promised to take care of it. So here we are."

"Who doesn't like good publicity?" Dudley asked.

"Not our job to ask, sergeant. Just make sure his name doesn't get out. If it does," he said ominously, "you and I will be talking again."

"I'll take care of it on my end, sir. No problem."

"Perfect."

The sergeant turned to Resnick, who clearly was ready to head back home. He was no longer in the mood for that pastrami sandwich.

"Mr. Smith," Dudley told him politely, "you're free to go."

Resnick flashed a pleasant smile. "Thank you, sergeant. You know how to reach me if it's absolutely necessary."

"Yes, sir, I guess I do. Nice work today."

Resnick nodded, then began walking south before any news crews showed up. The young woman called after him, but he pretended not to hear. He didn't need any complications in his life as a result of having done the right thing. Better, he thought, to leave this particular story out of his official biography.

Later that evening he did, however, watch a brief TV news account of the assault. The young Italian woman, Elisa DiConti, was shaken but fine. Ex-con Mo Tisdale was hospitalized with a fractured skull. And the other would-be rapist, Shaun Waxley, was in fair condition after surgeons had successfully reattached his left ear. The right ear, unfortunately, had been carried off by a seagull just before the ambulance arrived.

"But the big mystery remains," reporter Jenna Meyers intoned. "Who was it that came to Elisa DiConti's rescue? The police say the man disappeared before they could question him, and they are now hoping witnesses might be able to help them identify The Hero of 23rd Street."

Resnick shook his head in amazement as he thought back on all those early years when he craved publicity and worked fanatically to get it. Now when he neither needed or wanted it, publicity came looking for him.

Another of life's amusing ironies.

14.

Nazareth and Gimble felt they had wasted valuable time calling on the Russian consul general, so they decided to remedy that by paying a visit to novelist Feodor Sidorenko, a dissident whose profile was almost as high as that of the late Sergey Gerasimov. The meeting had been arranged by Prof. Alina Yesikova, who feared Sidorenko could be in grave danger if, in fact, whoever had murdered Gerasimov was already searching for his next victim.

As a young man Sidorenko had endured almost three years at a Soviet labor camp near Oymyakon, Russia, a tiny Siberian village whose record low temperature was nearly minus 90 degrees Fahrenheit. Reputed to be the coldest inhabited spot on the planet, Oymyakon was where you were typically given a grim choice: die of exposure or be worked to death by sadistic camp guards. Few prisoners left the place both alive and sane. Sidorenko was one of them.

He had been exiled to Oymyakon in part for expressing anti-Soviet views in his writing but mainly because he was deemed too smart for his own good. The Soviet bureaucrats of his day suffered from an incurable fear of intellectuals, especially those who openly expressed disapproving views about such things as government, law, and personal freedom. So men and women like Sidorenko were always at risk of being savaged by the system in a process that never varied: they were interrogated about their imaginary crimes, found guilty without even the pretext of a trial, shoved into an unheated boxcar, and sent down the tracks to some godforsaken outpost of the Gulag. It was not uncommon for those who survived the train ride to wish they hadn't.

What saved Sidorenko, ironically, was a camp guard's cruelty. One autumn day, when the temperature was several degrees below freezing, the guard ordered 25 of the male prisoners to work barefoot while unloading a rickety Bulgarian transport plane that had carried supplies to the outpost. After nearly an hour of laboring in severe conditions, some of the men began stumbling and falling, which in turn led to beatings. As the scene grew increasingly chaotic Sidorenko managed to slip under a canvas tarp in the plane's cargo hold. He was still hiding there when the aircraft took off two hours later for a return flight to Plovdiv, Bulgaria, where he began a harrowing but successful journey to Greece, then England, and finally the U.S., where he was granted political asylum.

Although Sidorenko professed to write fiction, everyone knew his novels were thinly disguised and achingly accurate representations of life under a repressive regime, and a long succession of Soviet and Russian leaders felt the sting of his words. But his latest book, the one that would perhaps clinch a Nobel Prize, had placed him dangerously at odds with Russian President Ruslan Kotov, whom he portrayed as a slobbering oaf who was overly fond of young girls. He named the character Boris Svinya -- свинья, or *svinya* for swine -- and in vivid detail made him look and act like the current Russian leader, who in fact was overly fond of young girls. Had Sidorenko still lived in Russia, he most likely would have disappeared late one night and never been heard from again. But since the author was safely situated in New York City, Kotov wisely decided not to have the man killed even though ordering his death would no doubt have made him feel wonderful.

When the detectives called on Sidorenko at his Upper East Side apartment they were immediately struck by the man's casual attitude toward the concern his good friend Alina Yesikova had expressed.

"Alina lives too much in the past," he said gently as he settled into a comfortable recliner. Nazareth and Gimble sat opposite him on a grand upholstered couch and sipped the cold Borjomi mineral water their host had set out for them. "She tortures herself with memories."

"How could she ever forget?" Gimble asked.

"Not *forget*," he corrected. "That's much too strong a word. Surely no one who experienced the Soviet horror will ever forget. But moving on is the only way to triumph over that madness. You must discipline yourself to look to the future instead of the past. This is absolutely necessary, detective, if you wish to enjoy peace in the present."

"So you don't think Prof. Yesikova should be worried about you after what happened to Sergey Gerasimov?" Nazareth wanted to know.

"I worry much more about crossing Fifth Avenue," he joked. "That is a far greater risk since I am no longer nimble enough to jump from the path of a speeding taxi." The detectives found the comment slightly at odds with reality since Sidorenko seemed exceptionally fit for a 73-year-old who had spent time in a Siberian labor camp. "I worry not at all about Russian assassins."

"What did you make of Gerasimov's death?" Nazareth asked.

"It lacked subtlety, and that's why I believe it could not have been ordered by Kotov. The man is a viper, deadly in the extreme. But he realizes the entire world watches what he does, so he keeps his dirty work hidden from view."

"If not a Russian assassin, who do you believe might have targeted Gerasimov?" Nazareth continued. He noticed without comment the antique rifle that hung in an expensive glass case on the wall behind Sidorenko.

"Why does anyone kill? Jealousy is the usual reason, detectives. Someone is jealous of your money, your position, your girlfriend, your success, and so on. But often," he added, "there is no clear motive at all. A madman with a gun decides to kill people, so he kills anyone who comes into view. This happens all the time in America, doesn't it?"

"More than we'd like," Nazareth answered, "but I get suspicious when the victim is such a high-profile figure. I'm not saying it can't happen, but it would represent a huge coincidence."

"And you don't believe in coincidences very much, do you?"

Nazareth smiled. "I'm paid to be suspicious, Mr. Sidorenko."

"And it no doubt serves you well in your line of work. But I believe you'll discover that in this instance you're dealing with random violence. My friend Gerasimov was killed by a crazy person who didn't really care whom he shot."

"I know you have some major appearances coming up," Gimble said.

"Always, yes. I speak more often than I would like," he chuckled, "but my publisher won't have it any other way. Book signings and TV appearances are draining but necessary. And then, of course, I am frequently invited to speak at universities throughout the United States. I do as many of those as I can because America's young people don't fully appreciate what things were like in Russia back then. Or today, for that matter."

"Are you active with Russian groups here in Manhattan?" Nazareth wondered.

"Dinner with friends," he shrugged, "and sometimes a larger gathering for a holiday or wedding anniversary. I avoid altogether those people who have a political agenda. Everything I need to know about politics is already in my head and in my books, so anyone who wonders what I'm thinking can find out quite readily."

"Mr. Sidorenko, we're concerned about your safety because some people believe you've pushed President Kotov too far with your comments about his interest in little girls," Gimble said flatly.

"Ah, but see, detective, this is hardly news to anyone familiar with the man. Everyone knows he has this problem, and he knows that everyone knows, so he ignores the topic completely. As far as he's concerned, if he doesn't respond, the problem doesn't exist."

"But what about people farther down the chain of command?" Gimble asked. "Isn't it possible someone would act on his own to protect Kotov?"

"Never. Kotov is in some ways unpredictable, but never when it comes to demonstrating ultimate power. Invading another country, starting a war, or having someone killed are the kinds of things he reserves for himself. No one would dare act without his approval."

"Which you believe Kotov would not have given in Sergey Gerasimov's case," said Gimble.

"Correct. Kotov is a remarkably evil and unbalanced individual, but he is an excellent manipulator of public opinion both at home and abroad. Murdering people like Gerasimov and me," he nodded, "would surely cost him support. Annexing a neighboring country, on the other hand, would actually bolster his standing with the average Russian."

"Understood," Nazareth said. "All I would ask, sir, is that you keep us in mind. If at any point in the near future you believe NYPD protection would be wise, all you need to do is call one of us."

"And I am profoundly grateful for this, believe me. Deep in my past was a police force that did everything *except* protect men like me. So having you and your colleagues ready to watch over me is a great blessing and comfort. That said, I feel quite safe here in New York City."

As soon as they reached the street following the interview Gimble asked the question that had gnawed at her for the past hour.

"What did you think of the gun on Sidorenko's wall?"

"Very impressive," he said. "Looked like an early Mosin-Nagant rifle, one of the most popular weapons ever manufactured in Russia. If Sidorenko's rifle is one of the originals, dating back to the late 1800s, it's probably worth a few bucks."

"Don't you think it's odd that a writer is into guns?"

"Not at all. I assume that when he was a young guy growing up in Russia he would have been a real oddball if he didn't hunt. And for the record," he grinned, "that gun didn't kill Sergey Gerasimov."

"Oh, I didn't think it did. But -- big BUT -- that doesn't need to be the only gun he owns. I'm not saying he killed Gerasimov," she argued, "but if he's the killer that would certainly explain why he's not afraid of being gunned down."

"Hey, you're even more suspicious than I am, Tara. This guy's being mentioned as a Nobel Prize winner for literature. That hardly seems like the assassin type."

"To quote Pete Nazareth, people aren't always what they seem to be."

"Okay, you've got me there. If you want to pursue this, I'm certainly willing to dig a little deeper into his background. But I think the gun is just an expensive relic that reminds him of his youth."

"You're probably right, but . . ."

"But you might be right too."

She laughed. "It's been known to happen."

15.

At 8:15 the next morning Deputy Chief Ed Crawford summoned the two detectives to his office and closed the door.

Nazareth put his hands up in mock terror. "Please don't make us drink the coffee, chief. We confess!" Gimble tried unsuccessfully to stifle a laugh.

"Hey, no problem," the chief groused. "You keep drinking that swill you buy out on the street corner, and I'll stick with the good stuff." He poured his fourth cup of the morning from the old electric pot behind his desk.

"But we're not here to chat about coffee, are we, chief?" Gimble asked.

"You must be a detective," he said seriously. "We've got a funny problem we need to discuss. And I'm not talking about funny as in ha ha." The chief's clarification was hardly necessary since he was known for not having much of a sense of humor, at least on the job.

"Okay, shoot," Nazareth said.

"There was a break-in last night at the Russian consulate, and someone stole what we're told were extremely confidential CDs. Very serious stuff, guys, especially since the U.S. and Russia aren't great pals right now."

"When did this happen?" Nazareth asked.

"About 1:30 a.m., they think. The consulate's security chief called it in, and we had officers from the one-nine precinct there for a couple of hours. But the real fun began at 6:30 this morning when I got a call from the forensics guys. Guess whose fingerprints they lifted from the crime scene."

"They got an ID?" Gimble asked.

"Yes, ma'am. Our very own Pete Nazareth."

Gimble was shocked, but Nazareth calmly said, "Then obviously someone at the consulate went to a lot of trouble to set me up."

The chief nodded. "Without question. Any ideas?"

"Oh, yeah. My guess would be Ilya Petrenko, the consulate's head of security. We had to check our weapons when we arrived," Nazareth explained, "and Petrenko must have lifted our prints for later use. Don't be surprised if Tara's turn up sooner or later."

"What do you think, Tara?" Crawford asked.

"Obviously Pete and I aren't dumb enough to break into the consulate," she offered, "but I can't imagine what Petrenko would gain by setting us up."

"Did anyone say specifically what files were stolen?" Nazareth asked.

Crawford shook his head. "Petrenko wouldn't say what was on the CDs, but they were somewhere in the consul general's private office."

"Okay, that would fit," Nazareth explained. "If the security chief didn't have access to those files but wanted them for some reason, he needed to set up someone else for the break-in."

"Why you?" Crawford wanted to know.

"Because we were there poking around, and that makes us plausible suspects. I'm sure Petrenko could sell that to his boss without much trouble since Vasilyev didn't seem all that happy about having us there."

"Or maybe they both want to keep us away for some reason," Gimble added, "and came up with this to discredit us."

"Either way," Crawford said, "it won't work. Maybe they thought we'd jump all over the planted evidence in order to maintain good relations with them. But that ain't gonna happen. We're not telling them whose prints we lifted, and they can't ask without implicating themselves."

"Since obviously they would have no way of knowing you found Pete's prints unless they put them there," Gimble added.

"Correct. I'm sick to death of all these goddamn diplomats in New York City who think they can get away with any crap whatsoever," Crawford huffed. "But this time they lose."

"If you want my gut reaction," Nazareth said, "this is all Petrenko. We didn't spend much time with him, but what little I saw I didn't like. He's an operator of some sort and has trouble disguising it. In any event the first thing I'd like to confirm is that something was actually stolen, and we should get that from the consul general himself, not from the security goon."

"I can call him right now if you want," Crawford said.

"No, I think a much better idea is to have Tara show up unannounced and ask for a quick audience with Vasilyev. If he'll see her," he reasoned, "I'm guessing Petrenko will sit in. It would be great to see how they're each reacting to this."

"You don't want to go?" Crawford asked.

"I'd love to go, but I can't while someone is trying to frame me for a burglary. Too many things could go sideways."

"For instance?"

"For instance they could lift my fingerprints from a doorknob today and compare them to the ones taken at the break-in. In that case," Nazareth argued, "they wouldn't need NYPD confirmation. They'd claim I was the person who broke in, right?"

"Okay, so Tara goes there and has the consul general confirm something was stolen. What then?"

"Two things. First, Tara pumps as hard as she can to find out what kinds of records were taken." He turned to his wife. "Are we talking personal emails or state secrets? That sort of thing. And second, she gets a read on Petrenko. What's really up with this guy? While she's doing that, I'll be getting some serious background on him from a friend in Washington."

"And you can do that quietly, away from official channels?" the chief asked.

"Absolutely. My friend wouldn't have it any other way."

An hour later Gimble left for the Russian consulate while Nazareth walked over to a small park across the street from One

Police Plaza. He sat in a shady spot on the stone wall that bordered the park's lush gardens and dialed Dalton Stark's private number in D.C.

"How's the weather in James Madison Plaza today, Pete?" Stark said energetically when he answered his friend's call.

"Just about perfect, Dalton, and I'm not going to bother asking how you know precisely where I am."

"Here's a hint. You're wearing a light blue button-down shirt, no tie, tan slacks, and a pair of cordovan penny loafers. Wait," he said, "let me guess. I'm going to say L.L. Bean loafers since you and Tara like all that outdoor stuff."

Nazareth would have been shocked had he been talking with anyone else, but he knew that the impossible was in all likelihood standard operating procedure with his mysterious friend.

"Can the satellite read my mind too?" Nazareth joked.

"What a fantastic idea!" Stark replied. He was in his office at the moment, seated comfortably at a large oak desk analyzing a field report that had just come in from Mashhad, Iran. On the wall behind him hung a tastefully elegant shadow box containing his Distinguished Intelligence Cross, the CIA's highest decoration, for his clandestine work in the agency's Special Operations Group.

"I could use some background on Ilya Petrenko, the security chief at the Russian consulate here in New York."

"Part-time security chief," Stark corrected. "I'll tell you something his boss the consul general doesn't know: Petrenko works for the SVR, Russia's foreign intelligence service. That much is gospel. What I believe is also true, but can't prove yet, is that he's involved in a rogue operation with a couple of Middle Eastern misfits."

"Terrorists."

"Possibly. Tell me what's going on."

Nazareth filled Stark in on Petrenko's game with the fingerprints and said he was dying to get his hands on whatever it was the guy had stolen from his boss's office.

"Tell you what, Pete. I don't have any resources to commit up there right now. But if you want to see what Petrenko's got, go take a look. I know you'll do it right."

"I'd love to do that, but if anything goes wrong and I'm caught..."

"You won't get caught. I know you. And if by some bizarre chance it goes wrong," he added, "I'll backdate your employment contract to my organization. You'll be untouchable."

"You're serious, aren't you?"

"Completely serious. I've got you covered. All I ask is that you let me know what you find. It's your op, Pete. But the information could be helpful to me."

"I'll give it some thought."

"Good man. Say hello to Tara."

"Will do."

"Oh, and go over and arrest the young punk in the gray hoodie. He just lifted that old guy's wallet."

By 2:30 that afternoon Gimble had met briefly with the Russian consul general and his security chief, both of whom had been cordial but somewhat distant. After returning to the office and comparing notes with her partner, she and Nazareth sat with the chief and laid out their assumptions.

"The consul general, Vasilyev, seemed more frightened than mad," Gimble began. "He couldn't believe someone would dare set foot on Russian property and steal *sensitive documents*. His words, not mine. As for Petrenko, the security guy, all he wanted to know was whether we had been able to identify the thief. And from the way he looked at me when he asked the question I could tell he already knew the answer."

"Good," Crawford nodded. "Let him wonder what the hell we're up to. But back to the consul general. You definitely got the impression that what was stolen was more than love letters to his mistress?"

"Absolutely. He worked hard at trying to look mad as hell, but to me he just looked plain scared. I have a strong feeling he's got a big problem on his hands because of the theft."

"And that's not the only problem he's got," Nazareth chimed in. "My friend in D.C. confirmed that Petrenko is much more than just security chief for the consulate. He's also a pretty high-level operative with ties to the SVR, Russia's foreign intelligence service. This is something the consul general doesn't know."

"Petrenko's a spy?" Crawford said.

"Certainly a spy," Nazareth replied, "and maybe an assassin as well. If he was ordered to kill a Russian dissident, I'd say he'd do it, no questions asked."

"That's just great," Crawford muttered. "We have a spy who may have stolen his own government's secrets in addition to murdering the most prominent Russian dissident in America, possibly on the planet."

"That's about it," Nazareth nodded.

"Okay, so where do you want to take this? We can't accuse him of anything without revealing what we know," Crawford said, "and what we know isn't enough to arrest him. Not that arresting him would matter since he's got diplomatic immunity."

"All correct, chief," Nazareth said, "but I think it's important to know exactly what's going on with this guy. He's a bad dude, trust me. He could be working for anyone."

"For instance?"

"Terrorists."

"Why terrorists?"

"Money."

"Pete, do you ever sleep at night, or do you just lie awake and think up complicated crap like this?" Crawford asked.

"It's really not that complicated, chief. IF Petrenko broke into his boss's files and IF he's a trained spy and IF he's as dirty as I think he is," Nazareth explained, "it's possible he was after information he could sell to the highest bidder. He wouldn't need to steal Russian secrets for the Russians, right? But maybe the consul general had documents that might be worth a ton of money to terrorists."

"I think that's a stretch, Pete," Crawford countered. "I can believe he set you up for the robbery, but that's a long way from thinking he's selling secrets to terrorists."

"Petrenko has a nice little home in Riverdale," Gimble smiled.

"And?" Crawford asked.

"Just saying," she replied.

He finally caught on to what she was thinking. "Oh, no. No way will you get a search warrant, and no way are you going to break in," he said sternly. "What an amazing headline that would be: **COPS BREAK INTO RUSSIAN DIPLOMAT'S HOME.**"

"Easy, chief," Gimble said. "We don't have to break in. Surveillance and a phone tap might be enough. If Pete's right and the guy is selling secrets to someone, maybe just watching and listening will give us what we need."

Crawford wasn't convinced. "I'll think on that, Tara. In the meantime, forget the international intrigue stuff and work on finding Gerasimov's killer."

"Who could very well be Petrenko," Nazareth added.

"For the moment how about we just assume the killer is someone other than Petrenko, all right?" The chief was obviously spooked by the thought of having the homicide case complicated by a possible terrorist plot. "I'll give this whole thing some thought while you two work on Gerasimov's murder. Period."

"Understood," Gimble assured him. Nazareth nodded in agreement. They had their marching orders.

But at home late that night, just before heading off to bed, Nazareth circled back to the subject of Petrenko. He liked doing things by the book, but he knew the Russian spy demanded attention.

"Here's what I think," he said to Gimble, who had already showered and now sat against the headboard of the king bed. She was thumbing through a well-used fitness book, searching for ways to improve her training program.

"About what?"

"Oh, right," he laughed. "You're not a mind-reader, are you? I meant here's what I think about Petrenko."

"Okay."

"The reason he used my fingerprints for the break-in at the consulate was to keep me away from the place. He knew I wouldn't go back there and risk having a new set of my fingerprints match those left at the robbery."

"Why would he focus on you? No, wait," she said. "I'll answer my own question. He ran your background and knows you're the type of threat he doesn't need anywhere near him. That makes sense."

"Whatever the reason, he succeeded in keeping me away. At least in theory."

"Meaning what?"

"Meaning I like your idea of visiting his house."

"Bad idea, Pete. It was a bad idea when I first thought of it, and it's even worse now that the chief has specifically told us to stay away. And we both know he's right. An illegal search of Petrenko's house could blow up in our faces. International incident, jail time for the NYPD's most famous detective, loss of pension, and all that."

"Highly unlikely. And if I find whatever it is he stole from the consul general's office, we may be able to crack a case that's much bigger than Gerasimov's murder."

"You're sold on the idea he's hooked up with terrorists."

"He wouldn't need to steal the documents for other Russians, right? And he didn't steal them for any U.S. agencies."

"You're sure he's not working for us?"

"Dalton Stark is."

"Good enough for me."

"So who does that leave? Answer: lots of potential buyers, but the ones we're most worried about are terrorists. This guy has gotten under my skin, Tara. I just feel as though he's really dangerous."

"Dangerous enough to risk our careers over?"

He thought about that. "Let me sleep on it."

That wasn't the resounding "No" she had hoped for.

16.

The university's auditorium was packed with a standing-room-only crowd. Students and faculty accounted for most of the guests, but event organizers had also managed to squeeze in nearly 200 members of the public who were eager to hear Feodor Sidorenko, the man widely assumed to be the leading candidate for the next Nobel Prize in literature. His title for the evening's lecture was "The Beast That Devoured the Dream," and everyone in attendance expected the master satirist to pull no punches in attacking Ruslan Kotov, Russia's president.

Throughout a series of internationally acclaimed novels Sidorenko had already portrayed his main character, a Kotov look-alike named Boris Svinya, variously as a murderer, a crook, and a defiler of young girls. More than this, the author had described in meticulous detail precisely how Svinya had single-handedly crushed the country's emerging democracy while establishing himself as a dictator through carefully orchestrated "free elections." So the evening's lecture promised to make headlines the next day, and the press was out in force.

Also in the audience were Pete Nazareth and Tara Gimble, who had snagged a pair of VIP tickets from the university's public affairs office. They had prime seats for the lecture as well as invitations to the private reception that would follow. Although the detectives weren't necessarily worried about a public assassination attempt, they welcomed the chance to see Sidorenko in action and to gauge the audience's response to his comments. Besides, they figured that with some luck they might even find a clue to Sergey Gerasimov's murder.

The auditorium lights went down as Sidorenko walked on stage to thunderous applause. He wore a nicely tailored gray suit, pale blue dress shirt, and maroon tie. In his right hand he carried a simple brass candle holder which he carefully placed on the lectern in full view of the audience. Without saying a word he reached inside his suit jacket and removed a red dinner candle, pressed it firmly into the holder, and held a butane lighter to the wick. He watched silently as the flame grew taller and began to sway tentatively in the auditorium's air currents.

"At the close of the 20th century," he began gently, "the fragile flame of democracy began to burn in my beloved homeland. It flickered in the wind, as this candle before me does. Then against all odds that flame grew taller and brighter and steadier, and in time shed its light across all of Russia. But where there is light, my friends, there are also shadows. And lurking within those shadows was the sinister countenance of Ruslan Kotov."

Sidorenko abruptly blew out the candle and watched the smoke curl from the glowing wick toward the ceiling. "Ruslan Kotov extinguished that flame of democracy, and with a heavy heart I watched the wisps of smoke that remained." Here he gestured with his right hand, imitating the smoke that rose slowly above the candle. "In the space of a few heartbeats the smoke, too, was gone. All that was left was an aching memory of what might have been."

He paused to let the words and images sink in, then began pointing here and there among the audience. "If you, and you, and you want to know how Ruslan Kotov rose to power," he said boldly, "simply follow the bodies. My friends, we have all heard that dead men tell no tales, but in this instance they do. If you follow the bodies of those who dared to stand in Ruslan Kotov's way, the trail will lead you to his fine office in the Kremlin. Tonight I will help the dead speak."

The audience sat entranced over the next hour as Sidorenko detailed what he believed was clear evidence of the Russian president's brutal crusade against freedom. At the same time every reporter in the room took furious notes while the legion of photographers shot thousands of images of the impassioned speaker. Among the photographers was Alex Resnick, easily the most famous of the bunch, whose pictures would undoubtedly end up on a magazine cover or on the front page of a major daily newspaper. In the photography world, after all, Resnick was royalty.

Nazareth nudged his wife just as Sidorenko opened the floor to questions. "Looks like we've got a feeding frenzy among the photographers." He was struck by the rudeness and aggressiveness that some of them exhibited as they jockeyed for position throughout the large auditorium. "Tough crowd."

"Yep, that's how it's done. A strong elbow helps get the best shot. Check that guy out," she pointed. "Alex Resnick."

"Name sounds familiar."

"Oh, Pete, come on. Probably the top nature photographer on the planet. He trained with Ansel Adams."

"Ah, okay. What's a nature photographer doing here?"

"Well, he's not just a nature photographer. He's also well known for images of people in action."

"Then he must have gotten some great action shots tonight. I'm amazed at how worked up Sidorenko was throughout his talk. When we interviewed him the other day he seemed pretty mellow, but tonight he was on fire."

"Oh, yeah. On fire big time. If I had to guess, I'd say tonight's speech will put him right at the top of the list for that Nobel Prize."

"You think so?"

"Sure, why not? I assume the selection committee weighs more than just the books when selecting a Nobel laureate. That was a pretty incredible performance."

"Also gutsy. He didn't act like a man with a bullseye on his back, did he?"

Gimble gave him a knowing look. "As I said the other day, Pete, he may be relaxed because he's the one who killed Gerasimov."

"No way I can get there, Tara. How in the world could someone who hates the strong-armed tactics of Ruslan Kotov turn around and kill a fellow Russian dissident?"

"Could be anything," she shrugged. "Jealousy, power, an old grudge, a woman. Sidorenko himself listed the typical motives when we met with him, right? I'm not saying he killed Gerasimov. All I'm saying is he doesn't seem afraid of getting whacked, which could mean he's the guy doing the whacking."

"I'll keep an open mind," he said with what his wife knew was a closed mind.

They ended their brief side discussion at the precise moment an audience member posed the very question that most bothered Gimble.

"Mr. Sidorenko, you've been even more outspoken tonight than usual. Are you not afraid of retaliation?" a young woman in the third row asked.

"Not at all, my dear," he replied. "Years ago, before Kotov ruled absolutely, he regarded anyone and everyone as a threat, especially those within Russia. But the times have changed. He now runs the country without opposition, at least within Russia's boundaries. And those of us outside the country, no matter how loud our voices, mean nothing to him. A fly may buzz around a bear's head, but the bear doesn't feel fear."

A young man across the room voiced a similar concern. "I'm sure you knew Sergey Gerasimov, who was murdered here in Manhattan some weeks ago. Do you think his death had something to do with President Kotov?"

"I knew Sergey," he nodded, "but only from having attended some of the same gatherings within New York City's Russian community. He was a galvanizing force for many people here, and perhaps it is true he hoped to replace Kotov as president. But let me tell you frankly that this never could have happened. He might one day have opposed Kotov on the ballot, yes. But he never could have been elected since elections are completely rigged. By this I mean the votes have been counted even before being cast. So, you see, Kotov had nothing to fear and certainly no reason to gets his hands dirty by ordering Gerasimov's death."

After another half hour of energetic discussion between Sidorenko and his admirers, Nazareth and Gimble joined the speaker and 50 important guests at a cocktail reception in a private room off the auditorium. The author immediately spotted the detectives and came over to greet them.

"Are you two now my official bodyguards?" he said, only partly in jest.

"No, sir, not at all," Nazareth told him. "My wife and I enjoyed meeting with you and were lucky to get tickets for tonight. You gave an excellent speech, sir, and I admire your willingness to stand up for democracy."

"Thank you, detective. I dream of having my words count for something in the struggle for justice," he said sadly, "but, alas, it is only a dream. I predict Russia will go backwards for many years before going forward again. Kotov is young and healthy, and he has no plans to step aside."

"As long as people like you continue to cry out for freedom," Gimble told him, "the flame won't die."

"I hope you are right, detective. I do hope so."

He shook their hands and rejoined the other guests, many of whom had begun clinking glasses of champagne, perhaps toasting Russia's future. Gimble studied his erect posture and confident stride as he walked away.

"He's too calm and cool, Pete. Either he's clueless about how much of a threat he represents to the Russian president, or he's the guy who killed Gerasimov. One or the other, period."

"Here's as far as I'll go, Tara. He carries himself surprisingly well for a man who sits at a keyboard all day writing novels that might earn him a Nobel Prize. I definitely wouldn't pick him out of a crowd as the writer," he said honestly. "But that doesn't make him an assassin."

"Well, that's progress, Detective Nazareth. You're willing to be at least a little suspicious of him."

"Maybe, maybe not. In any event, it's time for a glass of wine. I'm buying."

"How generous of you! I'll have a water with lime, please. While you're doing that, I want to say hello to Alex Resnick if he's still here."

"The famous photographer."

"Good boy. You were listening," she grinned.

Five minutes later he returned with their drinks and a small plate filled with hors d'oeuvres. "Did you find Resnick?" he asked.

"Nope, he must have split along with some of the other photographers and reporters."

"Deadlines, I guess."

"Yeah, I suppose so. But I was hoping to meet him."

"There's always another day."

They touched glasses. "To another day," she said.

17.

Volkov's tutors had long ago nicknamed him the Wolf for a variety of good reasons, none more important than his remarkable patience. Even as a boy he had possessed an uncanny knack for timing his attacks. Whether as a hunter, boxer, or competitive runner he had refused to strike until the moment was precisely right, and at that moment, like a gray wolf, he would swiftly claim his prize. So it was not surprising he had spent more than two months getting ready for Feodor Sidorenko. He had stalked, planned, and studied. He had even casually walked away from several good assassination opportunities while awaiting the perfect one. And here it was.

The traitorous author Sidorenko had a big night going for him. He had already addressed a sell-out crowd at Columbia University, and now he would spend several hours sipping fine wine and nibbling goat cheese tarts with a prideful collection of New York City's intelligentsia. Volkov was disgusted by the prospect. Did they intend to solve the world's problems over coffee and cognac? Would they congratulate themselves for being brave enough to insult President Ruslan Kotov from a distance of 5,000 miles? Would the VIP guests jostle to have their pictures taken with the great novelist, the man everyone assumed would soon take the stage in Stockholm to accept his Nobel Prize?

Volkov was normally a calm, thoroughly objective professional who went about his deadly work the way a neurosurgeon might dispassionately remove a tiny bit of a patient's brain. But tonight he couldn't disguise his hatred for Sidorenko. The man had made a laughingstock not only of Kotov but of Russia as well, and for this alone he deserved to die. Yet there was more. Volkov also loathed the man's regal manner, his way of making everyone around him feel like a lesser creature. He had heard Sidorenko speak several times in recent years, and he had found that the author had an unpleasant knack for making his listeners feel inconsequential.

Volkov had not gotten a phone call from his handler for over a month, the first such lapse in their decades-long relationship. Whether this meant Anatoly Bukarin was traveling or ill or dead he didn't know, but the old man's silence was now hardly relevant. After all these years Volkov could hear Bukarin's voice urging him on. "Eliminate the threats before the threats eliminate Russia," he liked to say. Names, dates, and circumstances might change, but never the mission. And the mission before the Wolf tonight was to eliminate Russia's greatest living threat, Feodor Sidorenko.

He vowed not to fail.

Volkov sat in his car across the street from Sidorenko's apartment building and watched the white-haired security guard struggle to keep his eyes open as he sat at the front desk. Four previous reconnaissance visits had revealed the same routine. Clearly the guard had grown too old for such serious work, and tonight the Wolf would turn this weakness to his advantage.

At 8:47 p.m. the guard's eyes closed. His head slowly sagged forward, and he began breathing through his mouth. Volkov turned to his Getac X500 laptop and shut down the building's closed-circuit TV system, which he had effortlessly hacked a week earlier with a bit of software appropriately called *Blind Eye*. Then he punched in the phone number for the apartment building's front desk and watched the guard jolt awake and fumble for the phone.

"Security, Len Baker here," the guy said, obviously groggy. "Can I help you?"

Volkov employed the Russian accent he had worked so diligently to mask decades ago. "Yes, this is Feodor Sidorenko. I'm afraid I left my car unlocked in the garage before leaving the building. Could you possibly check on it for me?"

"Oh, sure, Mr. Sidorenko, no problem," Baker answered. "I'll go down there right now and take a look."

"Thank you so much. I appreciate your kindness."

"Not at all, sir. Have a good night."

Volkov left his car as soon as the guard stood and made his way toward the elevator. By the time Baker had reached the underground parking garage Volkov had entered the lobby and stepped onto an elevator bound for the 15th floor. Once there he donned latex gloves and spent the next 17 seconds opening the door to 1501 with a small battery powered lock pick. Immediately upon entering Sidorenko's apartment he headed straight for the kitchen, opened the refrigerator, and studied its contents.

His eyes passed over the gallon of skim milk, the half-empty carton of orange juice, and the jar of blackberry jam. Then he saw what he was after. He reached in for a small bottle of Fiji water, one of three that occupied space on the center shelf. After a long night of excess wine, heavy food, and idle chatter what might Sidorenko want when he arrived home? Perhaps a cold drink? Yes, perhaps. Volkov was willing to place his bet on the designer water.

He carefully removed a syringe from his jacket and injected its contents into the plastic bottle just below the cap. Satisfied that the hole was too small to notice, he placed the bottle back on the shelf slightly in front of the others. If Sidorenko grabbed a water when he got home, this would likely be the one. If he wasn't thirsty tonight, well, tomorrow or the next day would be fine.

Volkov was always willing to wait.

After finishing up in the kitchen he went to the front door and checked the security peephole for hallway activity. Nothing. He slipped out and locked the door behind him. Before boarding the elevator he placed another call to the front desk.

"Security, Baker," the old man answered. "Can I help you?"

"Hey, we've got someone passed out near the elevator on five," Volkov shouted in his best Brooklyn accent. "Get up here right away!" Then he hung up. Thirty seconds later he had the main lobby to himself when he calmly strolled out of the building.

As Volkov drove home he considered how much more difficult his job had been during those early days in New York City. No cell phones, to begin with. Getting into and out of Sidorenko's apartment unobserved would have been a major challenge tonight had he not been able to make a couple of quick mobile phone calls to the front desk. Likewise, in 1975 there was no Internet to enable him to take control of the building's security cameras.

And, of course, back then there was no synthetic puffer fish neurotoxin, or tetrodotoxin, to eliminate traitors like Feodor Sidorenko. He had to acquire the natural product, and that always took time and sometimes great imagination. Yes, his handler had always gotten him what he needed eventually, but the process was cumbersome and highly imperfect, and more than one batch had been spoiled in transit. Today? Simply place the Internet order with a discreet supplier in the Middle East, wait five days, and retrieve the fresh supply from a P.O. box. The Wolf might be getting long in the tooth, but in this glorious age of high technology he found himself spending less and less energy to get the job done.

At this pace he could work another 20 years while hardly breaking a sweat.

18.

Professor Bradford Harlingen rolled his black 2008 BMW 135i to a stop in front of Feodor Sidorenko's apartment building and said goodnight as the tall author slowly unravelled himself from the cramped vehicle. A cab certainly would have been more comfortable, but he could hardly have turned down the professor's kind offer of a ride, especially near midnight when cabs were sometimes in short supply.

Sidorenko gave Harlingen a polite wave then walked through the lobby entrance a bit unsteadily. His legs, after all, were stiff from sitting in that tiny front seat. Well, he thought, perhaps he had also enjoyed a little too much wine this evening. He worked hard to keep himself in good physical condition, but he occasionally succumbed to the pleasant union of lively conversation and excellent cabernet. The author could handle his wine and vodka better than most men, so a modest overindulgence now and then did no lasting harm. Tomorrow morning he would jog for 30 minutes on the treadmill and take a hot bath.

The security guard shook himself awake from a light sleep as Sidorenko entered the lobby.

"Oh, hi, Mr. Sidorenko. Late night for you."

"Yes, this is far too late for me, Len. I may have to sleep in tomorrow morning."

"Well have a good night, sir. Oh, and everything's fine in the garage."

"I'm very glad for that," Sidorenko answered, not knowing why he should care about the garage. "Have a good night."

"You do the same, sir," Baker replied, wondering why the old man hadn't slipped him a five for checking on his car.

By the time Sidorenko reached his apartment those last two glasses of wine, a delightful 2012 Stag's Leap Cask 23 cabernet, had taken full effect, and he found himself floating pleasantly between moderately drunk and quite drunk. Yet he was alert enough to remember that the secret to avoiding tomorrow's hangover was to flush the body with plenty of clear water. He opened the refrigerator door. Ordinarily he would have turned to his beloved Borjomi mineral water, but he always avoided sparkling beverages this late at night. So a cold bottle of Fiji before bed would do nicely. He twisted the cap off and downed the water in a few refreshing gulps before heading to the bedroom.

After slipping into loose cotton pajamas and brushing his teeth he double-checked that the apartment's front door was locked. Even though this was known to be an extremely secure building, Sidorenko never took unnecessary chances. He had years of important work ahead of him -- words to be set to paper, wrongs to be set right. If he won the Nobel Prize in literature, as he fully expected, he would have a platform from which he could accomplish more than ever over the next 15 or 20 years.

As he walked back toward the bedroom he noticed an odd tingling in his lips. The wine, he smiled. Too much is too much, even if it's something as wonderful as the wine he had sampled tonight. What a gem the evening had been. His talk at the university had been extremely well received by an audience that seemed unanimous in its hatred of President Ruslan Kotov. And the reception, ah, the reception! It had been a glorious time with some of his oldest friends as well as new ones like the two NYPD detectives. He genuinely liked the young couple and appreciated their concern on his behalf. Tomorrow, perhaps, he would contact them and arrange for a nice Russian lunch at Mari Vanna on East 20th.

But suddenly it wasn't just his lips that were tingling. His fingers and toes seemed to be growing numb. Maybe this was a panic attack and not the wine. After all, he had experienced a number of panic attacks throughout his adult life. Always unpleasant but also short-lived. And then he noticed the sweating. Yes, the heavy sweating was a sure sign this was nothing more than a simple panic attack. One milligram of Xanax would solve the problem.

When Sidorenko reached the bathroom he found he couldn't open the plastic prescription bottle because his fingers refused to follow his brain's commands. He knew what he wanted them to do but lacked sufficient coordination. Then his heart ran wild. This was something he had never experienced before, and it frightened him. His heart rhythm, normally strong and steady, swung chaotically from fast to slow to fast again.

Heart problems had never troubled anyone in his family, and he took far better care of himself than his parents ever had. But he could not deny what he saw in the bathroom mirror. His lips and cheeks had a sickly bluish cast to them, and through the haze of his fading consciousness he noticed he was gasping like a fish out of water.

He reached the phone by his bed and managed to press 9-1-1 before the nausea hit him like a wave crashing on rocks. "Help . . . my heart," was all he managed to say when the operator answered. Then he collapsed on the hardwood floor.

The ambulance team that brought Sidorenko to the hospital had been unable to keep his heart from failing, and all that was left for Dr. Roland Schachter in the ER was to enter *sudden cardiac arrest* as the cause of death in the computer file. Contributing to the heart episode, he wrote, was a blood alcohol level of 0.28. The doctor had seen this sort of thing many times before, especially among elderly patients with a drinking problem.

Since Schachter had no reason to expect the presence of puffer fish neurotoxin in Feodor Sidorenko's bloodstream, he didn't look for it.

19.

On the morning after Sidorenko's speech Nazareth and Gimble huddled in a small conference room at One Police Plaza with two laptops, a printer, and enough coffee and bottled water to last until lunchtime. They were determined to nail down every detail they could about Ilya Petrenko, the Russian consulate's security director who, thanks to Dalton Stark, they now knew was also a spy. Stark had sent them all the information he had on the guy, but the detectives needed to add whatever public facts they could find as they tried to pinpoint why Petrenko had tried to set Nazareth up for the consulate break-in. Was it just a bit of sport, something he could laugh about over drinks one day with his fellow spies? Or was there a more complex reason for wanting to keep Nazareth away?

The classified files from Washington laid out the sanitized version of Petrenko's professional career. In Poland, Turkey, Germany, France, England, and the U.S. he had served as a mid-level bureaucrat who by all accounts seemed to specialize in pushing papers from one side of a desk to the other. Whatever his duties, in every case he had performed them while enjoying diplomatic immunity.

What secret role might Petrenko have played while acting as a legitimate Russian employee during his various embassy and consulate postings? Nazareth and Gimble devoted most of the morning to matching his foreign assignments with the deaths of Russian dissidents abroad. If dissidents had routinely died when Petrenko happened to be in town, he would immediately jump to the top of their list as a suspect in Sergey Gerasimov's murder.

That particular line of inquiry turned up nothing useful, but Gimble had noticed an interesting detail that might or might not be important to their investigation. Three countries -- Turkey, Germany, and France -- had suffered major terrorist attacks while Petrenko was in residence. If there was a connection between him and the terrorists it certainly wasn't obvious. What was perfectly clear, however, was that in each of the incidents the bad guys had somehow managed to arm themselves with highly sophisticated weaponry.

Remote-controlled vans, white-phosphorus grenades, and advanced surface-to-air missiles were hardly the sorts of devices generally associated with small terrorist cells. So their use in these attacks suggested the presence of a major arms dealer. Unfortunately, the Turkish, German, and French investigations had never agreed on a common source. The usual state suspects -- Iran, North Korea, and Syria -- had been mentioned in the reports, but no one could state for a fact that one of those three countries had supported the attacks.

"It's interesting that Petrenko happened to be serving in each of the countries when a terrorist attack took place," Gimble observed, "but I could easily chalk that up to coincidence. And I really can't imagine Russia supporting terrorists. Ruslan Kotov isn't my favorite foreign leader, but he's been fanatical about combatting terrorism."

"You know I don't believe in coincidences," Nazareth told her as he scanned the list of weapons used in the three foreign terrorist operations. "And maybe I'm guilty of shopping for evidence supporting my view that Petrenko might be working with terrorists. But I have to tell you, Tara, the kind of hardware used in these attacks could absolutely have been obtained by someone like him. He would have had easy access to the suppliers and would have had no trouble shipping the goods under diplomatic cover."

"I can't believe he'd be operating under orders from Moscow."

"Agreed. Ruslan Kotov has no use for terrorists and would never support them. So if Petrenko was involved in those three terrorist attacks, he was most likely doing it for money. *Lots* of money. And if he's hooked up with terrorists here in New York, he could be working on his biggest payday ever."

"I'm afraid to guess what kinds of weapons would produce a really big payday for him in Manhattan."

Nazareth studied his wife's face and said seriously, "Oh, I think you can guess. It's the thing we've all been worried about since 9/11."

"Nuclear?"

"That would be it," he nodded. "I figure the right nuclear device would net Petrenko many millions, and he'd live the rest of his life like a king somewhere the SVR would never find him."

"Son of a bitch."

"Right again," he nodded.

After breaking for a quick lunch they locked themselves in the conference room once again and organized all the facts, both classified and public, they had on Petrenko. Then they created a list of questions that still needed answering. At the top of the list was, *What was stolen from the Russian consul general's office?*

"If, as we assume, Petrenko was the thief," Nazareth offered, "whatever he stole holds the key to what he's up to here in New York. And on the chance he's up to something seriously bad, we need to see those CDs."

"However, there's no legal channel for getting anywhere near them, Pete, as you and I and the chief all know."

"I hear you. But this is suddenly a lot bigger than solving Sergey Gerasimov's murder. Suppose Petrenko actually has been providing arms to terrorists, and suppose he actually can deliver a nuclear device to terrorists in New York City?"

"Then you turn this over to Dalton Stark, fast."

"He can't build an operation on my suspicions, Tara. All I have right now is assumptions that even I have some trouble believing."

"Then let's keep digging."

"By waiting we might be digging a huge grave for everyone in Manhattan," he said as he shook his head emphatically. "Can't do that. I've got to know what Petrenko is up to."

"Even if getting caught means losing your job?"

"Even if," he assured her.

"In that case, let's make goddamn sure you don't get caught."

They spent the remainder of the day creating a plan built upon a useful fact their research into Petrenko's life had uncovered. For more than a year he had been romantically involved with Russian expatriate Darya Pushkina, a prominent socialite who owned a $6-million summer home set on 14 lavish acres in Southampton, just a short stroll from the Atlantic. Petrenko was known to spend long weekends at the gleaming white beach house whenever Pushkina's charitable activities in Manhattan allowed her to escape the city, and the detectives had learned that on September 23rd the couple would be at the Long Island estate hosting a large gathering of Metropolitan Opera donors. This meant Nazareth would have a prime opportunity to visit Petrenko's home in Riverdale while its owner was out of town.

"Help me here, Pete," Gimble said. "If this guy's out for money, why doesn't he just marry the rich Russian lady and live happily ever after? Why bother messing with terrorists?"

"There's money and then there's serious money," he answered. "A woman with a $6-million home in the Hamptons and a $15-million apartment in Manhattan probably can't compete with the money he'd get for delivering a nuclear warhead to Islamic terrorists. Besides, he'd have to take her and her money together, and he doesn't strike me as someone who wants to settle down with one woman."

"He's one sick puppy."

"In a world of many sick puppies."

"So when do you want to check out his house and see what we'll be up against?"

"Not we, I. We can check the place out together, but you won't be anywhere near me when I go in. If this goes wrong, at least you'll still have a job," he laughed.

"That's not funny. And I'm not really worried you'll lose your job. I'm worried you'll get killed by someone who's guarding the house while he's away."

"We'll know long before September 23rd whether he has security guards, Tara. And for the moment at least I'd bet he simply relies on electronics."

"Oh, is that all?" she kidded.

"You fight fire with fire and electronics with electronics. I'm not worried about getting in and out. I'm worried about finding whatever it is I'm after."

"Yeah, it's a pain when you don't know what you're after, isn't it?"

He smiled at her sarcasm. "I know you think this is a dumb idea, Tara, but I can't gamble on Petrenko's motives. The guy gives off really bad vibes. And you know I have a pretty good track record when it comes to reading people like him."

"That's the only reason I'm behind you on this. But I'm still nervous as hell."

"You help me work on Petrenko," he offered, "and then I'll help you with Sidorenko. I know you're convinced he killed Gerasimov."

"And I know you think I'm crazy."

"Not crazy at all. You're going with your instinct. Do we have a deal?"

"Deal."

They wrapped up the day's work shortly after 7:00 p.m. and on the way home decided to stop at Ruby's Cafe on Mulberry Street, where they each had a hamburger and a side salad. Once they reached their apartment they were both too tired and full for serious training, so they hit the home gym for some light cardio work and stretching. In the morning they'd get up early and pound the weights.

It was nearly 11:00 by the time they had showered, gone through the mail, and returned a few phone calls from family and friends.

"You going to watch the 11:00 o'clock news, Pete?"

"Yeah, might as well. I missed whatever happened in the world today, didn't I?"

"We both did, but the world didn't come to an end, did it?"

"Not that I'm aware of."

"Well, enjoy the news. I'm going to sleep." She kissed him goodnight and closed the bedroom door behind her.

After 20 minutes of half-listening to rehashed stories about geopolitics, terrorism, and Zika virus, Nazareth locked onto the phrase, "Meanwhile, here in New York City." What came next left him stunned on the living room couch.

"Feodor Sidorenko, the Russian-born author who was widely expected to be the next winner of the Nobel Prize for literature, died last night of a heart attack only hours after delivering . . ."

Nazareth dove for the phone before he heard the rest of the story. He had no time to waste.

Forty minutes and seven phone calls later he sank back on the couch and shook his head in disbelief just as his wife opened the bedroom door.

"You coming to bed soon, Pete?" She grew concerned when she saw the look on his face. "What's wrong?"

"Sidorenko died around midnight last night in his apartment," he told her. "He was gone before they got him to the ER."

Gimble could scarcely believe what she was hearing. "What happened to him?"

"They said it was a heart attack, but you and I know better. Somebody killed him."

"All right, then we'll get on it. If he was murdered, we'll find out."

Nazareth shook his head. "He's nothing but ashes, Tara."

"What? How the hell can he be nothing but ashes?"

"I just got off the phone with an extremely annoyed ME who doesn't like late calls at home. The doctor in the ER ruled it was a heart attack, plain and simple, and that was that. They contacted Sidorenko's attorney, who followed the instructions in the guy's will. He had the body cremated immediately and arranged for the ashes to be shipped to Petrenko's childhood home in Russia."

"Where the hell were the police while this was happening?"

"Except for the two cops who responded to the 9-1-1 call, there was no NYPD involvement since there was nothing suspicious. Just another old guy dropping dead." He reached for the phone.

"Who are you calling now?" she asked.

"Dalton Stark. It's late, but I need to bounce a few ideas off him."

"Want me to hang out with you?"

"No, you go back to bed," he smiled. "At least one of us should be awake tomorrow at the office."

Dalton Stark answered on the first ring. "Hey, Pete, what are you doing up so late?"

"Not having much fun, I'm afraid. Sorry for the late call."

"Not a problem. This week I'm working on Pakistani time," he said, "so right now it's not quite 9:00 a.m."

"You're serious?"

"Absolutely. Whenever I have something major going on in another country I work the same hours as the team that's in place. Helps keep things organized."

Nazareth explained the circumstances of Sidorenko's death and asked for Stark's assessment.

"Don't fault the doctor or the ME," he began, "because it's really easy to make a murder look like a heart attack. I can name at least 10 medications, plants, or chemicals that will get the job done every time. And unless you screen specifically for each of them, you'll never know the truth. Do you know if they saved the blood sample?"

"I was told they saved the results but incinerated the blood."

"That's too bad. Some hospitals keep blood samples for a few days, but I suppose they didn't think it was necessary in this case. We've still got a shot, though," he added. "If you get me a copy of the lab results, I'll have my guys take a closer look. In the meantime, I'd be willing to place two bets. One, this wasn't a heart attack. Your instincts are once again on target, Pete. Sidorenko pissed off the wrong people and was murdered for it. Two, the actual cause of death was most likely puffer fish neurotoxin or a synthetic version. The Russians have been in love with this stuff for decades because it works beautifully and is rarely discovered in the victim's bloodstream."

"You assume the killer is Russian?"

"I'd say it's a fact, Pete. You're dealing with someone very slick and highly trained. Maybe it's the security guy at the consulate, Petrenko, but I sort of doubt that. I don't see him getting involved in assassinations. He's got something else going on."

"Okay, so then it's back to square one. Whoever killed Sidorenko also probably killed Sergey Gerasimov, and for some reason he seems to be picking up the pace. Why the sudden spurt in murders?"

"Sidorenko and Gerasimov both called out Ruslan Kotov specifically," Stark answered, "and the Russian president certainly wouldn't be happy about that. But would he order their assassinations? No, I don't believe that. It's possible, though, someone has decided to protect Kotov by getting rid of his critics here in the U.S. Seems like a misguided strategy to me, but you won't know for sure what's in the killer's head until you arrest him."

"I don't see that happening anytime soon."

"If he stops killing, you're probably screwed, Pete, because a guy like this could remain hidden for years. So you need to hope like hell he's got other targets. Of course," he added, "it would be good to get to them before he does."

"Amen to that."

"Stay well, Pete. Gotta run now. I've got a call from Islamabad."

"Nazareth out."

20.

Nazareth was still up at 2:30 a.m. trying hard to make sense of the disjointed facts that ran loose inside his head. A second dissident, this time a potential Nobel laureate, had been murdered, and once again the killer hadn't left a clue. Meanwhile, the Russian consulate's security chief was possibly involved in a terrorist plot, but Nazareth had nothing more than guesswork on his side. Then there was the consul general, who didn't seem particularly interested in having the NYPD nosing around his turf. Why was that? What sort of game did he have going on?

Finally, there was Dalton Stark, who had offered Nazareth a free pass to break into a suspect's home while vowing to cover his butt if anything went wrong. Was that for real? Could Stark actually deliver on such a promise?

The search for clarity did nothing but raise more questions, two of which urgently demanded answers. First, should he tell his wife what Stark had said about burglarizing Petrenko's home? He didn't like holding anything back from her, but he worried about getting her involved in a covert operation that had no formal approval of any kind. How well, after all, did he really know Dalton Stark, his motives, or his capabilities? The second question was in some ways even trickier. Should he level with the chief about the nature of his Washington connection? Or would that only start a war between the NYPD and whatever organization claimed Dalton Stark as its own? Hell, did that organization even officially exist? He had no way of knowing.

He slipped into bed alongside Gimble close to 3:00, turned his brain off as best he could, and slept soundly until 5:20, when his wife got up and began dressing for some serious gym time.

"When did you finally come to bed?" she asked while lacing up her Nike cross-trainers.

"You don't want to know," he groaned. "I'm shot."

"Then why don't you sleep in this morning? You can work out tonight."

"No, actually I'm heading into the office early because I want to catch the chief before everyone else shows up. I need to bounce a couple of things off him."

"Then I'll go with you and work out tonight," she offered. "I can be ready in about 15 minutes."

"No, you stick to your schedule and drive in at the usual time. I'll take the subway and catch the chief myself."

"What time does he get in?"

"Before 6:00 for as long as I've worked for him."

"Okay, if you're sure." She wondered why her husband needed to see the chief alone but didn't pursue it. They had agreed early in their relationship not to play detective with each other. Sometimes secrets were necessary, even between a husband and wife. So if one of them didn't offer details, the other didn't ask.

"I'm positive. When you get there we can go get some coffee and talk about what's going on."

"Fair enough."

After a short subway ride to South Ferry with a handful of other sleep-walking commuters Nazareth hiked up to One Police Plaza and headed straight for the chief's glassed-in corner office. He was surprised to see all the blinds pulled down and the overhead lights off at 6:23 a.m. In fact, he was moderately annoyed. He thought about the extra sleep he could have gotten had he known Crawford was going to be late today.

Today? No, not just today. For the first time ever, probably. The chief was never late.

As he approached Crawford's office he noticed the door was open just a crack, so he peeked in. At the farthest corner of the room Crawford stood at a window with his back to the door. In front of him was a tripod onto which he had fastened a camera equipped with a fancy telephoto lens. The chief seemed to be lining up a shot of New York Harbor in the general direction of the Statue of Liberty. He pressed the shutter release, and the motor drive rapidly fired off six or seven frames.

Before Nazareth could walk away the chief turned suddenly toward the door and yelled, "Who's there?"

"It's Pete, chief. I didn't know whether you were in." Through the narrow opening Nazareth could see the chief looked as though he had just been caught with his hand in someone else's pocket.

"Uh, give me 10, Pete," the chief said sharply, obviously distressed.

"Sure. Sorry if I startled you."

"No, that's okay. Just give me a few minutes."

Nazareth had barely settled behind his desk when he saw the lights go on in the chief's office. A minute later the chief pulled up the blinds, opened the door, and waved Nazareth over. He stood at the credenza brewing a pot of coffee when the detective arrived.

The photography gear was gone. Since Crawford said nothing about it, Nazareth kept his questions to himself.

"You're in early today, Pete. What's up?"

"Feodor Sidorenko. Tara and I didn't hear about him until after 11:00 last night."

Crawford seemed not to recognize the name. "What about him?"

"He's dead."

"Fill me in. Do I know Sidorenko?"

Nazareth gave Crawford the 60-second version, all the while trying to remember whether he and Tara had already spoken with the chief about Sidorenko. Maybe not. So much had been going on lately it was certainly possible they had left Crawford out of the loop on the famous novelist.

"So you're thinking it was murder even though the hospital and the ME agree it was a heart attack?" the chief asked.

"Well, you know me," Nazareth smiled.

"Yeah, *suspicion* is your middle name. But if the experts say it was a heart attack, I suppose that closes the book on it. We'll never know for sure. I think you and Tara should just work the first Russian homicide."

"Sergey Gerasimov."

"Yeah, him. He's our priority. And as far as that security guy at the consulate goes . . ."

"Ilya Petrenko."

"Right. I don't know what he's into, but right now I want you and Tara to keep him the hell off your radar screen. We have nothing on him, and I don't need a goddamn diplomatic mess at the moment. Let's discuss him again after we have something going on Gerasimov."

"Understood."

"Want some coffee?" The chief offered a sinister grin. He knew that no one on the floor could stomach the mud he brewed behind his desk."

"I'm too young to die, chief."

"Your choice, my friend. Try to have a good day anyway."

By the time Gimble walked in at 7:20 Nazareth had tied himself up in knots over what he had seen earlier that morning. Crawford, he knew, was a grizzled old-timer who was all business all the time. Probably had been that way as a kid, he thought, whenever and wherever that was. Damn, another question mark! Where had the chief been born and raised? And exactly how old was he? Nazareth had never been motivated to ask. Crawford was the boss, and a good one. That was that.

"You look like hell, Pete," Gimble said cheerily.

"Nice to see you, too, sweetheart."

"Let's get you that coffee before you fall asleep at the desk."

"Somehow I don't think that's going to happen."

"Why's that?"

He shook his head. "Not here."

They strolled around the corner, got their coffee, and sat on a bench under a maple. Nazareth took a few sips before launching into his story. He looked up at the morning sky, still tinged with pink, and imagined Dalton Stark watching them via a top-secret satellite link. Let's begin there, he decided.

"I've debated whether I should tell you this," he said, "because I'm afraid it just ratchets up the career-risk level. But I've concluded that if there's fallout it's going to hit both of us anyway. So here goes."

Gimble listened intently as her husband described his conversation with Stark and the idea of breaking into Ilya Petrenko's home in Riverdale. Her face revealed nothing of the turmoil she felt inside, and she kept silent until he was finished.

"So that's the first half of this morning's agenda," he sighed, plainly relieved to have brought his wife into the loop.

"You mean this isn't enough? My poor heart may not be able to take anything else."

"Your thoughts?"

"We need to know for sure Petrenko doesn't have guards protecting his house."

"If he has guards, I stop. Let's assume he just has electronic security."

"Well, then it seems to me the risk boils down to one thing. Can Dalton Stark really pull you out of the fire if this goes all wrong? We don't know, and we have no way of finding out. So you need to take a leap of faith, Pete. How much do you trust him?"

He thought about that for a moment, then said, "He trusted me with his life once, and I felt then -- and still feel -- he can be trusted with mine. I just wish I had more facts."

"Your instincts are worth more than most people's facts, Pete. You've made your mind up. So stop second-guessing yourself. We should move forward on the assumption that Dalton's got you covered."

"I reach the same conclusion, Tara, but I'm glad to have you on board. So, about the second issue."

"You're sure I can handle this?"

"Yes, and I'll be brief." Then he told her about what he had witnessed at the chief's doorway earlier that morning. Seeing the chief take photos from his office window was about as odd as watching snow fall on Broadway in mid-August.

"It may not be relevant," Gimble noted, "but do you have any idea whether this was serious equipment? I mean not just amateur junk."

"The only fancy camera I've ever held in my hands was the one I got you last Christmas, but I'm guessing the chief's was certainly up there. And the long lens looked pretty expensive too."

"Did you happen to notice what he actually did with the lens?"

"Yeah, he twisted it with his left hand while he was looking into the camera."

"Okay, then it was a zoom telephoto lens, which is a lot more expensive than a fixed lens. Was it black?"

"No, it was white. That seemed unusual."

"Probably a Canon lens, very good equipment, worth a thousand or more."

"Not the sort of thing a rookie would be using."

"Definitely not."

"So now we've got two questions," Nazareth said. "Why is Crawford taking pictures with fancy cameras, and what the hell was he photographing out that window?"

"The simplest answer, Pete darling, is that he's got a hobby we didn't know about."

"That would certainly be the simplest answer, yes."

"But you're not buying it?"

He threw his head back, closed his eyes, and exhaled loudly. "Not this morning, Tara. This morning I'm seeing conspiracies everywhere I turn."

"Pete, the chief isn't a Russian spy."

"Do you know where he was born?"

"No, do you?"

"I sniffed around online before you got in this morning. He was born and raised outside Philadelphia and moved to New York City when he was in his early twenties."

"And this has you suspicious?"

He shrugged and looked at her sheepishly.

"You really are in bad shape today, aren't you?" she said calmly.

"Yeah, I guess I am. Let's go back and do some more thinking."

"How about I think while you nap?"

"That doesn't sound half bad, actually."

21.

Alex Resnick chose a glorious late-September morning to work on the "Home is Manhattan" photo essay he had agreed to create for Mayor Elliott Dortmund. He planned to spend three hours working the area around Battery Park, a busy spot at the island's southernmost end. Every day tens of thousands of Staten Islanders walked through this neighborhood as part of their ferry commute, and rarely did one of them notice the scenery. They were too busy jabbering on their cell phones or worrying whether the stock market would open up, down, or sideways.

But Resnick knew that for Manhattan residents with some time on their hands Battery Park and its surroundings provided a virtually endless array of sights and sounds worth enjoying. The first scene that caught his attention this morning was a young woman of 30 or so in paint-speckled jeans. Her wooden easel held a large canvas featuring the Statue of Liberty with a red tugboat in the foreground. She dabbed a few touches of titanium white at the boat's stern with a small brush, and the scene in oil suddenly looked almost as real as the one in the harbor.

He waited until she had finished that section of the painting, then handed her his business card. "Good morning," he said. "Lovely painting. Do you mind if I photograph you while you work? I'm doing a photo essay for the mayor's office."

"Heck, no," she smiled without even looking at the business card. "A little publicity always helps."

"The story I'm working on will feature Manhattan residents. Do you by any chance live here?"

"All my life. I grew up in Midtown, and now I live a couple of blocks from NYU."

He handed her a short photo release form allowing him to use whatever photos he might take. "Tell you what, if you give me permission to use the images, I'll make sure your name gets used in the mayor's ad campaign."

"Sounds fantastic to me." She glanced at the form and for the first time actually noticed his name. "Alex Resnick? You're Alex Resnick? Oh, my God. I love your work, Mr. Resnick. I'm Alice Turner."

"Very pleased to meet you, Alice. You and I obviously like the same kinds of scenes. The painting really is excellent."

"I'll gladly trade you the painting for one of your photos," she joked. "Of course, 10 of my paintings sell for about as much as one of your photos."

"Art is art, Alice. I'd gladly make that trade. When you're finished with the painting, give me a call," he told her, "and we can talk about what photo you want."

"Deal," she said energetically.

"Okay, then. We both need to get back to work. I'll take some photos and then leave you alone." He spent another 15 minutes capturing the artist, her canvas, and the harbor scene behind them. In one lucky, spectacular shot he caught the shocked look on the artist's face as a pigeon landed atop the easel and seemed to look at the upside-down painting. He knew instantly he had snatched a one-in-a-million opportunity.

"I can't believe that just happened!" the young woman giggled.

"Not the sort of thing you can plan, Alice. That one's going to be a classic," he assured her. "I'll make sure you have a copy."

He waved goodbye and strolled over to Castle Clinton, a splendid stone fort built just prior to the War of 1812, where he photographed a group of 18 elementary school kids playing a vigorous game of tag while two frazzled teachers tried to regain control of the morning. He managed to capture an especially revealing image of the frustrated park ranger whose face seemed to say, "Tour over. I'm taking early retirement."

During the next two hours Resnick took another 324 photos that wordlessly explained why Manhattan can be a great place to live, not just visit. Seagulls wheeled overhead in the autumn sunlight. A twin-masted tall ship with her sails unfurled cruised past Ellis Island toward the Narrows. Young mothers sat in the shade and chatted with each other while their children played among the chutes, bridges, and climbing equipment of Rockefeller Park. And towering above it all was the new World Trade Center, a symbol of America's strength and resilience.

Best of all, at least from Resnick's perspective, were the faces of people he encountered throughout his photo shoot. Of the 15 most interesting people he spotted, 11 turned out to be Manhattan residents. The 45-year-old guy in the $5,000 business suit and the 92-year-old woman who fed the pigeons from her wheelchair were of equal interest to the photographer, each revealing a shining facet of the gem they called home. Yet he remained somewhat baffled by the enthusiasm with which residents always described Manhattan. Most of them -- all but a few, in fact -- regarded their crowded island as the only place worth living in the entire universe. And after all these years he still didn't get it.

His uncomplicated viewpoint was that you live where you live. There's always sky above you and ground below. You've got a roof over your head, food in the pantry, and work. That's that. In the end, one place is like every other. Unless he could disappear into the wilderness, which was out of the question, he didn't care whether he lived in New York, Philadelphia, Chicago, Kansas City, or L.A.

All that mattered was the job.

22.

Early on the morning of Saturday, September 23rd, Ilya Petrenko slipped into his silver Porsche 911, put the top down, and backed out of his garage in the Bronx. He worked his way over to the Cross Bronx Expressway, then the Cross Island, and ultimately I-495, the Long Island Expressway, where he touched the gas pedal and rocketed from 60 to 110 in less than two seconds. The Porsche could do another 80 without difficulty but not on this particular day. Far too many *babushkas,* or grandmothers, out driving today, he thought, so the trip would take longer than he wanted.

As he blew past Hauppauge at 117 mph he saw the unmarked police cruiser accelerate into the lane behind him then fall back as soon as the cop noticed the State Department license plate. Yes, Petrenko could be written up for speeding, but he knew from long experience the police never bothered ticketing diplomats. The average trooper didn't have time to monkey around with a diplomat who wasn't going to pay the fine anyway. Unless the Russian ran someone over while drunk, he could pretty much do what he wanted on America's highways and get away with it.

The drive to Darya Pushkina's estate took just under two hours despite the moderately heavy traffic, and by mid-morning Petrenko and his part-time girlfriend were in their bathing suits alongside the Olympic-sized pool with its immense cascading waterfall and swim-up bar. Pushkina's fashionable guests wouldn't be arriving until 7:00 p.m., so the couple had the entire day to themselves.

Despite being a touch overweight Petrenko was a relentless swimmer whose sloppy form was more than offset by his remarkable endurance. He hit the pool several times each week at a Manhattan health club not far from the consulate, and he found swimming to be the one truly liberating activity in his life. No other form of relaxation allowed him to escape the conflicts and fears that gnawed at him all day every day. Yes, if his grand plans came to fruition he would be able to relax in comfort and grand style for the rest of his life. But between that day and today stood risks almost too great to contemplate.

After 25 minutes of swimming laps he had successfully cleared his mind of the dangers that awaited him. Pushkina, on the other hand, had begun to grow annoyed over the lack of attention. They hadn't been together for nearly two weeks because of her crazy schedule, and here she was sitting alone and thoroughly bored while Petrenko splashed his way through lap after lap and showed no signs of quitting. She stood and walked to the end of the pool as he approached the wall.

"Is this what you will do all day?" she asked with a mild edge to her voice. But he failed to hear her as he executed an awkward underwater turn. He had begun swimming back toward the far end of the pool when she yelled at him.

"Ilya! What is your problem?"

He swam another two strokes before Pushkina's voice connected with his brain, which had drifted pleasantly away from the present. When he looked up he immediately noticed her red face and pursed lips. Her blue eyes, often so tender, cut right through him.

"What?" he asked innocently.

"You can't even answer me?" she badgered.

"Answer when? What are you talking about?"

"I asked if this is what you are going to do all day!"

"How can I hear you when I'm swimming with my head in the water? What's the problem?" He was utterly bewildered.

"I've been sitting here all morning by myself. Tell me if this is your idea of spending time together," she demanded as he lifted himself onto the edge of the pool.

"Darya, I am swimming while you sun yourself. This is what we usually do."

"Not after we've been away from each other for two weeks," she huffed. "Did you not notice it has been two weeks?"

"Of course I noticed. What would you like to do? I'm ready."

"I want to walk on the beach."

"Fine, then we walk to the beach," he said gently, hoping to avert a serious argument. Her sharp tongue had always been an annoyance, one he tolerated only because of the perks that came with it. He loved the way she looked, the way she felt in his arms, the way she spent money on him, and the way she lived here in the Hamptons. What he didn't love was her moodiness and her occasional mention of marriage. No, marriage with her would never happen. If she had $50 million in the bank, well, then perhaps he'd risk waking up to her every day. But much of what she had was tied up in her two homes, leaving too little to fund the kind of lifestyle for which he hungered.

Pushkina dialed back her temper during the short stroll to the beach, where she bumped into a good friend and chatted for nearly 20 minutes while Petrenko stood by and nodded agreeably from time to time. Part of him wanted to run back to the house, jump in the Porsche, and head back to Manhattan. But the rest of him chose to stay and live the good life for at least a day or two. It seemed a small price to pay for such luxury.

By the time they finished their long surfside walk and returned home, Petrenko and Pushkina were holding hands, smiling, and once again enjoying each other's company.

"I need to take a shower," she said coyly, "and get out of this bathing suit."

"That is a splendid idea, Darya. I will gladly help you."

"You had better," she smiled.

The remainder of the day went exceedingly well until 6:45, just before the first guests were due to arrive for the soiree. A catering crew, most of them attractive coeds from local colleges, enjoyed a few precious moments of down time before their evening got crazy, and Petrenko chose the opportunity to chat up 20-year-old Eviana Fairhope. In his long and well-traveled life he had encountered few women worthy of the phrase "drop-dead gorgeous," but Miss Fairhope was one of them. She stood 5-6, had the body of a lingerie model, and wore her golden hair in a pony tail that swayed enticingly as she walked. As if this weren't enough to hold his attention, she was a senior majoring in Russian language and literature, and she was delighted to trade a few sentences with him.

Darya Pushkina, on the other hand, was not at all delighted by the interest Petrenko and Fairhope showed in each other, and she made this clear in characteristically blunt terms as she marched toward them with a tumbler of vodka in her hand.

"I ask for waitresses and they send me hookers," she said loud enough to be heard in Moscow. "Do you plan to take this little tramp for a walk in the bushes, Ilya?"

Fairhope was speechless, but Petrenko was furious. He turned toward Pushkina, who had been sucking down drinks for the past two hours, and decided to bid their turbulent relationship an overdue farewell.

"Darya, this woman is not only younger, prettier, and smarter than you," he told her, "she is also far nicer. Perhaps in time she will become, like you, a miserable bitch, but she has a very long way to go."

He walked away and left Pushkina screaming profanities in his wake. For him the affair was over, and if the traffic cooperated he would be back home shortly after 9:00 p.m., with plenty of time left to hit a couple of his favorite night spots.

The Porsche roared to life and leapt down the long driveway toward the Bronx.

23.

For three consecutive days at random hours Nazareth and Gimble had driven past Petrenko's home, a lovely red-brick colonial in one of Riverdale's finest areas, and not once had they seen a security guard. They had also gotten an important assist from their spy friend Dalton Stark in Washington, who had arranged for some nighttime satellite surveillance. This, too, indicated Petrenko felt he was adequately protected by the security company whose sign was prominently displayed next to the front stairs.

"This guy is no security expert, Pete," Gimble declared as they drove home after the final drive-by. "A pro wouldn't be using some mom-and-pop security service to protect his home."

"Agreed. He's a spy, plain and simple. I'm sure his staff does all the real security work at the consulate while he just signs off on it. As for his home, he probably sleeps with a Makarov 9mm under his pillow and figures that's enough."

"Which it probably is."

Nazareth grinned. "Not if he's partying all weekend in the Hamptons."

A week later, at 9:15 p.m. on September 23rd, Nazareth sat alone in a rental car across the street and a few doors down from Petrenko's house. He opened his laptop and called up the hacking software he'd be using for the night's mission. It took him less than five minutes to identify the wireless network that managed the home's security, including all the connected doors and windows. He memorized the code, 7651, and with one tap of the ENTER key disarmed the entire system.

He exited the vehicle with his laptop, walked confidently to Petrenko's front door, and rang the bell. While seeming to wait for an answer he used two slender tools -- a tension wrench and a diamond pick -- to unlock the deadbolt in less than 20 seconds.

He opened the door with his left hand and reached in with his right, making a great show of shaking hands with someone. The entire scene took less than 30 seconds and looked authentic enough to satisfy any curious neighbors who might be watching.

As soon as he entered the foyer he scanned for flashing lights, just in case the alarm system had somehow foiled his hack. Once satisfied he was clear, he locked the front door and headed upstairs to the four bedrooms on the second floor. He held a small LED flashlight in his teeth as his gloved hands quickly opened and carefully examined dresser drawers, night tables, and closets. After 15 minutes of fruitless searching he went back down to the foyer and pondered his next move. A small table lamp bathed the living room in soft light, and he quickly decided that what he was after wouldn't likely be hidden in such a public space. So he walked down the hallway and into the darkened dining room, where he briefly studied the shadowy shapes of a long table, tall wine cabinet, and massive china closet. Nothing in the room seemed relevant to tonight's mission.

On his way back to the foyer he stopped and smiled when he noticed the door on his left. It hadn't caught his attention on the first pass, but this time it practically screamed for attention. The locked deadbolt on an interior door told him all he needed to know.

* * *

Petrenko made decent time on the drive back to the Bronx until he hit a nasty stretch of I-495 just before turning north on the Cross Island Parkway. Since he never did this trip on a Saturday night he couldn't tell whether the heavy traffic was typical or the result of an accident. Either way, he was mad as hell. He was still seething over Darya's attack on him and the young woman, and now through the windshield he saw nothing but tail lights stretching off into the distance. Was it too much to ask for a simple drive home? All he wanted was to change into something more appropriate, then head off to celebrate his new-found freedom at Moskva, a hip nightclub on Manhattan's Upper East Side. Instead of being home by 9:00, he'd be lucky to make it by 10:00 in this traffic.

His mood grew uglier by the minute.

* * *

Nazareth made short work of the hallway door's double-cylinder deadbolt and found himself standing at the top of a wooden cellar stairway. He used the small flashlight to navigate his way down into what appeared to be a small home office that occupied the left half of the basement. The right half consisted of a chest-high cinder block wall beyond which was a cement crawl space where Petrenko had haphazardly stored a bicycle, tool chest, and a dozen large cardboard boxes he had never bothered to unpack after coming to the U.S.

Once again the detective looked for signs of an operative alarm system or perhaps security cameras Petrenko had placed in this obviously off-limits area. Finding none, he moved to the large metal desk in the far corner and tested the main drawer. Locked. He opened it with a small pick and gently sorted through its contents: documents in Russian, a Citibank checkbook, and two passports. Both passports contained Petrenko's photo, but only one of them bore his real name. The other had been issued to Konstantin Azarov. What this meant was anyone's guess, but Nazareth had no time to worry about it. He needed to find the missing CD and get the hell out.

* * *

Stupid Americans, Petrenko thought as he inched his Porsche past the source of the long delay. Twenty minutes of bumper-to-bumper traffic because ignorant people had to slow down and watch a man change a flat tire! You'd think they were watching someone set foot on Mars for the first time.

He jumped on the gas and fantasized about shooting those who had caused a major traffic delay over such nonsense. It would serve them right while at the same time teaching others a valuable lesson. Most of all it would make him feel a whole lot better.

Shooting someone always made him feel better.

* * *

Inside the bottom right drawer Nazareth found two pistols and a small metal box. The two guns were high-end items: a Glock 23 with a laser sight and a futuristic Kalishnikov PL-14 9mm handgun. It was a pretty safe bet these weren't Petrenko's only weapons. An even safer bet was that neither gun had been registered in New York, but Nazareth didn't give that a second thought. At the moment he cared only about the contents of the metal box.

He turned the box away from his face, prayed it wasn't rigged to explode when opened, and held his breath as he undid the small metal latch. His stomach did a huge backflip when he slowly opened the box and saw the CD in its hard plastic case. Someone had printed the words **озеро огня** on the case with a red marker. Nazareth didn't read Russian, but he had a strong feeling that what he held in his hands was the beginning of the end of Ilya Petrenko and whatever dirty operation he had underway.

He opened his laptop and prepared to burn a copy of the disk.

* * *

At 9:53 the tires on Petrenko's Porsche squealed as he fishtailed into the driveway and screeched to a halt just inches short of the garage. Still fuming over the long drive from the Hamptons, he slammed the car door behind him and walked hurriedly toward the front door. He cursed loudly when he dropped his car keys and managed to kick them under the shrubs alongside the walk. After rooting through the damp mulch with his bare hands he located the keys, threw them angrily against the front door, and cursed again. The whole world was out to get him!

Before the night is over, he told himself, someone will regret my foul mood.

* * *

Nazareth held his breath when he heard the squealing tires because they sounded way too close. He flew up the basement stairs, desperately hoping Petrenko hadn't come home but instinctively knowing that tonight's well-laid plan had fallen apart. From the foyer he saw the Porsche at the garage and knew his NYPD career hinged entirely on whatever happened in the next few seconds.

He punched in the security alarm code, 7651, saw the keypad flash red, and ran down the hallway for the basement door. Behind him he heard a loud metallic sound and thought he was finished. But the front door still hadn't opened by the time he locked the deadbolt from the basement side and hustled down the stairs. He replaced the CD in its metal box and quietly closed the drawer.

* * *

Petrenko picked up his keys at the front door, let himself in, and turned off the alarm system. Then he threw the keys again, this time leaving an ugly scar on a kitchen cabinet. The damaged cabinet further fueled his anger, so he kicked the hall closet's sliding door hard enough to snap the upper hinges. When the door slammed into the hardwood floor it left a deep gouge three inches long.

After a string of vulgarities in both Russian and English he stomped to the kitchen and calmed himself with four fingers of Stolichnaya Elit, at $60 a bottle something meant to be sipped rather than gulped. But the jolt of alcohol did the trick, and the frustration of this long day began to subside. He would change, yes, into something casual but impressive and see what, or perhaps who, awaited him at the nightclub.

Before going up to the bedroom, though, he walked down the hallway and unlocked the basement door. He switched on the overhead lights as he went down the stairs to his desk, where he opened the lower right drawer and removed the Glock pistol. After checking that it was loaded, he moved toward the stairs but stopped suddenly and looked back at the desk.

Cash. Yes, he needed more cash for tonight. Credit cards left too much of a trail when he went out on the town, and he didn't like people knowing where he had been or what he had done. He opened a drawer filled with neatly banded bills -- twenties, fifties, hundreds -- and grabbed some of each.

With enough cash in your hand, he smiled, you own the world.

* * *

After the basement lights went out Nazareth remained hidden behind the cardboard boxes in the crawl space, gun in hand. Over the next 15 minutes he heard Petrenko walk heavily up the carpeted stairs to the bedroom, then down again and out the front door. The Porsche rumbled to life and was gone.

When he felt confident Petrenko wouldn't be coming back right away, Nazareth went over to the desk, removed the computer disk, and copied its contents to his laptop. Five minutes later he was in his rental car heading for Manhattan.

Where this operation went next depended entirely on whatever he had just stolen.

24.

At 10:30 p.m. the line of smartly dressed patrons outside Moskva was quickly growing longer. Four massive, unsmiling bouncers in tight black muscle tees made sure everyone stayed behind the velvet rope and didn't block the sidewalk while waiting, and hoping, to enter one of Manhattan's hottest night spots. Now and then one of the crew members tapped an unattached pretty young woman on the shoulder and escorted her to the main entrance, where she was granted immediate access to the splendors within. No cover charge, no ID check. Anyone who grumbled about the unfairness of the system was invited to leave the line and told not to come back.

An older guy sporting a confident smile strolled past the throng up to the entrance. He was outfitted in a $15,000 silver-gray Brioni suit, an $800 burgundy silk shirt open to mid-chest, and $3,000 alligator loafers. The door manager immediately jumped from his seat.

"Good evening, Mr. Petrenko," he said in Russian as he bowed his head slightly. "What a wonderful surprise. We are delighted to have you with us."

As they shook hands vigorously Petrenko slipped the guy a $50 bill. "Thank you, Maxim. It is a pleasure to be here once again. How is the guest list tonight?"

Maxim grinned and said, "Some very lovely guests in need of a gentleman like you, Mr. Petrenko."

"Then I will do my utmost," Petrenko smiled, "to satisfy their needs."

The club's interior looked like an odd cross between a mid-seventies discotheque and the Komsomolskaya subway station in Moscow. But the mixture of flashing lights, soaring arches, and stunning laminated glass dance floor all worked somehow, creating an 80-decibel dreamscape in which Moskva's glittering revelers could leave the real world behind.

As soon as the floor manager spotted Petrenko he rushed over, greeted his important guest, and signaled for one of his men to bring a table. He held up four fingers, and in less than a minute a table for four had been nestled alongside the dance floor. A waiter appeared with an ice bucket containing a bottle of Stoli Elit vodka, and the manager poured the first glass.

"You always remember what I like, Oleg," Petrenko nodded.

"You have excellent taste in vodka, Mr. Petrenko," he said while palming the two $100 bills, "as you do in women. Would you enjoy some company this evening?"

"Yes, that would be very nice, Oleg."

He watched Oleg pass among the dancers who writhed and shuffled to the pounding beat of Pompeya, a popular Russian band the DJ always featured on his playlist. And then, as if by magic, the young women began arriving at Petrenko's table -- three of them, each beautiful, each wearing a tight, very short dress. Yes, they would love some vodka. Yes, they would enjoy dancing. And, yes, they would stay at his table and compete for his attention until the important man from the Russian consulate had decided which of them would leave the club with him tonight.

For the next hour and a half Petrenko and his delightful table guests danced, drank, and nibbled on thin crackers topped with Beluga caviar. What a glorious time to be free of that nasty bitch Darya! he thought. The young blonde to his right was running her shoeless foot up and down his leg while the brunette on his left would be in his lap if she got any closer. Yet he was primarily attracted to Tanya, the woman who sat across the table from him -- the one with the raven hair and smoldering looks who wore a tiny black cocktail dress with a V-neck that made his mouth water. She talked less than the others, but with her eyes she delivered a white-hot message.

Yes, she would be the one.

His cell phone rang just as he leaned forward to invite the dark-haired beauty to dance, and he angrily yanked it from his jacket. The timing could not have been worse. If this was Darya calling to beg his forgiveness he would tell her what to do with her self-pity.

"Petrenko," he growled. He recognized the voice immediately and adopted a more pleasant tone of voice. "Yes, I have what you need. Do *you* have what *I* need?" he asked calmly.

"We are prepared to pay $15 million," said a man with a Middle Eastern accent. "We believe that is more than enough."

The fuse that had been lit earlier that day in the Hamptons finally ignited Petrenko's vodka-fueled rage. "You are not even halfway to the right number, you raghead butcher. You do not decide what is enough. I decide! Do not call me again," he warned, "unless you have fifty." He hung up without waiting for a response and with a vicious backhand swatted his full glass off the table. The glass smashed into a neighboring table, spraying the young couple seated there with cold vodka and shattered crystal.

The young man who had just been doused with vodka immediately jumped to his feet and started for Petrenko. "You worthless old asshole," he screamed while his girlfriend plucked shards of glass from the front of her dress. "I'll break your neck."

Petrenko turned toward his attacker with murderous eyes and without saying a word delivered a ferocious right fist to the middle of the guy's handsome face, crushing his nose and shearing off three of his upper teeth. The young man fell backward onto his girlfriend, toppling her chair, and the two of them hit the floor covered with blood and booze.

Oleg the floor manager rushed over with two bouncers in tow. "Are you all right, Mr. Petrenko?" he shouted over the noise of the dance floor.

"This young punk attacked me, Oleg. He doesn't belong in polite company."

The bouncers silently awaited the command. Oleg pointed to the couple on the floor and aimed his thumb at the front door. "They never come back here," he commanded. "Have them pay for this damage, then throw them both out." Both men nodded dutifully and did as they were told. "I apologize for this, Mr. Petrenko. I am very sorry for the upset."

"Not at all, Oleg. As usual you have done everything perfectly. You can't control the behavior of everyone who comes here."

"Rest assured they will not come here again."

"And I appreciate that, Oleg. You are a fine man. Please, join us for a drink."

"Just one, Mr. Petrenko. Thank you."

Five drinks later Oleg escorted the blonde and brunette from the table and arranged for private cars to take them home. Petrenko, meanwhile, helped his raven-haired beauty into the Porsche, revved the engine, and popped the clutch. He was mad as hell that the big financial transaction had not yet closed.

But he was confident Tanya could help him forget about that until tomorrow.

25.

"Well, we've got it," Nazareth said softly as he and his wife stared at the large computer screen on his desk.

"Yeah, now we have to figure out what it is," she nodded.

Accessing the information taken from Petrenko's home had been easy, but the two detectives weren't at all sure what they were looking at. The first thing that had popped up on the screen was a number, SOVU809993, whose meaning was completely up for grabs. After that came an architect's rendering of what appeared to be a building, and a rather large one at that. But since all of the written details were in Russian, Nazareth and Gimble had no idea what the complex diagram represented.

Nazareth glanced at his watch. "Almost midnight. I hate calling Stark this late."

"He's probably up. Besides, he's the one who gave you the green light to go get this stuff. Why wouldn't he want to know what you found?"

"Yeah, I suppose." He dialed the number in D.C. and got Stark on the first ring.

"Hey, Pete, how's it going?"

"Great, I think. But you'll have to be the judge of that." He told Stark about his visit to Petrenko's basement, the writing on the disk's plastic cover, and the information he and Gimble had been staring at for the past hour.

"I can translate the Russian, no problem," Stark told him. "So why don't we start there and see whether that explains the blueprint. As for the number you're looking at, I have someone here who can probably tell us whether it's a product ID, serial number, or something else."

"Okay. How do we get this to you?"

"As we speak I'm sending you an encryption app that will take a few minutes to install on your computer. Once you've done that," he added, "download the information you got tonight and email it to me. Will you two still be awake an hour from now?"

"You bet."

"Great. I'll call you back."

Thirty-five minutes later Gimble grabbed the bedroom phone just as Nazareth picked up in the kitchen. "This could be a big deal, guys," Stark began, "but I'm not quite sure yet. The blueprint is for a tunnel we shut down years ago, something the Russians were still in the process of building. It was supposed to run from under their consulate to the reservoir in Central Park."

"How close to finishing it were they?" Gimble asked.

"Too close. They had spent huge money on the project, but until tonight we could never pin down the purpose. The CD you found seems to offer a clue. That printing you saw on the cover, **озеро огня**? A rough translation is *Lake of Fire.*"

"Not good," said Nazareth, shaking his head.

"Amen," Stark replied. "And there's more. The blueprint indicates that the tunnel was going to end in a chamber whose precise dimensions and construction materials were to be contained only in a separate document classified beyond top secret."

"So we still don't know what they were up to," Gimble noted.

"But we now have a better idea," Stark assured her. "All we had before was the actual tunnel as far as it had gotten. Thanks to this blueprint we now we have an insight into what the final product was supposed to look like."

"It was going to be a goddamn containment chamber, wasn't it?" Nazareth said angrily.

"You and I are on the same page, Pete. If that chamber near the Central Park reservoir was supposed to be constructed of steel and lead, I'd say there's a good chance they had planned to store nuclear material inside."

"Nuclear material as in nuclear bomb?" Gimble said.

"We're just guessing, Tara," Stark answered, "but that's what I'd say. I can't remember what nonsensical explanation they had given us for the tunnel at the time, but no one bought it. On the other hand, I don't recall anyone on our side mentioning a nuclear weapon. I think I would have remembered that."

"Okay, so the tunnel was never completed," Nazareth said, "and we never found a weapon. Does that mean the weapon never came to the U.S.?"

"Still too early for that question, Pete. We don't know for sure whether this was about positioning a nuclear device in Manhattan. That's just the three of us thinking out loud. I need to have some of the techies here in D.C. take a look at the plans. At the same time I want to find out what that number on the disk means. For all we know it's the shipping code for a case of vodka."

"Are you willing to bet on that?" Nazareth laughed.

"Hell, no. But I still have no clue what the number means. I'll give you a call by mid-morning."

After a shorter night's sleep than usual Nazareth and Gimble hit the office, coffees in hand, and headed to the conference room. They closed the door and pulled up the tunnel blueprint on the large wall monitor. Although they still couldn't read the Russian notes, they now knew what they were looking at.

"I can't believe they actually built this under the Upper East Side without anyone noticing," Gimble offered, clearly amazed by the scope of the project. "Wouldn't they have needed official blueprints of all the buildings in that area as well as detailed information on the subway system, Con Ed tunnels, water lines, and everything else?"

"Yes, they would have. And I'm guessing all those things are readily available if you're prepared to pay off the right people. But what's really scary is that we never could have anticipated something of this magnitude and complexity. I mean, who expects the impossible?"

"You."

"Sometimes, Tara, but I never would have dreamed up something this crazy. And they damn near got away with it."

The blueprint revealed an incredibly complex underground network that wormed its way over, under, or around every obstacle it encountered as it approached Central Park.

"Whoever designed this must have been a genius," Gimble noted.

"Also a sick SOB. If this was actually about planting a nuclear weapon in the park, someone was looking to take out damn near the entire city."

"You think that would have been possible?"

"Depends on a lot of things, mostly the size of the device. But I think even a relatively small bomb could finish off most of us."

Nazareth grabbed his cell phone on the first ring when Dalton Stark called in.

"Hey, Dalton. I'm at the office with Tara."

"Good morning, guys. Here's what I've got on that number you found on the CD," he told them. "It almost certainly represents a shipping container belonging to a former Soviet company called Morom Global Enterprises, or MGE, which folded in early 1992, just after the Soviet Union collapsed. On paper, at least, MGE was a legitimate business, but back then any Russian company could have been used by the state for any purpose at all."

"Including the shipment of a nuclear weapon?" Gimble asked.

"You name it, MGE would have done it as long as the right Soviet bureaucrat signed off."

"Is there any record of what happened to the shipping container?" Nazareth asked.

"No, but there should be. If the shipment had been delivered," Stark explained, "the container should have been released for future use. At the same time the number would have been closed out in the system. But as far as we can tell it never was."

"Dalton, how likely is it the Russians could actually ship a nuclear device to New York City?" Gimble wanted to know.

"Today, not very likely. We've had the Container Security Initiative in place since 2002, so for certain high-risk shippers we check all U.S.-bound cargo before it leaves the home port. But at the time MGE was operating," he added ominously, "there was essentially no security at all."

"Tara asked me earlier how much damage a nuclear device could do if it were detonated in Central Park," Nazareth said. "Did you happen to ask your team for an assessment?"

"I did, and it's grim," he said, "which is why we need to find that shipping container."

Gimble was shaken. "Wait a second, you think there may be a nuclear bomb here somewhere?"

"If we can't prove it's not," Stark replied, "we need to assume it is, Tara."

"Then why are we not already interrogating Petrenko?" she shouted.

"You know we can't touch him, Tara," Nazareth answered. "The evidence we have was obtained illegally, and we still aren't certain it's linked to a terrorist plot. If we go after Petrenko now he'll claim diplomatic immunity and be gone in a couple of hours."

"So what the hell do we do?" she demanded.

"I guess we start checking shipping containers," Nazareth said.

"I'd hold off, Pete," Stark said. "You'd actually need a small army to do that. Port Newark alone occupies nearly 300 acres, and they move nearly a million containers a year. Talk about a needle in a haystack."

"What do you suggest instead?" Nazareth asked.

"If Petrenko is attempting to sell a nuclear weapon, he needs to set things up very carefully with the buyer," Stark reasoned. "I'll have someone start listening to all of Petrenko's phone calls."

"How the hell long will it take to get a court order for that?" Gimble asked nervously.

Stark tried but failed to disguise his amusement. "Tara," he said, "I love your sense of humor."

26.

Nazareth and Gimble were nearly ready to leave the office for lunch when the chief waved them over. His face was more flushed than usual, and he wore a tight-jawed scowl typically reserved for his infrequent but sometimes spectacular bad moods. He motioned for Gimble to shut the door behind her as she followed her husband into the boss's office.

"Seems we have another Russian problem," he growled.

Nazareth had a sickening vision of his NYPD career swirling down the toilet. Obviously the chief had somehow learned of the break-in at Petrenko's house and was about to explode. Would the explosion take out just one career or two? Even though Gimble hadn't participated in the illegal search, she was certainly part of the conspiracy. Here's hoping Dalton Stark is actually capable of saving our asses, Nazareth thought as he glanced over at his wife.

"I just got a call from the mayor himself," Crawford began as he studied Nazareth's face, "and you know I hate when that happens." He seemed to be waiting for an admission of guilt before proceeding.

"What's the problem, chief?" Gimble asked innocently, already knowing the answer. By the time this conversation was over she and her husband would both be unemployed, maybe even in a holding cell for illegal search and seizure.

"Well, our illustrious mayor had just gotten off the phone with one of his big-shot campaign donors, Boris or Ivan something," Crawford said, "who's apparently the president of some Russian-American civic association we've all never heard of. Sounds as though the guy's son got his face punched in last night at an Uptown nightclub by the name of Moskva."

146

The heavy weight that had been pressing on Nazareth's chest immediately fell off. "Why'd he call you and not somebody Uptown?" he asked.

"Ah, I didn't tell you who did the punching. Apparently it was your boy Ilya Petrenko from the Russian consulate. So, naturally, since the mayor is a royal pain in my ass," Crawford complained, "he figured we should be in charge because we're investigating the Gerasimov and Sidorenko murders. I guess if a crime involves someone who either speaks or looks Russian it automatically comes to us from now on."

"I won't try to follow his logic," Nazareth said, "but the mayor may actually have lucked into the right call this time. Tara and I are still thinking there's a chance Petrenko murdered the two dissidents, and as you know we're certain the guy's a spy. But we have nothing solid on him yet."

"And if we go after Petrenko because he punched out some rich guy's kid," Gimble added, "we may succeed in having him sent back home without ever learning what he's up to."

The chief tapped a ballpoint pen on the top of his desk while he weighed the mayor's urgent call against the work being done by his two star detectives. If Crawford disclosed their interest in Ilya Petrenko, Mayor Dortmund would undoubtedly blab about it to someone and spoil everything. He had done that sort of thing before since his brain rarely kept pace with his mouth. But simply sitting on the mayor's request could prove disastrous. Crawford didn't feel like spending the rest of his career patrolling the City Hall grounds on the midnight shift.

"All right, let's do this," the chief said. "I'll kill a few days having the alleged victim and some witnesses interviewed. If I keep feeding Dortmund daily progress reports, maybe he'll leave me alone for a while. But eventually we'll have to interview Petrenko."

"If Petrenko punched some guy out," Gimble said, "I don't think he'd be surprised to have a detective visit him. It just can't be Pete or me. But whoever speaks with him has to make sure

Petrenko gets off the hook for this. Otherwise, he'll be flying back to Russia before we have a chance to nail him for something serious."

"I hear you. Of course, there's a small detail, right? You're not at all sure he's done anything wrong," Crawford replied.

"Pete and I are absolutely certain this guy is involved in something major," Gimble replied. "And we'll get the evidence. But if he's hassled over this stupid nightclub incident, we'll lose him for good."

"Okay, fine. But we don't have forever. You need to wrap this up as fast as you can. It goes without saying," Crawford added, "that Dortmund considers Petrenko guilty until proven innocent."

"Got it, chief. We'll push hard," Gimble assured him.

Crawford warily eyed both of them. "And remember," he said sharply, "*do not* go near Petrenko's home. We're not starting World War III over this."

"No World War III," Nazareth grinned.

The chief shook his head, sighed, and waved them out. Then he abruptly changed his mind. "Wait a second," he called after them. "Come on back and close the door again." He motioned for them to have a seat. Apparently this would take longer than a second.

"I've been at this police thing for a really long time, and I've mostly loved it. Not when the mayor calls," he laughed, "but there's nothing I can do about that. Anyway, over the past year or so my wife and I have talked about what we'll do when I retire. Where we'll live, how we'll spend our time, and all that. To make a long story short, I put my retirement papers in recently."

Nazareth and Gimble were flabbergasted. For the past several days they had worried that Crawford might be up to no good. Actually it was more than that: they reluctantly suspected him of being involved in something dirty. They had no explanation for why he was at his office window secretly taking photos of the Downtown area. When in doubt, they had agreed, assume the worst. That's what the job does to you.

"I don't know what to say, chief," Nazareth began. "I mean ..."

"Just listen first. When my wife and I agreed it was time for me to retire, we also agreed I had to find out what I'd do with myself. This job," he looked around the office at all the memorabilia he had collected during his storied career, "has been pretty much my entire life, and I've been really worried about what would happen to me if I stopped cold turkey. I'm not into gardening or rocking chairs or crossword puzzles. Know what I mean?"

"Absolutely," Gimble said sympathetically.

"So about a month ago I spent a small fortune on camera gear at 42nd Street Photo, enrolled in a digital photography class at the School of Visual Arts over on East 23rd, and started learning all about exposure and shutter speed and composition and all that other crap. When you saw me the other day, Pete," he continued, "I was doing the latest homework assignment: *The Statue of Liberty at Daybreak.*"

"How'd the pictures turn out?" Nazareth asked.

"The camera I bought will do damn near everything except brush your teeth for you, so the pictures were fine. But I wanted to keep this little project to myself because I wasn't ready to tell you guys about the retirement."

"Well, I think it's wonderful you've taken up photography," Gimble said brightly, "and you certainly deserve a great retirement after all the years you've put in. But Pete and I are going to miss the hell out of you."

"You're not rid of me yet," the chief said, allowing himself a half smile.

"So when does this happen?" Nazareth asked.

"It doesn't. I pulled the retirement papers yesterday."

"What happened?" both detectives asked at more or less the same time.

"I found out that taking pictures is about as exciting as watching mold grow on my basement walls," he told them. "I hate the camera, the tripod, the lenses, the class, and the pictures. Mostly I hate the idea of not being in the middle of the action. It's bad enough I spend most of my time at a desk. I'm not ready to park my ass on a bench in Central Park and take pictures of old men like me feeding pigeons. Just shoot me instead, please."

"If you're sure about this, then we're really glad you'll be staying, chief. No one else in the entire department would ever have done as much as you've done for us and the other guys," Gimble said.

Nazareth nodded as he shook Crawford's hand. "Really glad you're not leaving us yet."

"And you're really glad I'm not a spy, right?"

"I'd never think that," Nazareth lied.

The chief laughed. "That'll be the day when Detective Peter Nazareth sees something suspicious and doesn't think the worst."

"I was intrigued, not suspicious."

"Right, whatever. But, listen, I haven't told anyone else what was going on, so please keep this to yourselves, okay? And when the day really does come," he added, "I'll tell both of you before I start sneaking around the office."

"Deal," Nazareth said. "In the meantime, you can keep looking for the perfect retirement hobby."

"What I'm actually thinking about now is opening my own coffee shop. Speaking of which . . ."

"Uh, thanks anyway," Nazareth replied. "I think I speak for Tara as well when I say we've traveled that road and don't plan to again."

"In that case," Crawford said in mock disgust, "you two can get the hell out of my office. Go find out what this Petrenko character is up to."

Fifteen minutes later Nazareth and Gimble sat on a shaded bench enjoying their deli sandwiches. Corned beef on rye for him, tuna on pita for her. They shared a bag of reduced-fat potato chips that tasted remarkably like reduced-fat potato chips.

"Next time get the full-fat chips, Pete. These don't cut it."

"Yes, Tara, darling," he taunted. "My bad."

"And next time you suspect the chief of being an international spy . . ."

"Somehow I don't think that will happen again."

"Good. Then all is right with the world."

"Except that Ilya Petrenko might be trying to help someone blow it up."

"This is true," she agreed. "We definitely need to do something about that."

27.

Late that afternoon Nazareth took a phone call from Dalton Stark and got Gimble on the line. Their Washington friend had asked his tech guys to take a hard look at Feodor Sidorenko's blood test results and wanted to share the details.

"It's better to be lucky than smart," Stark said. "You're both going to love this."

"You found something in his blood results?" Gimble asked.

"No, not a thing. The written summary was useless. We needed an actual blood sample. But here's the deal. The hospital had bagged the guy's clothes along with his other personal effects, and we were able to isolate fluid samples from what he was wearing."

"How the hell did you do that?" Nazareth asked.

"With a mass spectrometer. First you vaporize the sample and . . ."

"No, I'm not talking about the actual test," Nazareth interrupted. "I mean how did you manage to get hold of his clothing from the hospital?"

"Friends in the right places, Pete. Anyway, we have a cause of death." Stark paused for effect. "And you won't be surprised. Sidorenko died of a fatal dose of tetrodotoxin, aka puffer fish neurotoxin. Unless he had some seriously bad sushi that night, he was murdered."

"Have you told anyone else yet?" Gimble asked.

"No, and I don't plan to. Whoever killed Sidorenko assumes he's gotten away with it, and that could work to your advantage. Maybe he'll get a little overconfident."

"Makes sense," Nazareth said. "There's no need to disclose the true cause of death yet since we're obviously the only ones who care. I like having the killer think we don't suspect anything."

"Unfortunately, we still don't have the first clue about the killer's identity," Gimble noted. "One murder with a high-powered rifle, a second with puffer fish neurotoxin. Are we even dealing with just one person?"

"I'd say yes," Stark told her. "A huge amount of meticulous planning went into the Gerasimov shooting, and it came off flawlessly. Same with Sidorenko's poisoning. We may never know exactly when or where the killer got to him, but we do know the plan went off without a hitch. I believe you're dealing with one professional, not two lucky amateurs."

"I still wonder whether the Russians planted someone at the consulate for these hits," Nazareth noted.

"Anything's possible, Pete, but I'd rate that as extremely unlikely," Stark answered. "The Russians know we assume that most or all of their diplomats are spies, so having one of them play hitman in New York City would be too risky. I do believe Petrenko may be working with terrorists, but I doubt he's your killer. I'm pretty well convinced you're working two separate cases. Let me keep monitoring Petrenko's phone calls while you two find the assassin."

The detectives spent the remainder of the day assessing next steps in the Gerasimov and Sidorenko murders. For the moment, at least, they were willing to assume they were after one assassin who had used two very different, though equally effective, methods of eliminating his targets. Like Dalton Stark, they were convinced the killer was a pro, which basically guaranteed he wasn't going to leave a simple trail for them to follow.

"Of the two murders," Nazareth reasoned, "the one that seems likeliest to provide us with a clue is Sidorenko's."

"Why so?" Gimble asked.

"In Gerasimov's case we have nothing but the result," he reasoned, "but with Sidorenko we have a verifiable chain of events we can break down and analyze bit by bit. We were there at his speech; we saw him at the reception; we know people were with him for at least a couple of hours after we left; and we know someone drove him home. Somewhere within that timeline he was poisoned, and it's possible -- or maybe even likely -- someone saw the killer at work but didn't recognize what was happening at the time."

"That's pretty optimistic, Pete. If one of the guests had seen someone spiking Sidorenko's drink I think he or she would have spoken up by now."

"Sure. But if we're dealing with a real pro, I doubt he would have made his move obvious. I'm sure there are plenty of ways to deliver poison without standing out in a crowd."

"I think it's a stretch, but I can't think of a better theory right now. So why don't we backtrack to the night of Sidorenko's speech and see what sort of guest list the university can give us."

"And while we're at it let's get as many photos as we can. You never know who was in the crowd that night."

"Absolutely. I'm sure the university's p.r. office has some pictures of its own, and we can also look at photos that were published after the event."

"Sounds like a plan," Nazareth said enthusiastically. "It'll be good to focus on Sidorenko's murder while Dalton keeps an eye on Petrenko for us."

"Speaking of Dalton Stark," she said warily, "does it not strike you as a little odd that he always seems to have the right connections?"

"Surprising but not odd. He's apparently higher in the spy chain than I had thought. So I'm no longer surprised by what he comes up with. I'm certainly glad to have him on our side."

"I hope he really is."

"On our side?" he said, puzzled by her suspiciousness.

"Yeah." Then she laughed. "Oh, God, I'm beginning to get as paranoid as my husband."

"Sometimes paranoia's a good thing, but in this case we're okay."

"Here's hoping."

"Seriously, Tara. Stark's an American hero."

Late that night, not long after Nazareth and Gimble had fallen asleep, they were jolted awake by the fax machine on the kitchen island. The thing hardly ever rang since few people knew the number, so the sound almost always meant something bad was on the way. They arrived in the kitchen just as the transmission ended and picked up the two-page document. It was a copy of an article the *Washington Post* had published a few minutes earlier in its online edition, and at the top of the first page someone had scribbled *FYI, guys* with a black marker. The first two paragraphs answered a question that had been on their minds.

CIA APPOINTS NEW TOP SPY

WASHINGTON, DC -- Late yesterday during a meeting with members of the House Intelligence Committee, CIA Director Preston Landers confirmed the agency has a new head for its Directorate of Operations, formerly known as the National Clandestine Service. The Deputy Director for Operations essentially orchestrates all clandestine activities across the entire U.S. intelligence community.

Although the CIA never officially discloses the identity of its Deputy Director for Operations, several mainstream media sources have identified him as Dalton Stark, whose government career includes service as a highly decorated Navy SEAL, leadership of a U.S. paramilitary program in the Middle East, and most recently as White House intelligence liaison.

After a moment of thoughtful silence Gimble gently nodded and said, "Well, I guess we don't need to worry about whose side Dalton Stark is on."

"I assumed he was up there," Nazareth said, "but I didn't assume he was running all U.S. covert operations around the world. This explains how he always seems to know everything."

"Except what Ilya Petrenko is up to."

"For the moment, Tara. Just for the moment."

28.

Russian consul general Grigori Vasilyev sat alone in his office at East 91st Street, a small brass desk lamp throwing just enough light for him to study the items contained in the thick red folder. Ordinarily he wouldn't be working at 1:00 a.m., but these were not ordinary times. President Ruslan Kotov was an early riser who took great delight in terrorizing his subordinates first thing in the morning, and Vasilyev knew that a call concerning Feodor Sidorenko's death would be coming one day soon. In fact, he was somewhat troubled Kotov hadn't called already.

The Russian president had, after all, been on the phone immediately after Sergey Gerasimov's murder, demanding answers that Vasilyev still hadn't provided. Surely Kotov was displeased by that. And yet he still hadn't phoned about Sidorenko, in some ways an even higher-profile dissident than Gerasimov. Was it simply that Sidorenko was said to have died of natural causes? Impossible. A man with Kotov's background would never believe the author had suffered a fatal heart attack within weeks of Sergey Gerasimov's shooting. During his years in the KGB Kotov had surely killed enough people to know that the official cause of death is almost never the real one. There were many ways, both commonplace and exotic, to create the illusion of a heart attack, and Kotov undoubtedly knew them all.

No, some other explanation, perhaps something sinister, accounted for Kotov's silence on the matter of Sidorenko. And Vasilyev wondered whether his own grave had already been dug in Russia.

From the red folder he withdrew a thick sheaf of papers containing all of the reports he had sent the Kremlin concerning Sidorenko's activities in New York City. There were 27 reports in all, beginning with brief notes on a chance meeting between Vasilyev and Sidorenko at the Russian Tea Room three years earlier and ending with a summary of Sidorenko's recent speech at the university. The reports in between painted a clear picture of a man who had used his worldwide fame as a novelist to indict not only President Ruslan Kotov but the entire Russian government.

In one particularly prophetic report, written four months prior to Sidorenko's death, Vasilyev had even raised the specter of an attempt on the author's life. "His comments," he wrote, "have managed to antagonize many here in New York City who are extremely loyal to Russia and who ask why something hasn't been done. I am not certain of what remedy they have in mind, but it occurs to me that some of these people, including the most dangerous ones in Brighton Beach, could easily do more than talk about silencing Feodor Sidorenko." Vasilyev was able to confirm that this message had been received in Moscow, though as usual his report had elicited no response from either Kotov or one of his worthless aides.

Next he thumbed through a stack of 8x10 photos capturing the many moods of Sidorenko's active life in Manhattan. In this picture the novelist scribbled notes to himself while seated on a bench near the entrance to the Central Park Zoo. In the next he danced an energetic but clumsy foxtrot with an elderly blue-haired heiress at a fundraising event. Here he cheered enthusiastically after a performance of *The Flames of Paris* by the Mikhailovsky Ballet at Lincoln Center. In the next image he waved to the camera at a New York Yankees game while eating a hot dog alongside the team's owner. And finally, of course, he addressed the huge university audience only hours before his untimely passing.

The dossier also included copies of Sidorenko's credit card bills, a list of his most frequently used phone numbers, medical reports in both Russian and English, and photos of all the women he had dated while living in New York City. Vasilyev smiled when he came to the picture of Veronika Belyakova, a stunning beauty who had come close to marrying the author before the FBI arrested her for being a spy. What a waste of time and talent that particular project had been! But at least he hadn't been implicated in the messy aftermath. Had the FBI truly failed to learn that the young woman was operating under Vasilyev's orders, or had they played dumb in the hope of nailing him for even greater crimes? He might never know.

By 2:00 a.m. -- 9:00 a.m. in Moscow -- Vasilyev felt certain the Russian president would not be calling on this particular day, choosing instead to let his New York City underling continue to wonder what loud message lay hidden within the silence. Part of him wanted to make the call himself and get this over with. The wait was making him half crazy. But he concluded that revealing his paranoia would be a grave mistake. Kotov, after all, preyed on weakness, hunted for it the way a pack of wolves seeks the single limping deer within a large herd. To be weak in front of Kotov was to be almost dead.

Vasilyev carefully reassembled the red folder and placed it in the desk's center drawer on top of his security chief's latest daily report on the break-in investigation and next to his RSh-12 revolver. Suddenly a wave of nausea hit him as it did every time he thought about the missing CD. If the disk wasn't found before President Kotov learned of its theft, Vasilyev would without question put the gun to his head and squeeze the trigger.

Suicide was much preferable to whatever alternatives Ruslan Kotov might offer.

29.

Nazareth and Gimble had once again commandeered the conference room on their floor at One Police Plaza and covered the long wooden table with photos taken at the late Feodor Sidorenko's university speech. Some of the photos had been provided by the school's public affairs office while others had been found either online or in magazines and newspapers. As Gimble examined each of the images with a large magnifying glass, hoping to notice something that wasn't quite right, Nazareth studied the event's VIP guest list.

"Lots of Russian-sounding names," he said, "but that tells me nothing. I don't know any of these people. Hell, I'm not even sure what I'm looking for."

"The name with *killer* written next to it," she wisecracked.

"Oh, is that how it's done? Gee, thanks, detective. I'll go back and start over."

"Always glad to help, Pete."

"What would really help is for you to find a photo that shows a guy in a black cape holding a bottle of poison."

"I've been looking," she smiled, "but so far no luck. You know what's odd, though? Out of all these pictures there's not a single one by Alex Resnick."

"The famous photographer you talked about?"

"Yeah. What does it mean that the most acclaimed photographer in America doesn't get a single picture published after Sidorenko's death? Weird."

Nazareth thought about that. "Maybe he wasn't covering the speech for a specific publication. He was probably just adding to his files for when Sidorenko won the Nobel Prize."

"That's possible," she nodded, "but I don't see why he'd pass up a chance to have a few more photos published, especially after

Sidorenko died. I've got to believe his work would have been in demand."

"If you're suspicious, ask him."

"I think I'll call the university first. Maybe someone in the public affairs office knows whether Resnick was representing a specific publication." Two phone calls and eight minutes later she had her answer. "The guy running the event didn't even know Resnick was going to be there until he saw him working that night. He wasn't on the list of people who had requested press credentials."

"Then how did he get in?"

"I'm sure he had loads of other press passes," she reasoned, "and there's probably a good chance whoever let him in recognized the name."

"Did the guy at the university seem upset that Resnick was there?"

"Not at all. He was delighted, in fact. He figured some major coverage would follow."

"But instead," he replied, "nothing followed."

"Nothing by Resnick, for sure."

"Then it's probably worth paying him a visit. Nothing to lose."

"I hate treating him like a suspect just because he didn't have any photos published. I'm sure there's a perfectly innocent explanation."

"I agree. So tell him we're visiting some of the photographers who attended the event to see if we can find a picture that shows us something useful. You're a big fan of his, so it was perfectly understandable for you to notice him at Sidorenko's lecture."

"That actually sounds plausible," she smiled.

"Sure it's plausible. Just speak the truth. You've found nothing in all the published photos," he told her, "and you know there might be hundreds of good pictures that didn't get used. Who knows what we'll find?"

Gimble caught Resnick at home, and he seemed genuinely eager to assist the NYPD. He did quite a lot of work for the mayor, he told her, and in fact was working on a major project for City Hall at the moment. The two detectives could meet with him at his apartment in an hour.

"Nothing sounded off about him?" Nazareth asked her.

"Nope. He's doing a photo essay on people who both live and work in Manhattan, and Sidorenko made the short list. Nothing like having a Nobel laureate in the mix, right?"

"Absolutely. Does he have photos for us to look at?"

"About 150, all digital. He'll put them on a large computer screen so that we can look as hard as we want." Gimble was obviously more relaxed than she had been just a few minutes earlier. "Resnick sounded really happy about helping us, and I'm glad for that. I didn't like thinking maybe he was a bad guy. Your suspicious nature keeps rubbing off on me, Pete."

"Suspicious always beats naive, Tara. I'd rather be guilty of suspecting the innocent than not suspecting the guilty."

"I guess. But still, I didn't want to imagine someone like him being up to no good."

"Can't disagree."

By the time they got to Resnick's place he had uploaded all the pictures onto his computer, ready to be displayed on a $5,000 photo-editing monitor whose 32-inch screen would make reviewing the images a piece of cake. Definitely no need for Gimble's magnifying glass. The detectives declined an offer of prosecco and went instead with chilled bottles of Fiji water.

"Most of the shots are of Mr. Sidorenko," Resnick explained as he called up the first image, "but I'd estimate there are at least 50 that show the audience. Several of those images include people I recognized, and I can point them out unless you'd rather view the photos by yourselves. Your choice."

"That's very kind of you, Mr. Resnick," Gimble said. "If you can spare the time we'd love to have you help us out." When

Nazareth nodded in agreement, the photographer pulled up a chair next to them.

"Unfortunately, I don't have any photos of the VIP reception that followed the speech," Resnick offered, "because that was a private event, and I hadn't asked for an invitation. Being there that evening was actually a spur-of-the-moment decision. But since the speech was open to the public I felt comfortable attending."

"Tara and I were surprised you didn't have any of your photos published after the event," Nazareth said.

"I focus primarily on nature, as you may know," Resnick offered, "so the speech wasn't the sort of thing I would normally cover. But the mayor's project has me looking in all sorts of directions right now, and it occurred to me that Mr. Sidorenko was a fine example of those who both live and work in Manhattan. I now suspect none of these photos will be useful to that project under the circumstances."

"Did you know Mr. Sidorenko?" Gimble asked.

"I never had the pleasure of meeting him. I have, however, read all of his novels, and I greatly regret he will not be writing others. This is a terrible loss."

The first few dozen photos revealed nothing unusual, but Gimble grew excited when the next image appeared and she spotted Ilya Petrenko in the audience. He sat in the fifth row at the center of the auditorium and seemed completely absorbed in what Feodor Sidorenko was saying at the moment.

"You know him?" Resnick asked.

"Yes, we've met him," Gimble said. "He's the security chief at the Russian embassy."

"Ah, interesting. I suppose the Russians like to keep an eye on someone as famous and outspoken as Mr. Sidorenko."

"We suspected as much," Nazareth told him, "but here's the proof. It certainly doesn't mean Ilya Petrenko is guilty of anything, but it's helpful to know he was in the audience that night."

"If you'd like," Resnick offered, "I can crop the image and enlarge that area for you."

"That would be great," she said.

Resnick worked on the image for a few seconds, hit PRINT, and handed Gimble a color 8x10 showing Petrenko and those seated to his left and right.

"Do you know any of these others?" Resnick asked.

Gimble shook her head. "I don't think so, but we can run them through facial-recognition software just in case."

"Well, let me help you out," Resnick said. "The lovely young woman to his right is the daughter of Russia's ambassador to the U.N. I've never met her, but I remember her face from an event at Gracie Mansion. And the man to her right -- you can see he is holding her hand -- is the French Ambassador to the U.N., Yves Lemaire. Him I know because he helped arrange an exhibition of my work in Paris."

"The three of them must be there together," Gimble said. "It's too much of a coincidence for the Russian U.N. ambassador's daughter to be sitting next to the Russian consulate's security chief."

"Let's look at the next few images," Resnick suggested. "Maybe they'll give us a clue." But only two images contained all three people, and at no time did Petrenko seem to be interacting with the couple to his right.

"Unless a later photo shows us something different," Nazareth offered, "we'll have to assume Petrenko wasn't with the other two. I'm not sure it would matter anyway, but it's an intriguing combination of players, isn't it?"

"Yes, it is, detective," Resnick answered, "but I'm afraid my photos won't be shedding any further light on this small mystery. Once I'm finished photographing a particular element of a large scene, I don't go back. I simply keep moving. So I don't have any other photos of these three. But here, let me show you something else."

He advanced slowly through eight or nine more images, then stopped at one he knew would prove interesting to his guests. It showed two well-dressed older men who occupied adjoining seats. The one on the right had leaned toward his neighbor and appeared to be speaking angrily.

"Do you know these men?" Resnick asked. The detectives didn't. "The unhappy man on the right is Semyon Voznesensky, one of the most powerful mobsters in Brighton Beach. I know this because two years ago, when I was having dinner at the River Cafe in Brooklyn, he came over to my table quite drunk and said he wanted several of my most important photographs."

"And did you sell to him?" Gimble asked.

Resnick laughed heartily. "No, detective, he didn't want to buy them. He thought I should be honored to have my work hang in the home of such a great man. The photographs were to be gifts from me to him."

"What did you say?" Nazareth wanted to know.

"I didn't have to answer. The man to his left here in this photograph came over, took Voznesensky by the arm, and gently led him back to his table. After they had left the restaurant," he continued, "someone told me who they were. The man on the left here, whose name I was never given, is apparently the one who does Voznesensky's dirty work. Precisely how dirty is anyone's guess."

"I'm glad you're still here with us," Gimble said seriously.

"As am I, detective. On the other hand, it was flattering to think that a leader of the Russian Mafia loved my work."

"As long as he doesn't love you to death," Nazareth quipped.

"I agree with you there, detective. Too much of a good thing is never healthy."

The three of them spent another 45 minutes analyzing each of the images, with Resnick occasionally pointing out someone he recognized: a deputy mayor, an opera star, and a TV talk show host among them. But no one came close to piquing the detectives' interest as much as Ilya Petrenko and Russian mobster Semyon Voznesensky. It was relatively easy to imagine circumstances under which either of those two might have wanted the author dead.

"This has been extremely helpful, Mr. Resnick," Nazareth said as he offered his hand. "We really appreciate the time you've given us."

"Not at all, my friends. I am glad to help in any way I can." He handed Nazareth a business card. "My cell phone number is on here, and you can reach me no matter where I may be traveling. Please don't hesitate to call if I can be of assistance."

As the detectives inched along toward One Police Plaza in heavy traffic Nazareth was uncharacteristically silent, generally a sign that something was troubling him. Gimble had seen this many times before, often just before Nazareth seemed to pluck a brilliant idea out of thin air. So she waited and left him alone to his thoughts.

"That picture of Petrenko alongside the Russian ambassador's daughter," he said while jumping on the brake to avoid a yellow cab that had just swerved in front of him, "got me a little sidetracked. I've been thinking too much about what sort of connection there might be between the two of them."

"So what's your conclusion?"

"That they bumped into each other that night and decided to sit next to each other. That's all. She's not involved in some sort of bizarre criminal conspiracy, especially when she's sitting there holding hands with the French U.N. ambassador. So I vote we stop thinking about her."

"Okay. I can buy that."

"The key is that Petrenko was in the audience, and that means he most likely could have gotten close enough to Sidorenko to poison him. He wasn't on the VIP reception list," he added, "but that means nothing. It wouldn't have been too difficult to sneak in, spike the guy's drink, and bail."

"And what about the mobster from Brighton Beach?"

"We can get some background on him to see if he's so pro-Russian that he'd consider killing someone for speaking out against the homeland, but I can't imagine him showing up and actually killing Sidorenko. He'd never put himself anywhere near the crime scene."

"So it's Ilya Petrenko at the top of the list."

"Maybe two lists," Nazareth continued. "Arming terrorists and murdering dissidents. Tough double, eh?"

30.

Long after midnight the two detectives were sound asleep in their apartment when the phone on the night table jolted them awake. Nazareth grabbed it and mumbled a half-hearted greeting.

"Sorry to wake you up, Pete, but something big is about to go down." Dalton Stark sounded more businesslike than usual, and the urgency in his voice was unsettling.

"No problem, Dalton. What's going on?"

"Open your front door, and I'll tell you?"

"You're outside our apartment?"

"Would I lie about this?"

Nazareth went to the door dressed only in boxer shorts emblazoned with the U.S. Marine Corps logo while Gimble wrapped herself in an oversized fleece robe. Stark's mood lightened just a bit when he saw his friend's get-up.

"Semper Fi, Pete. Once a Marine, always a Marine."

"Oh, these. Tara gave them to me. I have matching socks if you want to see them."

"I'll pass on that opportunity. Is Tara here?"

"She is," Gimble said as she came around the corner from the bedroom. "Are you actually here, or is this just part of some crazy dream?"

"Nightmare is more like it, guys. I landed at LaGuardia 20 minutes ago," he told them, "and we all need to be someplace in a hurry. I apologize for the short notice, but I'll explain on the way."

Fifteen minutes later they were powering through the Holland Tunnel in a black armored SUV driven by a scary looking guy whose chest threatened to rip apart his camouflaged T-shirt. He was quiet, armed, and clearly dangerous.

"This here's D," Stark said from the front seat. "D, Detectives Nazareth and Gimble." D nodded but kept his eyes moving rapidly between the road ahead and the three rearview mirrors.

"Remember that phantom shipping container we talked about? Well, about an hour before I showed up at your apartment," Stark began, "we intercepted an encrypted phone conversation between Ilya Petrenko and an unknown suspect with an Arabic accent. At 11:00 o'clock tonight, or roughly 21 hours from now, they'll be exchanging $50 million for a nuclear weapon presently stored in a shipping container at Port Newark."

"Dear God!" Gimble responded. "I can't believe this."

"Believe it, Tara," said Stark. "This is about as bad as it gets."

"Have you located the container?" Nazareth wanted to know.

"Yes, thanks to you two. That code number you found on the stolen CD was easy to trace once we hacked Port Newark's system. Looks as though the container has been there for a very long time," he noted, "and fortunately for us it's located right near the water where we can easily access it."

"But I thought we screened shipping containers for radioactivity!" Gimble exclaimed. "How does a nuclear bomb sit there for years without being detected?"

"Too soon to say," Stark explained, "but in all probability both the weapon and the container have been shielded. In that case, unless you go inside, you'd never know."

"Could the bomb still be operational after all this time?" she asked.

"Absolutely. We need to assume the device has been connected to an electric current the whole time, in which case it's ready to go."

"Okay, so what happens tonight?" Nazareth wondered.

"First of all, this is now a federal operation," Stark replied. "Officially your role is to help us identify Petrenko. Unofficially, of course, you deserve to be here, since you got this teed up for us. Second, after we've removed the weapon and replaced it with a dummy, we'll arrest Petrenko and whoever comes with him to take possession of the bomb."

"Any idea what type of nuclear weapon it is?" Nazareth asked.

"Unless Petrenko was lying to the buyer," Stark said, "which is never a good idea when dealing with terrorists, it's a variable-yield portable device that probably weighs no more than 300 pounds."

Nazareth's jaw tightened. "How variable is *variable-yield*, Dalton?"

"You always ask the right questions, Pete. At the low end I'd say, oh, probably 10 kilotons. At the top end maybe 100 kilotons. To give you some perspective on that, the bomb dropped on Hiroshima was 15 kilotons."

Gimble was shocked. "You're telling me the Russians had originally planned to put a 100-kiloton bomb in that tunnel under Central Park?"

"We can't rule that out, Tara," Stark answered. "We may never really know what they were up to. In fact, it's possible they had still planned to use it on us. But the issue before us today is keeping that device from falling into terrorists' hands because we all know what would happen next."

"What the hell would a 100-kiloton blast do to New York City?" she persisted.

"If they got the weapon above ground before detonation," he said, "which is probably the idea, then basically you'd have no more Manhattan. You'd also lose a large chunk of Queens and a significant portion of New Jersey along the Hudson. And that would only be the immediate damage. The longer-term consequences are unquantifiable."

"But millions of people would be dead," she said soberly.

"More than 15 million is our current guess. And believe it or not the economic and cultural impact would be far greater than the loss of lives. The United States would never be the same."

According to Stark the plan agreed upon by Petrenko and his terrorist colleagues was already very much in motion. An empty 18-wheel container trailer bearing the name PennFast Trucking had already left a secluded terrorist training compound deep in the woods near Tannersville, PA. The driver would make frequent stops en route to Port Newark, each time waiting for a coded message before completing the next leg of the journey. If all went as scheduled he would have his rig idling at the Grover Cleveland service area on the New Jersey Turnpike at 10:30 p.m., leaving only a short drive to Port Newark for loading around 11:00.

Once the bomb had been armed by the team's weapons expert the driver would roll north to the Vince Lombardi service area near the top of the Turnpike and park until 4:30 a.m. During that time he would prepare himself for the suicide mission with prayers, a final meal he had carried with him, and one last study of the route map. Unless he received a no-go order, he would drive over the George Washington Bridge, patiently work his way to Times Square, and wait. The nuclear blast would occur at precisely 5:30 a.m., as programmed the night before.

Is there any chance the terrorists could arrive early and steal the weapon without paying off Petrenko?" Gimble asked.

"Zero. They don't know which container they're after," he told her. "All they know is it's at the Port Newark Container Terminal, which covers nearly 200 acres and is piled to the sky with steel boxes."

"Any idea how many terrorists will be coming?" Nazareth asked.

"Seven, if they stick to what they said on the phone. Petrenko will meet them about two miles from Port Newark with a small moving van," Stark explained. "The lead terrorist, whose name is still a mystery, will sit with Petrenko up front. A weapons expert and four armed guards will hide in the back. The driver of the container carrier makes seven when he shows up."

Stark's SUV rolled into Rutkowski Park on the western shore of Bayonne, N.J., where D nodded through his open window at an armed guard who stood at the park's entrance alongside a sign that read *Closed for Emergency Repairs.* Less than a minute later the vehicle was parked alongside four other black SUVs at the edge of Newark Bay. A dozen men dressed in camouflaged battle gear stood next to a pair of inflatable boats, both of them Zodiac F470 combat raiding craft that had already been prepped for action.

"Jack, this is Pete and Tara," Stark said as he walked over to a tall guy who, like his colleagues, wore no rank or service insignia. "Pete and Tara, this is Jack. He's commanding tonight's operation."

Jack nodded to his new acquaintances and motioned them over to a tripod that held a small fortune in classified equipment, including a high-res day/night video camera and a 15-inch LED viewing monitor that showed a crisp close-up image of a blue-and-red shipping container.

"That's a live shot of the target," he said, "located at the corner of Port Newark about 20 meters from the water and roughly 1.5 miles from where we're standing. You'll be able to see and hear everything that's going on. Our time on the ground will be no more than 18 minutes."

Gimble seemed concerned as she studied the screen. "Is it really this light over there?"

Jack shook his head. "It's actually pretty dark over there. Perfect for what we'll be doing. What you're seeing on the screen is the computer's modified version of the scene as it appeared about a tenth of a second ago."

"Your boats can handle the weight of the package?" Nazareth asked.

"Max payload is about 2,500 pounds," Jack assured him. "Piece of cake."

Stark gave Jack a thumbs-up. "Let's do this," he said.

"Yes, sir." Jack waved his troops toward the water. Twenty seconds later the two Zodiacs, each holding six warriors, silently entered Newark Bay and disappeared in the night.

31.

"Kazi, please stay with me," she cooed from the bed. "It's only a little after midnight. I have more vodka and more love for you tonight."

Kazimir Malinovsky wanted desperately to crawl back under the satin sheets with Marta, the 25-year-old graduate student who always made him feel decades younger. No, it was more than that. She made him feel desperately wanted again. When he was 25 he had been handsome, athletic, and always in the company of beautiful women, most of them married. But that was decades ago. Now he was a man with responsibilities, among them two teenaged children and a wife who had already threatened him more than once about his wandering eye.

"Tonight I cannot, Marta," he said gently, turning away from her as he reached inside his leather attache case for a pistol that he tucked under his belt. He slipped into a dark blue Burberry blazer that looked fabulous over the pink Ralph Lauren polo shirt. "You know I would if I could, don't you?"

"Promise me you will stay for good soon," she pleaded.

He leaned over and kissed her on the top of her head. "You have my word on this, Marta. Soon."

"Not soon enough," she pouted.

He locked the apartment door behind him, then stood there like a lovesick schoolboy agonizing over his decision to leave. The long night in Marta's arms had been magical, and it could continue to be so if he simply unlocked the door. But in another hour he must be with the others. There was no changing this. Not tonight.

The group he was meeting with drew its strength from his presence, his courage, and his powerful voice. And he could not risk tarnishing the image he had cultivated. One small crack is all it takes sometimes. One crack in a foundation grows deeper and wider until the entire structure crumbles, and he could not have that. Not when he was so close to crushing his enemies. He pocketed Marta's key and walked to the elevator.

Malinovsky was no ordinary Russian dissident. The others, including the two who had recently died -- Gerasimov and Sidorenko -- were overly fond of being safe. They spoke and wrote brave words from the comfort of their living rooms or university lecture halls. But Malinovsky had always been a man of the street. Face to face he had recruited like-minded Russian immigrants, and they in turn had recruited family members and friends, and finally after four years of impossibly dangerous work he had built an organization capable of threatening President Ruslan Kotov's regime in the homeland.

The group that Malinovsky headed met twice each month, always in a different place and always at an odd hour. Tonight they would gather at 1:00 a.m. in the home of a wealthy physician, a man who practiced in Brooklyn and who had kept his anti-Kotov sentiments secret until he was touched by Malinovsky's passion and commitment. Also in the group of 25 Russian emigrés were scientists, business leaders, professors, retired generals, and former government officials whose connections could make things happen back home. If these people chose to strike the match, the resulting firestorm would surely overwhelm Ruslan Kotov and his supporters, and the day of reckoning was fast approaching.

As Malinovsky slipped into his Mercedes E500 the tall man with a compact air pistol in his right hand quietly emerged from the black sedan parked directly across the street. Before Malinovsky had time to pull the car door behind him the Wolf reached inside the vehicle and fired at his victim's face. Then he calmly shut the door with a gloved hand, walked back to his own vehicle, and drove off.

A dose of hydrogen cyanide gas will often prove rapidly fatal, as it did in Kazimir Malinovsky's case. The faint odor of bitter almonds was followed almost immediately by the total failure of his heart, brain, and lungs. He was quite dead before he slumped back on the leather seat, where he would remain until Marta found him early the next morning on her way to class.

Shortly thereafter Malinovsky's wife would learn from a doctor at Lenox Hill Hospital that her husband had succumbed to a heart attack. She was not terribly surprised that a man his age could die suddenly, but she could not explain why he had been parked alone on a dreary Downtown side street at the time.

32.

Nazareth, Gimble, and Stark watched the entire operation on the computer monitor. As soon as the two Zodiacs reached the dark shadows alongside the Port Newark docks four men scrambled ashore, two in combat gear and two in black hazmat suits. One of them spent less than 20 seconds unlocking the target shipping container while the others stood guard. Then the two in hazmat suits slipped inside.

Two minutes later the door opened, and one of the men gave a silent all-clear signal that set the entire team in motion. Four large guys ran from one of the Zodiacs to the shipping container, went inside, and came out carrying the disabled weapon. Meanwhile, four more men hoisted the dummy weapon from the second boat and placed it in the container. After making the exchange they locked the door behind them, returned to the boats, and shoved off.

"Damn, 13:47," Stark said as he shook his head in amazement.

"What's that?" Gimble asked.

"Jack estimated 18 minutes on the ground, but the entire op took 13:47."

Nazareth had led combat forces himself, and he was much impressed. "Something tells me these guys have done this sort of thing before."

"Oh, yeah. But never when the stakes were quite this high," Stark replied. "This was huge."

"And all without a single shot being fired," said Gimble.

"Well," Stark told her, "this was the quiet part of the program. Things may get noisier tonight when the bad guys show up."

"Please tell me we won't have to watch that on a video screen," Nazareth pleaded.

"No chance, Pete. I want both of you with us when we take Petrenko down."

The detectives smiled at each other. They were doers, not watchers, and they couldn't wait to get their hands on the bad guys.

As soon as the two Zodiacs returned to Rutkowski Park four members of the team carried the nuke to one of the SUVs while Jack, the commander, briefed Stark and the detectives on what had been found.

"Fully operational device, for sure," he began, "but no radiation leakage, so we're okay to roll without additional containment. The weapon was neutralized without difficulty, and now we can examine it to see just how powerful the thing is. Rough guess at this point is above 100 kilotons, but don't hold me to that."

"Great work, Jack," Stark said. "How does the dummy weapon look inside the shipping container?"

"It's certainly not a perfect match for the real thing," he answered, "but even to a trained eye it looks pretty damn good. Once they take a close look at it, though, they'll know it's a fake. We installed a small remote camera and speaker near the ceiling, so you'll get the whole show on tape."

Stark replied with a thumbs-up. "Okay, you and your guys be back here at 2130 hours. Shut down the park again. No lights or sirens. And be in the boats at 2200 just in case things start early. Once the action begins," he noted, "your only job is to make sure no one escapes by water. That's it. My team will make the arrests on land."

"Understood. But if things get out of control for some reason," Jack added, "we'll be ready."

"I'd rather not have us firing at each other in the dark," Stark smiled, "but we'll do what we have to do. I don't want any of these bastards to get away." He turned to Nazareth and Gimble as Jack walked back toward his team. "I'll drop you off at your apartment now and pick you up again at 6:00 tonight. Just stay close to your cell phones in case our plans change."

"Sounds good, Dalton. How much should we be saying to our chief about this?" Nazareth asked.

"Nothing yet. This is a federal operation," he told them, "and I'll bring him in at the appropriate time. Ball's in my court."

Nazareth and Gimble were back in their apartment well before sunrise, and they grabbed some much-needed sleep before tackling what promised to be a long day. A few hours later, while downing a late breakfast of scrambled eggs and multigrain toast, Nazareth checked his voice messages for the first time that day. The message the chief had sent at 9:17 a.m. was hardly the sort of news he wanted to hear. He sat at the table staring at the phone and shaking his head.

"What's up, Pete?" Gimble asked when she caught the look on his face.

"While we've been working on terrorists," he told her, "another big-name Russian dissident left this world. Kazimir Malinovsky."

"Murdered?"

"According to the chief it was a heart attack, or so says the hospital. Guy sitting in his car all alone apparently. Someone found him this morning."

"Should we let Stark know?"

"You bet. We would never have known the cause of Sidorenko's death if Dalton hadn't gotten involved, so we need to have him check this one out for us."

"If this is Ilya Petrenko's work, he's even busier than we had imagined. He's out murdering dissidents even while he's selling a nuclear weapon to terrorists."

"Somehow I think this will all get sorted out tonight, Tara. In the meantime, I'll call the chief and let him know we'll add Malinovsky to our list."

"Our growing list."

"Our fast-growing list."

33.

That evening at 6:00 sharp Nazareth and Gimble climbed into the back of the armored SUV. Stark sat up front with D, the same driver as earlier, though this time he was outfitted in black battle dress. He wore a Glock 19 pistol on his right hip and had an FN SCAR assault rifle tucked in a scabbard on the passenger side of the shift console. Whatever the evening called for, D was prepared.

In heavy traffic it took them nearly an hour to get from Manhattan to a dilapidated warehouse in a trashed industrial park about three miles from Port Newark. Stark opened a side garage door with the remote as they flew inside at 40 miles an hour. D yanked hard on the hand brake and screeched to a halt after executing a flawless 180. The garage door had already closed behind them.

"You never know who might be driving by," Stark grinned, "so we like to get in and out of here fast."

"I think my neck will recover in a few hours," Gimble laughed. "But I have to say it was fun."

"Well, that may be the last fun of the day," he said, "except for dinner. We do have a nice dinner."

Gimble warily eyed the dreary surroundings: broken windows high on the corrugated metal wall, piles of worn tires, and sprawling grease stains everywhere. "You really know how to show a girl a nice time," she said.

Stark winked. "Follow me."

He punched in the code for a heavy steel door, and they walked into a pristine suite of offices that would have looked completely at home in a fancy Manhattan tower.

"It's a little home away from home," he said casually. "Let's eat while we go over tonight's operation." D set a large brown bag on the conference room table and began passing out overstuffed sandwiches from Katz's Deli on the Lower East Side.

Stark's plan was predictably audacious. Earlier that day a nondescript gray shipping container had been driven to Port Newark and deposited diagonally across from the Russian container that now housed the dummy bomb. Inside the newly arrived container was an air-conditioned HABX-8 troop shelter capable of supporting its six heavily armed occupants for two weeks under extreme combat conditions. Among other things the lightweight composite structure contained an advanced communications system that allowed them to monitor the area by satellite, thermal imaging, and radar.

"The terrorist who's driving in from Pennsylvania with the container hauler will be the first to arrive," Stark explained. "Then a few minutes later Petrenko will get there with his crew. We're assuming, and hoping, Petrenko will go inside the nuke container with the weapons expert and the lead terrorist. As soon as that happens, my team will exit the HABX and neutralize the remaining terrorists. My preference," he added quickly, "is to capture them alive, but I'll settle for dead if necessary. Then we'll arrest Petrenko and the other two as they exit the container. By that time we will have videotaped their transaction, so we'll have more than enough evidence to make the charges stick."

"What do you want us to do?" Gimble asked.

"You, Pete, and I shouldn't need to do more than watch until it's time to arrest Petrenko and his buddies," he answered. "Between my men in the trailer, the guys on the boats, and D here, we'll have 19 combat troops in place. I'll put these 19 up against anyone else's 190 any day of the week."

"Sounds good," Nazareth said. "Then after this has all been wrapped up we just need to figure out how we explain everything to our boss."

"I've got you covered, Pete. Chief Crawford has already been told to expect an 8:00 p.m. call from the U.S. secretary of homeland security, who'll tell him your participation is required in a highly classified operation. The NYPD is going to score big points for this mission."

For the remainder of the evening they studied aerial photos of the target site and periodically listened to live reports from members of Stark's team, some of whom had eyes on Petrenko while others tracked the empty container truck that was on its way to Port Newark to pick up its nuclear cargo. Based upon his long combat experience, Nazareth felt that the mission was as much under control as it could be. Which basically meant not at all. Any slight change in behavior by Petrenko or the terrorists could turn all of Stark's carefully constructed plans upside down. But this, he knew, is how battles go.

The winner is the one who most efficiently adapts to change.

34.

At 10:30 p.m. sharp D started the SUV's engine and they all strapped in. Fifteen minutes later one of Stark's men elsewhere in Newark called to say Petrenko had just picked up his passengers in a yellow Penske rental truck, now code-named *Canary*, and was driving slowly toward Port Newark. So far so good.

Then came the first glitch. Another of Stark's men called from the N.J. Turnpike to say the terrorist vehicle from Pennsylvania was stuck in traffic caused by a minor two-car accident in the northbound lanes. The truck would be at least 10 minutes late arriving at Port Newark.

Stark spent a few seconds processing what he had just heard, then quickly modified the op. Four combat troops from the boats were to proceed undetected to Port Newark's main gate. Once Petrenko's truck and Stark's SUV had passed through, the troops would secure the entrance and stop the terrorists' container hauler when it arrived. Other than that the mission would go as planned.

D opened the garage door and turned the SUV toward Port Newark. Timing was critical because they needed to arrive at the main gate just after Petrenko had rolled in. A few seconds too early, and they might be spotted. A minute too late, and they could miss the start of the operation. And Stark definitely wanted to be on hand when his troops confronted the terrorists.

The call came at 10:57: *Canary in the cage.* Petrenko had just cleared the terminal's main gate and would be pulling alongside the target container in another minute or so.

"Hit it, D," Stark ordered, and they were all pushed back in their seats as the SUV sprang from 25 to 75 in half a heartbeat. "The guard at the front gate is one of ours, by the way," he told the detectives. "We made that switch about an hour ago, just in case Petrenko had arranged some inside help."

"So you'll have five men at the gate when the terrorist rig shows up?" Nazareth asked.

Stark nodded. "Four of whom are ready for war."

"I sure hope so," Nazareth replied, "because a truck that size can really screw with us if it gets through."

"Not to worry, Pete. Once he stops at the gate he won't be moving again."

D skillfully guided the SUV into the main entrance at something close to 50 miles per hour, killed the lights, and let the speed bleed off as they coasted toward the target. They parked 40 yards away and took the rest of the distance on foot, moving silently within the shadows of steel containers until they got within 20 feet of *Canary*.

With guns drawn they watched Petrenko open the driver's side door of the yellow truck and step down to the pavement. A few seconds later a bearded man in an ill-fitting black suit walked around the front of the truck and joined the Russian.

"Hafiz al-Harbi," Stark whispered to Nazareth. "Head of ISIS in the U.S. This is like hitting the Powerball, Pete. Super big prize."

Together Petrenko and al-Harbi walked to the back of the rental truck and rolled up the steel door. The first man out, most likely the weapons expert, wore casual Western clothes and carried what appeared to be a small metal tool box. Behind him came six armed terrorists in camouflage gear.

Stark was tight-lipped and powerfully annoyed. "Six, not four," he said. The terrorists had added two men to their security team, which meant Stark's guys in the HABX would be matched one for one. On the other hand, Stark, Nazareth, and Gimble each had handguns while D carried his beloved assault rifle, which could pound out 625 rounds per minute. The situation was still very much under control.

Petrenko and the two high-value terrorists unlocked the container and went inside while their six armed troops took up defensive positions, three on each side of the massive steel box. This was good. Now when Stark's troops emerged from the HABX they would immediately confront only three of the enemy combatants. Piece of cake.

The offsetting negative, however, was that the three other terrorists would have several tons of steel between them and the good guys, thereby increasing the likelihood of a firefight. But this was the hand they had been dealt, and Stark had no choice but to play it. He waited 60 seconds, then punched in the four-digit attack code on his cell phone.

Stark's men sprang from the HABX as one, trained their assault rifles on the three terrorists, and ordered them to surrender. One of the terrorists appeared ready to comply, but his colleagues raised their weapons instead, triggering a massive response from the U.S. troops. Each terrorist caught eight or more rounds before hitting the pavement.

Back at Port Newark's main entrance the terrorist who had driven in from Pennsylvania panicked when he spotted four men in combat dress taking positions on both sides of the gate. Maybe they were fellow terrorists, but maybe they weren't. When in doubt, he told himself, assume everyone is your enemy. He hit the gas, swung into the terminal at high speed, and began accelerating.

Inside the nuke container the terrorist weapons expert had required less than a minute to determine that what he was looking at was fake. He turned angrily to his leader and shouted the bad news in Arabic just as the shooting began outside. Believing Petrenko had set them up, al-Harbi pulled a small revolver from his jacket, jammed the muzzle against the Russian's temple, and pulled the trigger. Petrenko was dead before he slumped sideways onto the dummy nuclear bomb.

Back outside one of the three remaining terrorists ran from the rear of the container with his rifle on full auto, but Nazareth put a round in his forehead before the guy could do any damage.

"Two left, two left," Stark yelled while motioning for his men to surround the container.

A few seconds later one of his guys called out, "They're gone. I say again, they're gone. We're in pursuit."

The six soldiers fanned out and began working their way through the huge terminal, leaving Stark, D, and the two detectives to take down the bad guys in the Russian container. Before they could close in, however, the weapons expert kicked the door open and began firing. Although he bought enough time for al-Harbi to slip out and run behind the container, he also took a dozen rounds to the torso and was blown backward to the pavement.

Gimble spotted al-Harbi's exit, and she called back to Nazareth as she ran toward the container. "He's in back, Pete. I'm going in from the right."

"No, wait!" he yelled. But she had already covered most of the distance and didn't plan to slow down. Just as she reached the end of the container al-Harbi flew around the corner and raised his gun toward her face. She immediately dove low and slammed her right shoulder into his chest while locking her powerful left hand on the weapon and ripping it away. In the process, however, she dropped her own gun.

Al-Harbi staggered briefly, then recovered and locked both hands around her neck. Gimble immediately grabbed the lapels of his suit jacket, planted her right foot on his midsection, and rolled backwards onto the pavement. With a flawlessly executed *tomoe nage* judo throw she launched the terrorist into the air .

Al-Harbi landed hard on his back in time to see the 20-ton truck bearing down on him. He struggled to one knee just as the massive front bumper connected with his chest and snapped him like a twig. When the terrorist driver saw Stark's troops he veered left toward them but lost control at high speed. The truck rolled on its side and flipped twice before toppling into 60 feet of murky water.

Stark lit up Newark Bay with portable spotlights but after 15 minutes decided the driver hadn't escaped. Neither had the two terrorists who fled the firefight earlier. Both had thrown down their weapons rather than become martyrs, providing Stark with a fresh source of intelligence on ISIS operations in the U.S. He would have much preferred to leave with al-Harbi in handcuffs, but knowing the terrorist leader had died an ugly death made him feel somewhat better.

"What were you thinking, Tara?" Nazareth asked her when things finally calmed down.

"I was afraid he might get away," she shrugged.

"We have an entire army here, for God's sake. He wasn't getting away."

"Well, I wanted to make sure."

Stark overheard the exchange and walked over to them with a broad grin on his face. "If you two are going to fight," he joked, "I'm taking my men someplace safe."

"We don't fight," Nazareth laughed. "We just disagree now and then, like when Tara decides to go Rambo on me."

"What he really means," she added, "is that only big tough Marines like him are allowed to play Rambo. Not little girls like me."

Nazareth brushed the comment aside. "That's not what I mean at all."

"Well here's what I mean," Stark said. "I could really use both of you on my team. Not just part-time like tonight. I mean full-time."

The detectives looked at each other and smiled. "Are you going to tell him," Gimble asked, "or should I?"

"You're in charge of this one," he answered.

"I'm pregnant, Dalton," she said. "I think my days of chasing down terrorists are nearly over."

Stark knew just about everything, but he definitely hadn't seen that coming.

35.

Russian President Ruslan Kotov had for several weeks seethed over the deaths of the two dissidents in New York City. It's not that he would miss either Sergey Gerasimov or Feodor Sidorenko, a pair of devoted troublemakers who had done their best to make his life difficult. But getting rid of them was his prerogative, no one else's. That someone within the Russian chain of command had taken this sort of action without his approval was infuriating. It was without question a treasonous act punishable by death.

He had choked back his anger, waiting impatiently for the guilty party to be brought to him. Yet that hadn't happened. Why? Had Vladimir Krupin, his SVR chief, not understood the direct order he had been given? Or was he, in fact, the traitor? Had Krupin for some insane reason decided he could snatch the reins from his boss? In Russia, Kotov knew, anything was possible.

Alone in his grand Kremlin office Kotov grew edgier and more suspicious day by day, became obsessed with this intolerable challenge to his authority. But it was the sickening news of Kazimir Malinovsky's death in New York City that pushed him over the edge. He rejected as laughable, of course, the report that Malinovsky had died of a heart attack. No, Malinovsky had been assassinated, and Kotov knew it. So he decided it was time to send a message.

He picked up the phone and ordered the immediate arrest of Vladimir Krupin, who was promptly delivered bound and gagged to a state-owned farm 23 miles east of Moscow. There in a tumbledown barn once used for slaughtering pigs, Krupin managed to withhold his confession during a half hour of torture. He finally saw the error of his ways when a titanium drill bit turning at 1,500 RPM was placed against his forehead. At that precise moment he pleaded guilty to the full list of accusations:

plotting against the president; spying for the United States; ordering the assassinations of three dissidents in New York City; and embezzling state funds. He was willing to confess to anything as long as the pain would cease.

The moment the confession had been signed Kotov picked up the drill, placed the bit in Krupin's right ear, and bored a hole straight to the middle of his brain. The result was predictably unpleasant though not immediately fatal. Krupin was still breathing, just barely, 20 minutes later when the president ordered him strangled with a length of rusty barbed wire from the barn floor.

Kotov's mood improved noticeably after the execution. Although Krupin may have been innocent of the assassination charges, he was surely guilty of something else. So why quibble? Besides, the president clearly understood that spilling a bit of blood now and then was the surest way to instill fear in one's enemies, and more fear was always preferable to less.

The one thing that Krupin's murder would not change, of course, was Kazimir Malinovsky's death in America, and that represented a major setback for the regime. Malinovsky, a highly prized Russian spy, had been working under deep cover directly for Kotov and had spent four grueling years winning over a group of key dissidents in New York City. Worse, he had been only days away from arranging one final meeting at which everyone in this band of revolutionaries would be abducted and eliminated.

Now? Nothing. Four years wasted.

Kotov promised himself that whoever had killed his man Kazimir Malinovsky would regret ever having been born.

36.

Nazareth and Gimble sat in Chief Crawford's office sharing with him the details of the successful Port Newark operation. The story that Stark had leaked to the press was interesting but far too commonplace to merit much coverage. According to this version a pair of NYPD detectives had helped shut down a local drug smuggling ring. The reality, Crawford soon learned, was that his two star detectives had helped prevent terrorists from wiping Manhattan off the map.

"I knew this had to be big when I got a call from the director of homeland security," he told them, "but I had no idea several million lives were at stake. How in the hell did you two connect the dots between Petrenko and a nuclear weapon?"

Nazareth tilted his head back and studied the ceiling while trying to come up with a plausible answer. Did the chief really want to hear about the break-in at Petrenko's home and the stolen disk? Or was that more than he needed to know?

"Well, it's a complex answer," Nazareth finally said.

"And I probably don't want to hear it, do I?"

"Possibly not."

"Well, regardless of how you did it, you obviously did it right," he said. "Too bad you didn't get al-Harbi alive."

"Yeah, if Tara hadn't thrown him under that truck . . ." Nazareth grinned.

"You probably would have shot him in the head," she countered, "the way you did that other guy."

"You both did what you had to do," Crawford said, offering them an energetic thumbs-up. "I wish you could get the public recognition you deserve."

"That's not a problem," Gimble assured him. "Pete and I agree completely that this needs to be kept confidential. It would serve no good purpose to let people know we almost lost New

York City to nuclear terrorism. What's much more important is for guys like Dalton Stark to make sure this was the one and only nuclear device hidden someplace in America."

"But you doubt that's the case, don't you?" the chief asked.

Nazareth nodded. "I'd say the odds are against it, but I've got my fingers crossed."

"Maybe Stark will get some useful information from the two terrorists who surrendered," Crawford added. "What happened to them?"

"Officially they no longer exist," Gimble said coolly. "They were driven away in a black SUV, and I doubt they'll be on the street anytime soon. I also suspect they'll give up whatever they know. Stark can be pretty persuasive."

"Speaking of Dalton," Nazareth said, "his tech people have now confirmed that the two most recent dissident deaths were murders. Feodor Sidorenko was killed with puffer-fish neurotoxin, and Kazimir Malinovsky was killed with vaporized cyanide."

"Any chance this was all Petrenko?"

"We have no other suspects at the moment," Nazareth answered, "but I seriously doubt he would have been thinking about assassinations when he was so close to finishing the deal of a lifetime with al-Harbi."

"I'm keeping an open mind about Petrenko," Gimble said firmly, "but I'm certainly willing to look for other suspects. For the moment Pete and I are going to focus on people who were photographed at Sidorenko's speech because it's possible the killer was in the audience that night. If not Petrenko, then someone we haven't considered yet."

"If you need help interviewing people, let me know," Crawford told them. "I still have the mayor busting my chops over two dead dissidents, and I guess I'll be getting a call about the third."

"Probably," Nazareth smiled. "But at least you can tell him Ilya Petrenko won't be assaulting rich kids anytime soon."

"Damn, I forgot all about that. What can I tell him about Petrenko?"

"Same thing the Russian consul general has been told," Nazareth said. "Petrenko was shot and killed by a drug trafficker during a deal gone bad. For security reasons the feds refuse to provide any more details."

Crawford nodded thoughtfully. "Yeah, I suppose he'll have to accept that. In the meantime, you guys tread carefully. Obviously you're after someone who's very slick and who seems to enjoy killing. You do understand that, right?"

Gimble nodded. "That's precisely why we need to get him."

"What we believe could be helpful right about now," Nazareth added, "is a little publicity."

"What do you have in mind?" Crawford asked.

"Leaking a story to the *Times* linking the three deaths," Nazareth explained, "and suggesting that the second and third killings were most likely assassinations."

"And this accomplishes what?"

"First, it gets other dissidents looking over their shoulders," Nazareth replied, "and that's not a bad thing under the circumstances. Second, maybe it triggers a memory in a key witness -- someone who saw something suspicious but didn't think anything of it at the time."

"We had hoped this guy might get sloppy if he thought we didn't know about Sidorenko's murder," Gimble added. "Obviously we were wrong. So it's time we let the public know we're looking for a serial killer. It's the only way people will start feeding us leads."

"Then why not arrange a press conference?" Crawford wondered. "The commissioner is always up for that sort of thing. He loves seeing himself on TV."

"Stark wants to stay out of this," Nazareth said, "so we can't mention his forensics help. Plus a leaked story will help keep this thing sounding a little fuzzy to the killer, assuming he reads the *Times.* He won't really be sure how far along the investigation is."

The chief weighed the proposal. A leaked story on a murder investigation would no doubt get the mayor riled up once again, and Crawford would be the one to bear the brunt of his anger. But a *Times* story might be the only way to break the investigative logjam that Nazareth and Gimble currently faced. "Can you get this to the *Times* without having it traced back to us?"

"Absolutely," Gimble assured him. She didn't mention that both she and Nazareth had family connections at the newspaper and didn't fear being exposed as the source.

"Okay, then go with it. Just shut this guy down before we have a fourth murder, all right? Seems to me he's picking up the pace."

"He definitely is," Nazareth agreed. "And I wish to hell we knew why."

37.

For only the second time in his life the Wolf was adrift. He vaguely remembered the feeling from his childhood after being ripped from his home, his parents, and his village to be raised as a servant of the state. But back then he had the benefit of time on his side. Ahead of him were decades filled with great promise, and alongside him were dedicated, sometimes fanatical tutors whose sole job was to nurture the Soviet Union's future heroes.

Now he was alone, this time without the expectation of a long life ahead. Yes, Volkov had grown old. His mind remained razor sharp, and he was in wonderful physical condition for a man approaching his seventh decade. But fitness for duty, he knew, is an absolute. You're either ready or you're not. And he didn't need to look in the mirror to see how far from the top he had fallen.

He was a highly capable old man playing a life-or-death game meant only for the young.

The burden of old age had begun to weigh on him in recent years. But whenever he had questioned his continued usefulness, his mentor Anatoly Bukarin had been there, only a phone call away, to brush aside the doubts like so many irrelevant cobwebs. Over the decades Bukarin had grown to be more like a proud father than a spy handler. He had offered praise, counsel, and encouragement in equal measure, always guiding Volkov along the safest path to his goals. And now he was gone.

Too many weeks of not hearing from his handler finally drove Volkov to visit the public library at 5th and 42nd. After three hours of working his way through back issues of *Izvestia* he found the brief mention of Bukarin's death. There were no high-sounding testimonials from Russian officials, no impressive list of medals, and no recounting of his storied career. A man named Bukarin had lived, then died. That was that.

As Volkov prepared to leave the library that day he glanced at a copy of the *New York Times* someone had casually tossed at the end of a table. The words **Russian Assassin** in the headline made him feel slightly disoriented, as though a car crash outside his apartment window had awakened him from a sound sleep in the middle of the night. He desperately wanted to walk away and lose himself in the crowd on Fifth Avenue. But he could not.

He sat and read.

It was a small headline on the lower left of page one: **NYPD Links Three Recent Deaths to Russian Assassin.** The article by Madelyn Jensen quoted the customary "unnamed source close to the investigation" as having verified that both Feodor Sidorenko and Kazimir Malinovsky had been poisoned. Combine these murders with the shooting death of Sergey Gerasimov and you had the plot of a Cold War spy novel, except that the Cold War had ended decades ago and the story wasn't fiction. According to Jensen the deaths of the three prominent dissidents was considered "highly likely" to be the work of a Russian assassin. What's more, the NYPD now believed the murderer had been operating in New York City for quite some time and might be responsible for the deaths of numerous other Russian dissidents dating back 10 years or more.

Volkov knew how to hide his feelings, especially in public, so as he moved toward the lobby he carefully maintained his posture, deliberately walked more slowly than he would have liked, and wore a faint smile. But the storm that raged within was unlike anything he had ever experienced. The double blow of Bukarin's death and the **Russian Assassin** article had brought him to the brink of panic, a place he had never been before. All he wanted was to get home, lock the door, and think.

Would the police be waiting for him? Against all odds they had learned that Sidorenko and Malinovsky had been poisoned. Had they also somehow traced the poisons to his apartment?

Stop and think, he told himself. The *Times* story was written last night. If the police had identified him as the killer they would have come for him by now. Okay, so they still didn't know who they were after. But why did they assume the assassin was Russian? How could they be sure of that? Answer: they couldn't. They're simply assuming it's a Russian agent because that would make some sense. Yet they have no proof whatsoever. And if they are, in fact, looking for a Russian, what are the odds they would ever focus on him? In the New York Tri-State area there are more than 1.5 million Russian-Americans, 600,000 of whom live in New York City. Talk about finding a needle in a haystack!

Logic prevailed. By the time Volkov reached his apartment he was satisfied that the NYPD had no reason to suspect him. Furthermore, if he stopped killing dissidents for some period -- six months, a year perhaps -- whatever faint trail the police might have discovered would vanish without a trace. Yes, all he had to do was wait. Or maybe even stop for good.

Stopping wasn't an option, and he knew it. He hadn't been sent to America to live the good life, though he had certainly done so in order to cover his tracks. No, he had been told at the outset that this was a lifetime job, something he would do until he no longer could. If he died, as some of the others had, only then would he be freed from his duty. Otherwise, he would be expected to continue eliminating threats like Gerasimov, Sidorenko, and Malinovsky.

He naturally assumed that someone in Moscow would be taking over Bukarin's duties and would soon contact him about the ongoing mission in New York City. So until then he would carry on or perhaps risk becoming a casualty himself. After all, Bukarin had warned him many years ago that someone would always be watching. Always!

Volkov knew better than to doubt this.

38.

Leonid Zaitsev, a square-jawed, 45-year-old former Spetsnaz officer, showed up unannounced at the Manhattan office of Russian consul general Grigori Vasilyev early one morning. The special forces veteran cut an imposing figure in his tailored gray suit: broad shoulders, narrow waist, tastefully long blond hair, and piercing steel-blue eyes that missed nothing. Vasilyev looked up but remained silent as the younger man walked over and placed a letter signed by President Ruslan Kotov on the desk. The stranger wore a slight grin as he said, "I am your new security director."

Only four days ago Vasilyev had reported Ilya Petrenko's death to the president, and already here was a new consulate security chief. This was alarming, of course, since things did not normally move so quickly within the Russian bureaucracy. What's more, the careful wording of Kotov's letter of introduction was profoundly disturbing. "Leonid Zaitsev will manage all matters relating to consulate security," it said in part, "and will report directly to me." Vasilyev struggled to find the right words. He wasn't quite sure what it meant to have a staff member who reported not to him but to the president, but he knew it couldn't be good.

"This is most unexpected," he finally said, hoping his nervousness didn't show.

"Precisely what is unexpected?" Zaitsev asked. Vasilyev could tell it was more than a simple question. It was a challenge, delivered with much the same tone of voice that Ruslan Kotov himself used with underlings.

"That President Kotov acted so quickly in replacing Ilya Petrenko."

"Ah, of course. Well, you see, the president is not pleased that someone here in New York City is acting without authority. He hopes it is not someone within your consulate." His eyes seemed to bore through the consul general's skull and examine his darkest secrets. They were the eyes of a predator, menacing and cold. Vasilyev didn't need to be told he was in the presence of someone who had killed often, had enjoyed doing so, and hungered for more.

"It is not a member of my staff," Vasilyev insisted. "On this I would stake my life."

Zaitsev smiled knowingly as he settled onto the handsome 18th-century sofa to the right of the desk. He motioned for Vasilyev to join him. Once the two men were seated next to each other Zaitsev removed a small leather notebook from his jacket and flipped through several pages.

"Are you familiar with the name Anatoly Bukarin?" Zaitsev began. "Old man, former KGB, now dead."

"I may have heard of him," Vasilyev replied warily, "but I can't be certain."

"No matter. Someone close to the president attended this man's funeral not long ago, and while there he spoke with Bukarin's son. The son told him an interesting story about the old man's final hours and how he had hallucinated over a Kirov wolf." Zaitsev paused and studied Vasilyev's face, hoping the mention of the wolf would elicit a response. When it didn't, he moved on.

"The wolf meant nothing to the son," Zaitsev continued, "but for the president's acquaintance it triggered a frightening memory. The man wisely reported it to President Kotov later that same day. Soon afterward I interviewed the son and concluded we have a serious problem on our hands."

After weeks of meeting with graying old men who had once been important Soviet insiders, Zaitsev had pieced together the fascinating bits of an outrageous story: Anatoly Bukarin had somehow managed to create a top-secret operation that not even Kruschev had known about, and as part of that program had sent a number of assassins abroad, the Kirov Wolf among them.

But this was as far as Zaitsev's investigation had gotten. All traces of the assassins had been meticulously erased by the time they were turned over to their handlers. And as the handlers died, their links to the assassins died with them. Incredibly, no one in Russia knew whether these men still existed or, if so, where they were stationed.

"So these assassins could all be dead by now?" Vasilyev said.

Zaitsev smirked. "Have you failed to notice the trail of bodies here in New York City?"

"If you mean the three men who died recently . . ." Vasilyev began.

"I mean," Zaitsev snapped, "the three who were assassinated recently as well as the scores of others who have been eliminated over the past 20 or 25 years. The police seem to have done their homework on this, while you have obviously been busy doing other things. Yet President Kotov made it abundantly clear he wanted you to get to the bottom of this."

Vasilyev was indignant. "I am not a professional investigator."

"On this we agree," Zaitsev nodded. "That explains my presence."

"And I will certainly help you to the best of my ability."

"You can begin by showing me to my office and then arranging for me to see the employment file on every member of the consulate staff." He thought for a moment then added. "You need not include yours. That one I have already studied."

"Yes, of course," Vasilyev mumbled. He thought about the pistol in his desk. Would he be using it on Zaitsev? Or on himself?

39.

"Let's suppose you're in the Amazon rainforest, where there are roughly 400 billion trees," Stark said. "And let's further suppose most of them are palm trees, which happens to be the case. Now let's say one of those palm trees -- just one -- is fake, an almost perfect replica made from vinyl, and you guys need to find it. That's the sort of problem you're up against."

Nazareth and Gimble had called Stark from One Police Plaza to float their theory about the Russian assassin. They had tentatively ruled out Ilya Petrenko and now believed they were searching for a highly effective, and so far completely invisible, deep-cover operative. But the story they had planted in the *New York Times* had not produced a single lead. Crackpot calls, yes. Serious leads, no.

"We're still hoping the *Times* article causes the killer to do something that makes him stand out in the crowd," Gimble reasoned, "but honestly, Dalton, we're not sure what that would be."

"Only three possibilities make any sense," Stark replied. "One, he goes into hibernation, in which case you'll lose him forever. Two, he sticks to business as usual, and you keep following the bodies until you find him. Three, he gets rattled by the newspaper article and does something stupid."

"I don't think hibernation is an option," Nazareth declared. "He's been more active than ever lately, and that tells me he's under some sort of pressure."

"Any thoughts on what that pressure might be?" Stark asked.

"We've kicked around lots of ideas," Nazareth said, "but here's the one that grabs me. If this guy has been assassinating Russian dissidents in New York City for 20 or 25 years, he's at least middle-aged. But it's also quite possible he's been operating

200

here much longer, in which case he could actually be fairly old. If he feels he's running out of time, he may want to work faster."

"Makes sense, Pete. Let's assume he came here during the Soviet era," Stark said. "The Russians would have sent a tested veteran, not some rookie, to cover New York City. That much I can guarantee you. So let's say he was 25. If he got here in 1980, he's now over 60. But for all we know he's pushing 70."

Gimble was highly skeptical. "A 70-year-old assassin? Why in the world would the Russians have an old man running around killing people? That just doesn't make sense."

"Actually it makes very good sense, Tara," Stark offered. "I can tell you the U.S. frequently relies on agents who are 70 or even 80. If someone that age can still handle the pressure, he or she is an amazing asset. Our enemies aren't looking for senior-citizen assassins. That's a fact."

"We actually have agents as old as 80?" she asked.

"The oldest right now is 87 and irreplaceable," he nodded. "But here's another thought. I know of at least one case of a U.S. deep-cover operative who basically got lost in the system. As a matter of fact, several years ago we had to completely revamp our command-and-control structure because of the incident. This guy operated completely on his own in China for quite some time, and no one in D.C. even remembered his name until he showed up in Langley one morning."

"How the hell does something like that happen?" Gimble wondered.

"This was around the time CIA analyst Aldrich Ames was convicted of being a KGB mole, so everyone started building secret operations inside secret operations, sort of like those toy nesting eggs that fit inside each other. In this instance," he explained, "only one person knew about our agent in China, and he died in a traffic accident."

"So you think we may have a Russian agent who's completely off the grid?" Nazareth asked.

"Not likely but possible," Stark shrugged. "More than anything I think this guy is just really good at what he does. Trust me when I say it can take decades to get someone like this established in a foreign country, so the Russians need to use him while they can. The fact that you still have no clue to his identity tells you he's extremely well hidden in plain sight."

"Like the vinyl palm tree in the Amazon?" Gimble laughed.

"Precisely. As I'm sure I told you once before, this guy almost certainly looks, sounds, and acts American. You will not recognize him when you see him unless he makes a mistake."

"Which might be his first one," Gimble noted.

"Most likely, yeah. On the other hand," Stark noted, "he's never read about himself on the front page of the *New York Times* before, and that could make him just a little crazy for a while."

"So all we need to do is look for a crazy person in New York City," Nazareth joked.

"Especially one who's dressed like a palm tree," Stark nodded.

40.

At 8:15 on a Friday night Gimble was at an Italian restaurant four blocks away from the apartment, dining with three college friends who were in town for a few days. Nazareth relaxed on the living room couch with a protein shake watching a PBS special on America's natural wonders, among them Glacier National Park in Montana. One of the show's most interesting segments, captioned *Eye of the Beholder*, was a brief history of work done at the park by Ansel Adams and other famous American photographers. Included in the two dozen images was a breathtaking black-and-white photo of Chief Mountain taken five years earlier by Alex Resnick, the photographer who had recently helped Nazareth and Gimble search for Feodor Sidorenko's killer. The mountain's crowning feature is a gargantuan block of stone that towers over the Great Plains like an ancient fortress, and in Resnick's image the snow-covered monolith was bathed in shafts of winter sunlight that streamed through an opening in storm clouds.

He hit PAUSE and studied the photograph. Christmas was still a few months away, but Nazareth had just found the perfect present for his wife. She loved nature as well as Resnick's work, so a large print of Chief Mountain was a natural fit. They could showcase the picture on the living room's far wall and be dazzled every time they walked by it.

When he was finished watching the show he went online to see about purchasing a print. He had briefly thought about calling the photographer directly, but he was reluctant to do so for fear Resnick might think he was being hit up for a gift. And that was a game Nazareth would never play. If he didn't pay for it, he didn't want it.

He began his search on Resnick's gorgeous website, which offered detailed information about hiring him for photo shoots but contained nothing about purchasing prints. Interesting.

Apparently famous photographers sell only through galleries, Nazareth concluded, so he continued looking. After several misses he found the photo he was after for $1,500 at the Sylvia Mathers Gallery in Manhattan. The price was pretty steep, but he figured that one of Resnick's original prints might actually gain in value over the years. In the meantime, the photo would be the artistic highlight of their apartment.

Before entering his credit card information he noticed a link to Resnick's biography, so he clicked over for some background on the photographer's long climb to fame. He was surprised to find lots of words devoted to critical acclaim but nothing that might truly be called biographical other than the mention of Resnick's college. Perhaps this too was standard practice among famous photographers, Nazareth thought. If you're up there at the top, you're free to assume everyone knows how you got there.

But Nazareth, ever the curious detective, now felt challenged to learn more about Resnick's life. By the time his wife returned home from dinner two hours later he had more questions than answers.

"How was your dinner?" he asked as she walked into the kitchen.

"Food was A+, as always," she smiled, "but the company ranged from B- to D."

Nazareth was surprised to hear that since Gimble's three friends had been close to her since they had been freshmen together at Stanford. "That's odd," he said.

"Things have changed, Pete, apparently starting with my pregnancy."

"How so?"

"Well, Sherry is married more to her career than her husband," she began, "and has no interest in kids. So she sort of withdrew once I told them I was expecting. As for Marissa and Jenn, they're devoted bachelorettes who want nothing to do with marriage, let alone kids. They spent the entire time coming on to a couple of guys at the bar."

"So you're now the symbol of their rejected lifestyles."

"I suppose."

"Are you sad?"

"Yeah, sad for them. My life is precisely where I want it to be."

"Glad to hear it, Tara. Because mine is too."

After Gimble had showered and changed for bed she sat on the living room couch next to her husband. "So did you spend your entire evening working out?" she asked.

He hesitated a beat too long before saying, "Not really. I also did some reading, but we can leave it for tomorrow."

"Meaning we can't talk business at night?" she smiled.

"This is actually part personal . . . and maybe part paranoia as well."

"Let's have it, Pete. You know I'm not going to drop the subject."

"That's probably true, isn't it?"

"It's absolutely true."

He told her about the PBS show but didn't mention the idea about buying her one of Resnick's prints. All he said was that he suddenly had an urge to learn more about the photographer's career.

"And something you learned is bothering you?"

"A little, yeah. It's actually what I *didn't* learn that has me . . ."

"Suspicious? Gee, why doesn't that surprise me?" Although she greatly valued his instincts, she knew that every now and then he worried about problems that didn't actually exist.

"Okay, listen to this. After two hours of searching online I now know almost everything about Alex Resnick since the time he studied with Ansel Adams. But all I know about him before that," he said, "is that he was born in 1951 and attended two schools."

"Should anyone really care about what he did before studying with Ansel Adams?"

"I think so," he nodded, "yeah. Number one, he graduated from Wellner High School of the Arts in 1969. The school went bankrupt and closed in 1982."

"And this makes you suspicious?"

"Number two, in 1973 he graduated from Lankton College, which operated from 1898 to 1993 before folding."

"The high school and the college both closed?"

"Yes, ma'am."

"Okay, and what does that mean to you?"

"You know how much I hate coincidences, and here you have a highly improbable coincidence. The same person attends a high school and a college that both go out of business. And, by the way, that means if I want to check his student records I can't. The schools no longer exist."

Gimble ran that notion through her head then said, "I do think it's an odd coincidence, but I'm sure we could still get some information if we wanted to."

"Well, we could search for people who knew him as a student and interview them, but that would be ridiculously difficult, wouldn't it? We'd have to track down the names of people who either worked at the schools or attended at the same time he did, and then we'd have to find them someplace in America if they're still alive."

"That *would* be a challenge, wouldn't it?"

"You bet."

"But that's what you want to do, isn't it?"

"You bet."

"What exactly are you thinking, Pete?"

"I'm thinking that a man who has no past is a man who deserves watching," he said seriously. "Nothing more than that. Alex Resnick didn't materialize out of thin air, Tara. I'd like to know his full story."

"Then we'll find it. I'm not suspicious, but I'm certainly curious."

"Fair enough."

"But we don't need to start this tonight, right?"

"Correct. We need our beauty sleep."

"Something we definitely agree on, Detective Nazareth."

41.

It took Leonid Zaitsev, the Russian consulate's new security director, less than a week to unearth a mountain of damning evidence. Under his relentless questioning several frightened employees either hinted or flat-out claimed that Consul General Vasilyev had a long history of taking kickbacks from U.S. companies headquartered in Manhattan. Want to build that new plant in Vladivostok? For the right price Vasilyev could open certain doors. Want to break into the Russian banking market? Vasilyev was a close friend of the minister who would make that happen. Want to peddle U.S mansions to Russia's megarich? With one phone call Vasilyev could put you in business.

Zaitsev now figured that these and similar "courtesies" had made the consul general an extremely wealthy man. About this he had absolutely no doubt. But there was another enterprise, this one merely rumored to exist, that had Zaitsev salivating. A young secretary, plainly eager to please, had wondered aloud during her interview whether the consul general had been collecting protection money from certain Russian émigrés.

"You have actually heard that Consul General Vasilyev received money in return for protection?" Zaitsev had asked the young woman. She could see that this important and attractive man from Moscow was greatly interested in what she had to say, and it occurred to her that he might be her ticket to a dream job back home.

"As a rumor," she said softly, "yes. This is what I have heard."

"And why would people need to buy his protection?"

"Well, you know people have died here. Even the *New York Times* has said a Russian assassin is at work."

"And you believe the consul general might have been selling protection from assassination?" Zaitsev was firm with her, but not so firm as to scare her off. He didn't want her to back away from her story.

"This is what some people think," she whispered. "I have heard this spoken of here at the consulate."

"I value your honesty and your courage," he told her. "Anything that could tarnish Russia's reputation is of concern to all patriots, and I can see that you are one of them."

She blushed and went back to her desk, certain she had just made a wise career move.

Zaitsev didn't waste valuable time distinguishing between fact and rumor when he phoned the Kremlin to report his findings the next morning. By then he had connected the dots to his own satisfaction and was prepared to slip the noose over Vasilyev's head. First he told the president about the consul general's bribery scheme, and based on Kotov's reaction he knew that Vasilyev would, at a minimum, soon be residing in a labor camp somewhere above the Arctic Circle. This emboldened him to wade into the turbulent waters of the recent assassinations, presenting his theory as the only reasonable explanation.

"Based on what knowledgeable people have told me, Mr. President, I am confident the consul general is deeply involved in the recent murders. As for motive," he continued, "I must assume that the three dead men had refused to pay for Vasilyev's continued protection and were therefore eliminated."

He then recounted the story of the Kirov Wolf, both man and myth, and the ultra-secret operation that had sent him to America. "I believe it is highly likely that Vasilyev has been using the services of this so-called Wolf," he argued. "I am not certain of this yet, of course, but I suspect Vasilyev will enlighten us if asked properly."

"Then let's ask him properly," Kotov hissed. "I'll make the necessary travel arrangements."

"I'll await word from you, Mr. President," Zaitsev grinned. Things were moving rapidly in the right direction. Perhaps it would soon dawn on Kotov that a highly skilled security expert could make a fine New York consul general.

At 5:00 the next morning Zaitsev and two immense Russian security agents quietly let themselves into Vasilyev's apartment, injected him with midazolam, and carried him unconscious to the waiting SUV for a short ride to Teterboro Airport in New Jersey. Halfway into the 9-hour flight to Moscow on a private Gulfstream G500 the consul general awoke to find himself handcuffed to a seat at the back of the aircraft. Zaitsev and the two agents, meanwhile, were up front dining in style at a mahogany table set with linen and fresh flowers. A young flight attendant in a pale blue uniform poured vodka for them.

"What are you doing?" Vasilyev screamed. The roar of the jet's two Pratt & Whitney engines dampened the sound of his voice, so there was no risk of spoiling the pleasant meal at the far end of the aircraft.

"We're enjoying dinner, as you can plainly see," Zaitsev called back. The other men chuckled while sucking down their drinks.

"I order you to release me!"

"The only person who gives orders is President Kotov," Zaitsev replied coolly, "and he has ordered us to bring the traitor home."

"I am no traitor," Vasilyev protested. "This is a mistake."

Zaitsev shrugged to the others, reluctantly set down his knife and fork, and walked to the back of the plane.

"I will interrupt my dinner only this once, Vasilyev, so listen very carefully. I have in my possession bank documents we found in your apartment," he said, "and together they show you have more than $2 million from bribes sitting in four different New York banks. I also now have clear evidence of your involvement in the assassinations of Gerasimov, Sidorenko, and Malinovsky."

"Are you crazy? I have killed no one in my entire life. You're making a terrible mistake." Vasilyev wore the look of a tiny animal with its paw caught in a large steel trap. "You must believe me."

"No, the person who must believe you," Zaitsev told him as he turned away, "is President Kotov. Convince him of your innocence, and all will be well."

The private jet landed shortly before midnight at the Kubinka air base 47 miles southwest of Moscow. At precisely 12:30 the Russian president walked into the dimly lit maintenance shack where Vasilyev had been shackled at the back of the room. Kotov wore a black leather jacket, jeans, and well-polished military boots. As he walked past the lone lightbulb that hung above a cluttered workbench his eyes seemed to glow, and Vasilyev struggled to keep his intestines under control.

"Here is our rich friend from America," Kotov growled. Zaitsev and the two security guards were greatly amused by the president's sarcasm. "How many millions are you worth today, Vasilyev?"

"Mr. President, I have used this money only to support official programs," the consul general vowed. "Not one penny has been used for my personal needs."

"I am delighted to hear that, Vasilyev. But now we must make this truly official." He beckoned for Zaitsev to bring him the bank documents. "You may now transfer your assets to the consulate." Vasilyev eagerly signed the papers, hoping the nightmare would now end.

"Mr. President, there has been a terrible misunderstanding," he began, "and I am grateful for this opportunity to discuss it with you in person. I assure you I am guilty of no impropriety whatsoever."

Kotov studied him with those cold reptilian eyes. "When you murdered Malinovsky," he said, "did you know he was an agent of the Russian Federation and that he worked directly for me?"

"Mr. President, I have killed no one. I don't know why anyone thinks otherwise."

"Let's not quibble. When I say you killed Malinovsky," Kotov continued, "I mean you had the Wolf kill him for you. Is that not true?"

Vasilyev was utterly befuddled. "The wolf? I don't know what you mean by the wolf, Mr. President. I beg you to believe me. I have no idea what you're talking about."

"This is what I know, Vasilyev. You have been using a Russian agent called the Wolf to assassinate people who refused to pay you for protection. This is fact. All I want from you tonight is your confession and a heartfelt apology."

"I have killed no one," Vasilyev argued, daring to raise his voice for the first time. "Where is the evidence? Who is my accuser? I have a right to know these things. I have a right to a fair trial."

"A trial? You don't need a trial," Kotov said soothingly. "You simply need to confess and apologize. I first want you to explain why you had Gerasimov, Sidorenko, and Malinovsky murdered. After that, tell me you are sorry for betraying my trust."

Vasilyev shook his head and turned away from his accuser. He was prepared to carry his silence to the grave if necessary, but he would not confess to murders he had neither ordered nor committed. Yes, he had taken bribes, as no doubt had every consul general before him. But he had not killed anyone.

The brave silence ended at 12:47 a.m. when one of the security agents slowly pulled the fingernail from Vasilyev's left index finger with a pair of grimy pliers. Once he stopped screaming he signed the typed confession that had been set before him.

"I accept your confession, Vasilyev," Kotov said pleasantly, "and now await your apology."

Vasilyev's entire body shook uncontrollably and his voice cracked as he said, "Yes, of course, I am truly sorry, Mr. President. I will never do anything like this again."

"That is quite true," Kotov said flatly. He turned and nodded to Zaitsev, who motioned for the two security agents to conclude the evening's festivities. They half carried, half dragged Vasilyev to a construction zone alongside the main runway and tossed him into a deep drainage ditch, which they then backfilled with the help of a massive Chetra bulldozer. They parked the tractor parked on top of the grave for good measure.

"In case he wants to climb out," Zaitsev joked to President Kotov, who laughed at the pleasantry.

"Yes, absolutely. Leave nothing to chance, Zaitsev," the president replied. "That advice will serve you well as our new consul general in New York."

Zaitsev bowed slightly as he shook the president's hand. An exceedingly long day had ended exceedingly well.

42.

Dalton Stark's periodic phone calls almost always turned the world upside down for his detective friends in New York, and this latest one would be no exception. He caught them just as they were about to leave the apartment for One Police Plaza.

"I don't have final confirmation of this yet," he began, "but it appears that Consul General Vasilyev was executed in Russia late last night." His words were met by stunned silence. "You guys still there?"

"Yeah, but we're both sort of speechless, Dalton," Nazareth said. "I won't ask how you got the information, but I can't imagine why Vasilyev would have been executed. And when the hell did he even leave New York?"

"I've got some very good people in Russia," Stark offered, "and what I've been told is that Vasilyev was accused of killing Gerasimov, Sidorenko, and Malinovsky. Apparently some Russian security goons grabbed him yesterday in Manhattan, flew him to an air base outside Moscow, and executed him after he signed a confession."

"He confessed to all three assassinations?" Gimble asked, astonished by what she was hearing.

"I didn't have anyone right there at the scene," Stark told her, "so I need to tighten this up a bit. But, yes, it appears he confessed to the murders. Of course, Kotov could probably get both you and Pete to confess to the murders if he wanted to."

"I agree the confession means nothing," Nazareth said, "but I can't imagine why Kotov would think Vasilyev was the killer. That makes no sense at all. What possible motive could he have had?"

"Unless he was ordered to do it by Kotov," Gimble suggested, "and then was killed to shut him up."

"Nothing in Vasilyev's background suggests he would have been used as an assassin," Stark argued, "so I don't think that's it. What's possible, but still pretty unlikely, is that he had hired someone to get rid of the three dissidents. As for why he would have done that, I have no clue."

"Since I'm usually the most suspicious guy in the room," Nazareth said, "I'll throw out this idea. Suppose Vasilyev was, in fact, part of the plot to kill the three men and that he was acting under orders from Kotov. Isn't it possible we're being fed a story about his execution? Maybe this is just a smokescreen designed to cover Vasilyev's tracks."

Stark took a moment to consider that possibility. "Could it be? Yes. But I hope to hell not. I got this report from my most senior agent in Moscow, and if he was deliberately fed a bogus story it means his cover has been blown. In that case," Stark concluded, "he's as good as dead."

"So what should we do?" Gimble asked.

"Sit tight," Stark said, "until we know for sure what we're up against."

The detectives headed to the office and spent the next two hours considering the likeliest combinations of players: Vasilyev and Petrenko working together; either man working with a hired killer; or a third man, the mysterious assassin, operating on his own. Less than 48 hours earlier they had convinced themselves they were looking for a lone assassin, but the shocking report from Russia had rattled that comfortable theory. The game contained far too many moving parts to yield an easy answer.

Not long after they had finished their brainstorming session Stark called to update them on his earlier report.

"My guy in Moscow is safe, thank God," he told them, "and confirms that Vasilyev was executed last night. Only four people on the planet should know this, so you can't use the information in any way without putting our agent at risk."

"Understood. And you're sure they executed him because he supposedly killed the three dissidents?" Gimble asked.

"That, yes, plus financial crimes," Stark said. "He was accepting bribes from U.S. companies that wanted to do business with the consulate or that were trying to buy their way into the Russian market."

"That much we already knew about," Nazareth responded. "Vasilyev had been selling favors for quite some time, and that's actually the main reason I can't imagine him getting involved in murders. He had a really good thing going, Dalton. He didn't need a sideline."

"Can't argue the point, Pete. Maybe he was just a scapegoat. Kotov has a long history of getting rid of people for little or no reason," Stark explained, "so it wouldn't be out of character for him to waste Vasilyev on a whim. If that's what happened, of course, then your real killer is still out there."

"Which is what my gut tells me," Nazareth shot back. "I don't care why Kotov killed Vasilyev. The person we're after is still on the street planning his next hit."

"Then you need to hit him first," Stark said seriously.

"That's Plan A," Nazareth assured him. "As soon as we know who he is."

43.

Nazareth sat at the conference table, chin resting on his fist, and stared at the half-empty coffee mug. He was unaccustomed to being completely stumped after weeks of working a murder case, yet here they were without the first clue to the assassin's identity.

"All of the homicides you and I have solved so far had one thing in common," he told Gimble. "They involved amateurs -- very smart, pretty careful, but ultimately amateurs. And they each made a big mistake. But in this case we're dealing with a highly trained assassin who's possibly been at this longer than you and I have been alive."

"And if Dalton is right," she replied, "he doesn't look, sound, or act Russian. If, in fact, he's Russian."

"My brain is fried, Tara. I don't know what to try next."

"The only thing I can think of is going back to the beginning. We create a new list of Russian dissidents and interview every single one of them. If we do that," she said, "maybe we'll turn up something or someone that connected the three victims. Maybe it was their hometown in Russia, or jobs they'd held, or causes they'd supported."

"It's a shot in the dark, but I don't have anything better. But we could be talking about weeks of interviewing, and that could mean several more bodies."

"If there's another way, Pete, I don't see it. We interview as many people as we can and maybe show them a bunch of photos from Sidorenko's speech. I still think there's a good chance the killer was in the audience that night. He either poisoned Sidorenko right there or followed him home."

Nazareth nodded. "I still agree that Sidorenko's murder is the one that puts us closest to the killer. But you and I didn't see anyone in the audience who looks good for this."

"And neither did Alex Resnick, who obviously recognized more people than we did."

"Yep, that's true. Which reminds me: I still want to learn more about Resnick's background. I refuse to believe someone as famous as him could be missing a childhood. Something's not right."

"I think you're overstating the case just a bit. What has you spooked is that both his high school and college went out of business."

"That, yes, but also the fact that I haven't been able to find anything at all about his life before he became famous." Gimble gave him a disapproving look. "I know, I know. You think I'm a little off the wall about this. But how does a young guy from nowhere suddenly become apprenticed to Ansel Adams? Why haven't I found a story about how that happened? That's a pretty big gap in the record, Tara."

"Tell you what. A year or so ago at a Women of Achievement dinner I sat next to the editor of *Coastal America*, which is a really first-rate nature magazine. Her name is Kerri Marchant, and I know she's used a lot of Resnick's work. In fact," she continued, "we ended up talking quite a bit about him because Kerri was one of the first editors who latched onto him after he trained with Adams."

"Okay, then let's try this. I'll start pulling together a list of dissidents for us to interview while you track down Kerri and see what she can tell you about his background. But try not to make it sound like a police investigation."

"No problem. I'm sure she'll remember our conversation, and I can tell her I'm just doing some extra homework before you and I buy one of his photos."

"One of his very expensive photos."

"Hey, we're worth it. And, for the record, I think one of his photos would look fabulous in our apartment." He nodded knowingly. Great minds think alike, he thought.

44.

Under Kerri Marchant's leadership *Coastal America* had become widely regarded as perhaps the country's classiest nature magazine. The design was simple and elegant, the production flawless, and the photography breathtaking. On this last point Alex Resnick had exercised quite a bit of control as both a paid photographer and as what he liked to call "the unofficial volunteer assistant editor." What he meant was that he and Ms. Marchant had been dating exclusively for the past four years, and she relied heavily on him each month when it came time to select the best images by some of the country's top photographers. Although their relationship was by no means secret, they also didn't go out of their way to advertise it, so it wasn't something that would have come to Gimble's attention.

Yes, Marchant remembered Detective Tara Gimble from the women's dinner and was delighted to take her call. After catching up on each other's careers for a few minutes, they turned to the subject of Alex Resnick.

"My husband and I were extremely fortunate to get some help from Alex recently on an investigation we're handling," Gimble explained, "and I came away thinking it's way past time for us to own one of his photographs. I'd like to surprise Pete with one for Christmas, but I'd also like to give him something about Alex's career -- a book, if there is one, or maybe a reprint of a magazine article that tells how he came to be the best-known outdoor photographer of our time."

Marchant was highly enthusiastic about the idea. "The photograph would make a stunning gift," she gushed, "but someone still needs to write the book you've got in mind. So far Alex has refused to put it on his agenda. He's had plenty of offers from publishers and authors, but he's just not interested yet. I assume he'll get around to it when he stops traveling so much."

"Do you know of any magazine articles that did a good job of talking about his childhood or how he first became involved in photography?" Gimble asked.

"The best article was in *Time* about three years ago," Marchant said, "but it was focused entirely on his work since training with Ansel Adams. Alex has mentioned to me that his childhood was in some ways uncomfortable, and he doesn't like talking about it. So I've dropped the subject."

"Understood. Then I'll track down the *Time* article and maybe have it framed so it can hang near the photograph. Fortunately I have plenty of time to pull this together before Christmas."

"If you do decide to buy one of his photos, I recommend you visit the Brenton Smythe Gallery in SoHo," Marchant offered, "and ask for Adriana. Tell her I sent you, and you'll get the best service as well as the best price. She sells more of Alex's work than anyone else, so he gives her preferential treatment."

"That's very kind of you, Kerri. I absolutely will work with Adriana when the time comes. Actually I can't wait," she laughed, "because I'm still in the process of transforming Pete's man-cave into a home for two."

"And one of Alex's photographs would be a significant step in the right direction, Tara. I wish you well. Let's get together for lunch sometime."

"I'd love that. In the meantime, stay very well."

"You too." As soon as the two had hung up, Marchant speed-dialed another number.

45.

Before comparing notes on their latest efforts, Nazareth and Gimble walked outside One Police Plaza to visit Sameer Khan's hot dog stand, perhaps the most popular wheeled restaurant in Manhattan. Khan and the detectives were old friends, and he had once helped them foil a terrorist attack that would have claimed hundreds of lives. After word of his heroics had spread, every cop within 50 blocks began stopping by his cart at least once a week, and some were even passing out Khan's business cards to tourists. He wasn't a rich man, but on most days he had more police protection than the mayor.

"Good afternoon, detectives," Khan called to them. "It's good to see you today."

"Always great to see you, Sameer," Nazareth replied. "Tara and I decided we were in the mood for some fine dining."

"Then you have come to the right place." He handed a cardboard tray of eight hot dogs to a young father who stood alongside the cart with his wife and three children. Then he began serving four other customers who were enjoying the sunshine while awaiting their turns. "I'll be right with you."

When it was their turn the detectives ordered two hot dogs each -- chili on Nazareth's, sauerkraut on Gimble's. Two bottles of water and a bag of chips brought the total to $10, which included the discount Khan gave to every police officer who visited. "So how are things going, Sameer?" Gimble asked.

"Wonderful, as always," Khan replied. "I have the best regular customers in New York City, this is for sure. I did have one very bad experience yesterday, but this sort of thing is rare."

"Why, what happened?" Nazareth wondered.

"A beautiful car pulled up next to my cart," he explained, "and the driver rolled down the passenger window. A very nicely dressed and pleasant man in his thirties, I would say he. He asked for two hot dogs and a bottle of water. When I passed everything to him inside the car, instead of paying me he laughed and drove off."

"I hope you got his license plate," Gimble said.

"I was too shocked to think of it, detective. Nothing like this has ever happened to me in all these years. My wife says the man might have been desperate for food," he said, "in which case I would have helped him. But he didn't look like someone who was desperate for food."

"I'd say he was just a dirtbag, Sameer," Nazareth told him. "Lots of people in this world look like decent, honest folks but inside are really bad. You can't always tell by their looks."

"Yes, but it's disappointing, isn't it?" Khan said wistfully. "From now on I suppose I will ask people to pay before I give them their food."

"Especially when you're dealing with Pete here," Gimble joked. "In some parts of Manhattan he's known as the Hot Dog Bandit."

Khan had a good laugh over that. "No, never Detective Pete Nazareth," he said. "I know that what you see in this man is what you get. He is one of the best people God has ever put on this Earth."

"And Sameer never lies, Tara," Nazareth grinned. "You're a lucky woman, aren't you?"

"Oh, help me," she groaned as she turned away. "The check's on him, Sameer."

The detectives settled on a bench to enjoy their lunch, but first Gimble reacted to something she had just heard. "What you said to Sameer is quite true, you know."

"What's that?"

"A person's looks don't tell you what's inside."

"Oh, that. Well, it's true, but that's not news."

"But it sort of grabbed me after the conversation I had with Kerri Marchant," she told him.

"Ah, so how did that go?"

"Very nice, friendly conversation, but she really doesn't know anything about Resnick's background. She says he once told her he'd had a tough childhood, but that's all he'd give her."

They both considered that as they ate. Finally Nazareth said, "Everybody has a story, Tara, even if it's one they'd rather forget. But what could be so terrible in Resnick's story that no one has ever heard it? To me that's a big red flag waving in the wind."

"I'm still a lot less worried about it than you," she replied, "but I have to admit it's odd. I'd feel a lot more comfortable if I could fill in the blanks. When we met with him he was charming and friendly, and he really seemed to want to help us. So I'm puzzled about the secret childhood."

"What you see isn't always what you get. This could be nothing, but it could be something big. And I think we need to know for sure."

"Yeah, I guess we do."

"We do, Tara."

She nodded. "Agreed. So how did you make out identifying other Russian dissidents we should interview?"

"I spoke again with Professor Alina Yesikova, since she's the one who had put Feodor Sidorenko on our radar screen, and she gave me the names of nine people she's worried about."

"Okay, then. We can start on those right away. Did she have any feelings about who might be behind the killings?"

"She's convinced it's someone who was sent here by Ruslan Kotov," he said, "given how good this guy seems to be at what he does. But here's the really interesting part: she's convinced we'd never recognize this person as a Russian assassin. She believes he's hiding in plain sight and most likely passes as a non-Russian."

"So basically she's on board with Dalton Stark's theory?"

"Yep. That's interesting, isn't it?"

"Frustrating is more like it," she answered.

"You know, Tara, Alex Resnick doesn't look or sound Russian."

"Oh, come on, Pete. Now you think he's an assassin? Really?"

"We're desperate, Tara. Desperate times require desperate measures."

"And what exactly do you have in mind?"

"Unfortunately, I think we have no choice but to pay Resnick another visit. And at the risk of offending an innocent man, we need to question him about his missing life story."

"We could come away from this looking really stupid, you know? He's a rock star, Pete."

"We'd look a whole lot dumber if we didn't ask," he said, "and Resnick turns out to be a killer. Hey, I can go see him alone, Tara. That's okay."

She sighed and stared at the sky for a moment. "No, we're in this together. If someone has to look dumb, it might as well be both of us. But can we at least try one other thing before we call him?"

"What's that?"

"Track down some alumni from his high school and college. Someone's bound to know a person as famous as Resnick, right?"

"Will this take years, Tara?"

"No, just give me a few hours. I can think of several online tools that can help -- Facebook, Classmates, LinkedIn, and a few others."

"Okay. We hold off calling him."

"Thanks, partner." She offered Nazareth a half smile. "Why do I have a really bad feeling about this?"

46.

Resnick immediately picked up the phone in his home studio when he saw it was Kerri Marchant calling. "And how are you this fine day, my love?" he asked.

"Absolutely wonderful. Autumn is without question the best time of year."

"I completely agree. In fact, I was thinking maybe you and I should get away one day soon and spend some time up in the Adirondacks."

"That sounds excellent, as long as we'll be staying in a hotel," she snickered. "I don't do tents."

"No tents. I was thinking about the Whiteface Lodge in Lake Placid," he told her. "It's a five-hour drive, and it should be a lovely trip if we go on a weekend."

"You've twisted my arm, Alex."

"Good. I'll check some dates later today and see what works best for you."

"Fabulous. In the meantime," she added, "I have some good news for you. I spoke a little while ago with a woman I met last year at an award dinner, and she wants to buy one of your photos for her husband as a Christmas present. I suggested she call Adriana at the gallery."

"You're my marketing secret weapon, Kerri. I've lost count of how many buyers you've sent my way."

"Well, this one was already coming your way, so I didn't have to do much. Actually you met her and her husband recently: Tara Gimble and Pete Nazareth."

Resnick was a bit surprised the two young detectives could afford his work, but he was also flattered. "Yes, a lovely young couple. I tried to help them with an investigation they've got in progress, but I don't think I accomplished much. Did she say which photograph she was thinking of?"

"No, I don't think so. But she was also hoping to find a book about you."

"A book?"

"Yes, along with the photograph she'd like to give her husband something that tells the famous Alex Resnick's life story. See," she said playfully, "I've been badgering you to have someone write your biography."

"Well, there are certainly plenty of magazine articles out there," Resnick replied coolly. He pulled a bottle of Tums from his desk drawer and popped two in his mouth. This delightful conversation was suddenly headed in an unappetizing direction.

"She's already looked at some of those articles, but as you and I both know they don't show anything at all about your younger years. People really are interested in that sort of thing, Alex."

"*Some* people," he corrected, "but my difficult childhood isn't something I wish to discuss right now." He could feel his heart rate picking up speed. "I'll think about it when I retire."

"That's up to you, hon'. But in the meantime your fans are searching on their own, and that should make you very happy."

"It certainly does," he lied. "I'm shocked that people find me so interesting."

"You know I do," she said sweetly.

"And you know the feeling is mutual."

"Yes, I do. I've got to run. Give me a call tonight, okay?"

"Absolutely. Enjoy the rest of your day."

After hanging up he went over to the large window facing the Hudson and tried to calm himself with a series of slow, very deep breaths. This kept him from slipping into full panic mode, but for one of the few times in his life he was truly rattled. Resnick had always been in control, had always mastered detail after detail so that the desired outcome would never be left to chance. More to the point, he had recently handled the two detectives with what he believed was exceptional skill. He had actually worked alongside them! What better way to deflect their attention?

So why in God's name were they now poking around in his life?

Instinct told him that Gimble's interest had nothing to do with buying one of his photographs. No, what she was really after was his background, and that was something he could not allow her to have. Others had been interested in his life's story for a variety of harmless reasons, but they all had politely dropped the subject when he told them he wasn't ready to talk. Is that what the two detectives would do?

Not likely.

He wondered what had attracted their attention. In the end, though, it didn't matter, did it? They were interested. Period. And that wasn't good.

Early in his career he had been forced to eliminate several threats that had crawled ominously from the shadows, and he would do so again if that's what was necessary. He remembered in particular the scare he had in April of 1985, when he spotted Eduard Denikin while having lunch at a Midtown deli. An uninvited ghost from the past, Denikin had once been the vulgar, much-feared Party chief in Kirov, and he represented a serious threat. The presence of a potential adversary who could identify him was intolerable, so he did what needed doing: he tracked Denikin to his Long Island home and on a chilly moonlit night left him floating in South Oyster Bay.

Other threats had come along over the years, each of them efficiently addressed. Would it be different when dealing with two NYPD detectives?

47.

Gimble's online research produced the names of three dozen people who had attended Resnick's high school or college around the time he would have been a student. Of that number she selected eight people who lived in one of the city's five boroughs and began making phone calls. The first five had graduated from Wellner High School of the Arts in the early 1970s, and not surprisingly they all recognized Alex Resnick's name. Yet no one recalled a connection between Resnick and Wellner High School.

"The school had a big fundraising campaign just before it closed for good in 1989," one woman recalled, "but it was a complete flop. Believe me, if Alex Resnick had been a Wellner alum, they would have built the fund drive around his name, and it probably would have been a huge success."

Gimble then reached two Lankton College graduates, only one of whom recognized Resnick's name but thought he was either an actor or a singer. After that she succeeded in tracking down three people who had worked at the college before it went bankrupt in 1993. One of them, the former admissions director, had been there for nearly 25 years and vowed he would have remembered if Alex Resnick had been a Lankton student.

"I have certainly seen Resnick's photographs," the man said. "Who hasn't? But I have never once heard anyone say he attended Lankton. He wasn't there while I was on the staff, for sure. I would have remembered someone like that."

By the time Gimble finished her calls she had reluctantly concluded that Alex Resnick had doctored his resume as successful people -- doctors, politicians, and business leaders among them -- often do. But she wasn't ready to believe he was an assassin working for the Russian government. Her suspicious husband might be able to get there, but she couldn't.

"We need to handle this tactfully," she told Nazareth. "If Resnick fudged his resume, which seems to be the case, he's got plenty of famous company."

"Understood. I won't hold it against him unless it turns out he's been killing people."

"Oh, come on, Pete. Enough already! You can't seriously believe one of the world's most famous photographers is a murderer."

"On the contrary. I absolutely believe anyone can be a murderer," he insisted. "An assassin? A serial killer? Probably not. But until we're certain he's clean, we have to assume Resnick may be living two lives. We can't not check this out."

"Okay, then we'll check it out. I'll call him and say we need some more help with the photos, and then while we're there we can steer the conversation toward his background."

"Why not just drive over?" Nazareth asked. "We don't normally call suspects for an appointment."

"I don't consider him a suspect."

"Then what is he?"

"A famous man who values his privacy. Look, maybe he dropped out of college. Or maybe he never even enrolled," she argued. "Early in his career he felt he needed credentials on his resume, so he manufactured them. This happens all the time."

"But not usually with someone as famous as he is."

"He wasn't famous when he fabricated the details, Pete. But now he's stuck with them. I'm sure he never thought the police would care about his childhood."

Nazareth thought his wife was being too soft on a legitimate suspect, but he recognized that what she was saying was highly plausible. "Okay, give him a call and let him know we need to stop by again. But please tell him it has to be today, okay?"

"Yes, I will. I'm sure he'll be happy to cooperate."

As soon as Resnick picked up the phone Gimble knew he was not, in fact, happy to cooperate. He sounded edgy, maybe even a touch annoyed. She wasn't prepared for this.

"I certainly would like to help, Detective Gimble," he said warily, "but I'm not sure I can add anything to the conversation we had the other day. I've looked the photos over again and don't recognize anyone else."

"We would also like to learn more about some of the other photographers who covered Sidorenko's speech," she countered, "and maybe you can steer us to the right ones."

"What do you want to know about them?"

"We're not really sure. I suppose it's possible one of them saw something that might help with the investigation."

"Then why not go to them directly, the way you did with me?" As he spoke he fumbled through his cluttered desk drawer. "And I have to say this really isn't a good day, detective. I've got a lot going on."

"We won't need more than 15 or 20 minutes, Mr. Resnick," Gimble replied gently. She was growing frustrated, and she could tell from Nazareth's face that he was itching to fly out the front door. "This would really be helpful."

Resnick found what he needed: a business card for the private car service he generally used for airport trips. "Well, look, if this cannot wait for another day," he said more kindly, not wishing to alarm her, "let's do it about two hours from now. Until then I'll be working on some prints. But we really will need to keep the conversation short this time, detective. Later this week I'll give you all the time you need."

"That's fine, Mr. Resnick. We'll stop by in two hours. I appreciate your help."

Nazareth was already pulling his jacket on as Gimble hung up.

"I take it you don't plan to wait two hours," she said.

"I'm okay with not knocking on his door for two hours, but until then I want to sit right outside his apartment building. You do agree he's not crazy about seeing us, right?"

"He's not dying to see us, but maybe he's just really busy."

"No problem," he nodded. "We won't bother him for two hours. I'm fine with sitting in the car drinking coffee while we wait."

Gimble couldn't disguise her frustration. A crazy idea had grabbed hold of her husband, and he wasn't about to let go of it. "All right, Pete, let's go sit outside his apartment and drink coffee."

Eighteen minutes later they were sitting in their unmarked sedan on Fulton Street, less than five blocks away from One Police Plaza, hopelessly stuck behind a delivery van that had swerved in front of a speeding yellow cab and gotten T-boned. Behind them a dozen drivers leaned on their horns, apparently believing the noise would cause the two surly tow truck drivers to work faster.

There were times when Nazareth hated Manhattan. This was one of them.

48.

Resnick threw the empty suitcase on his bed and turned toward the large mirrored dresser. The man who stared back at him today was no longer the celebrated photographer whose work had graced the covers of prestigious magazines around the world. Instead he saw the lined face of an aging assassin, a man who had been groomed by his Soviet masters to perform a great service for the state and who had never been freed from his sworn duty.

The years had been kind to him in many ways. He had enjoyed good health, a satisfying life in the company of a few close friends, and as much adulation as an artist could ever desire. Yet the guiding force of his life was, and would always be, the vow he had taken as a young man. He was Borya Volkov, the Wolf, and his work would end only when he stopped breathing.

How easy it would be to eliminate the two young detectives, to invite them into his apartment and be rid of them for good. Inside a closet safe he possessed a smorgasbord of poisons that could easily do the trick: potassium cyanide, thallium, tetrodotoxin, scopolamine, atropine, chloral hydrate, paraldehyde, and more. But if he killed them the world would be too small a place in which to hide. The NYPD, he knew, would never rest until the cop-killer had been hunted down.

His alternative? If he simply vanished the detectives would eventually have no choice but to forget him. In time the case of the dead Russian dissidents would fade as new headline-grabbing homicides came along, and the NYPD wouldn't have time or money to squander on the man everyone knew as Alex Resnick.

Abandoning his comfortable New York City life would be difficult, of course, but staying was no longer an option. So as he began stuffing the large suitcase with necessary items he devised what seemed like a reasonable exit strategy. First he would have the car service deliver him to the United Airlines terminal at Newark Airport. Instead of catching a flight he would rent a vehicle for a long, leisurely drive to Los Angeles. Once in L.A. he would spend a couple of weeks changing his appearance so that it matched the photos on his alternate passport and driver's license, each in the name of Francis Benton. He had never needed to use the documents before, but now he congratulated himself for having planned ahead.

Finally, on the appropriate day he would catch an Aeroflot flight to Russia and present himself at the offices of the Foreign Intelligence Service in Moscow's Yasenevo District. Once he proved he was the late Anatoly Bukarin's agent from New York City he would undoubtedly receive a hero's welcome. In fact, he could easily imagine being given use of a country estate in consideration of his long and distinguished service to Mother Russia. Yes, that would only be fair. And with the money he had wisely placed in a variety of foreign banks he could live without a care in the world.

He was enormously energized by the thought of returning home after so many years and spending the rest of his life photographing the glories of Russia. Although his New York life was ending more abruptly than he had expected, maybe that was for the best. He was growing tired of the hunt. The Kirov Wolf had earned a long rest.

When the suitcase was full Volkov turned to the metal camera case, knowing he faced painful choices since he couldn't bring all of his precious gear with him. The three newest digital cameras would come because together they had cost over $200,000. But he struggled with almost everything else, in particular the old Pentax K1000 35mm camera that sat in a glass display box on the bookcase. It was the first camera he had purchased after coming to America, and he had done enough with it to convince the great Ansel Adams to take him on as a humble apprentice. He wrapped it in gray packaging foam and slipped it into the gear case.

His old Canon A-1 wasn't as lucky. It's the camera Volkov had used during his first hiking tour of the Adirondacks, and after two weeks in the wild he had returned with the images that would reward him with his first *National Geographic* photo essay. Sentimentality went only so far, though, and the Canon remained on the shelf. He hoped someone would see its value, but more than likely it would be tossed out along with the rest of his belongings once he skipped town.

The last thing he saw as he closed the apartment door behind him was the framed 8x10 photo that occupied a prominent place on the hallway console table: a striking black-and-white image of Kerri Marchant and him at the summer home they had rented near Gibson Beach in Sagaponack. Volkov had taken the shot himself using a wireless remote on the last day of their vacation two years ago, and he had done a magnificent job of capturing the handsome couple's bittersweet moment. They were returning to Manhattan after a joyous time together, and their smiles were tinged with unmistakable sadness.

He had room for the picture in his suitcase, but what was the point?

49.

With an assist from his vehicle's flashers and a few piercing blasts of the siren Nazareth finally inched past the fender bender on Fulton Street and weaved his way over to West Street. He drove north toward Resnick's apartment near the corner of Bank Street and made good time until he reached 11th Street, where two dozen moderately out-of-control schoolkids were crossing West Street in the company of three overwhelmed teachers, all headed over to the Hudson River Greenway. One of the students, a girl of about nine, stumbled and fell in the crosswalk, where she lay wailing over her scraped knee.

"I cannot believe this," Nazareth muttered. "Should it really take a whole day just to drive a few blocks?"

"Stay cool, Pete," Gimble told him. "I'll get out and speed things up for us."

"Great idea," he said as he lit up the flashers to help protect the intersection.

"Yes, I thought so," she smiled. Gimble stepped onto the pavement and approached the young teacher who was trying unsuccessfully to convince the injured girl to get off the highway. Before she could identify herself as a detective, however, she happened to glance a block ahead, where a uniformed doorman hoisted a large suitcase into the trunk of a black sedan outside an apartment building. That's when her eyes met Volkov's. He stood alongside the rear door and stared at her. Then he climbed into the back seat, and the car sped off.

Suddenly Nazareth was at the crosswalk lifting the injured student from the street and carrying her gently to the grassy median. "I'm a police officer," he told the girl softly as he studied her knee. "Your teacher will wash off the scrape, and you'll be fine." Meanwhile, Gimble kept traffic stopped until her partner could return to the vehicle. "You saw him?" he said excitedly as they sped off. "Resnick?"

"Yes, in the black sedan. Quick, pull up by the doorman."

Nazareth slammed on the brakes, and Gimble held her shield out the window. "NYPD. Where was black limo headed?" she yelled to the guy who had just loaded the trunk.

"Newark Airport," he called back. "United Airlines."

The doorman never heard Gimble thank him because Nazareth roared away from the curb, tires screaming. "Damn, damn, damn," he shouted. "I see three black sedans up ahead, Tara. No idea which one is his."

"Then pick the one that's going fastest. That's my bet."

Despite the siren and lights Nazareth struggled to work his way through the heavy traffic. For every Manhattan driver who pulls over for a police vehicle there are three who keep texting or talking on their cell phones. After swerving behind a large delivery truck Nazareth hit the fast lane but could now see only two black sedans ahead.

"One of them turned off, Tara," he yelled.

"I'd still go for the one that's out front, Pete. But it's your call."

"All right, hold on. We're going for the fast one."

50.

Volkov was rapidly approaching full panic mode as he watched the unmarked vehicle through the rear window. He had lost control of events and desperately needed a lucky break. It arrived on cue when Nazareth pulled behind a delivery truck and momentarily dropped out of sight.

"Turn right! Turn right!" he screamed from the back seat. The livery driver instinctively followed Volkov's command and in the process nearly ran down a young woman pushing a baby stroller.

"What the hell's wrong?" the driver yelled angrily, his heart pounding as he barreled down West 17th Street.

"The guy that was behind us is out to kill me. He's already killed three other people, and now he's after me."

"That guy who's been killing all those Russians?"

"Yes," Volkov shouted. "I accidentally took a photograph of him, and now he's trying to kill me."

"Did he turn behind us?" The driver was badly shaken and didn't know what to do next.

"No, he went up West Street. Go down to 8th Avenue, then head uptown."

"Let's just go to the police," the driver whimpered.

"No! I've got to get out of town!" Volkov shouted. "Just do as I tell you."

The driver made a hard left on 8th Avenue and joined the other crazies who were speeding north. Four red lights and six near collisions later they were almost to Central Park.

"Take a left on 55th, then go up 10th Avenue," Volkov ordered.

"But what if that guy goes all the way up to the Henry Hudson?" the driver argued. "He could be waiting for us near the GW Bridge."

"No, he'll turn off when he can't find us on West Street, so he'll be somewhere in Midtown. You and I are heading north. Forget about Newark Airport."

"You're the boss, Mr. Resnick, but I hope to hell you're right."

"Trust me, I know this guy. He'll be in Midtown looking for us. But even if he does go to the GW Bridge, he won't come anywhere near us on 10th Avenue."

"I still think we should just go to the nearest precinct."

"No!" Volkov screamed. "This is *my* life we're talking about. Just drive."

Again the driver did as he was told, taking 55th over to 10th Avenue, hanging a hard right, then stomping on the gas. Volkov ordered the driver to go all the way up to 181st Street before turning left toward the Henry Hudson Parkway. At that point they would be well beyond the entrance to the GW Bridge. So even if Nazareth and Gimble went as far as the bridge -- something Vokov thought highly unlikely -- they would be out of luck.

"Okay, here's what we're going to do," he said after a frantic online search with his cell phone. "You'll drop me off at the Doubletree Hilton in Tarrytown. I have a friend there who can take care of me. Then you'll head back to Manhattan."

"Unless I get shot first," the driver said nervously.

"You're not going to get shot. But you *are* going to pick up a $500 tip."

The driver grew courageous at the mention of a $500 tip and was now fully on board. The pieces of a bold new plan had clicked into place.

The Wolf was back in business.

51.

The detectives closed rapidly on the two black sedans until an 18-wheeler pulled out from West 27th Street and got hung up making a tight right turn, forcing the driver to back up and try again. By the time Nazareth was able to resume the chase both sedans had disappeared around the bend at 30th Street. Once he finally hit top speed alongside the Javits Convention Center at 34th Street he could see only one of the cars four blocks ahead of him. Had the other one turned onto a side street, or had it already rounded the next bend in the highway at 42nd Street?

"We lost one of them, Tara. I don't know whether it turned or it's farther ahead."

"He shouldn't turn off if he's going to Newark Airport," she answered, "so I'd keep going, Pete. Maybe we'll pick up both of them when the road straightens out again."

But at 45th Street they could still see only one black car, now two blocks ahead of them in the left lane and traveling well above the speed limit. Even after Nazareth had worked his way directly behind the vehicle the driver was slow to respond to the lights and siren, and he didn't pull over until he reached DeWitt Clinton Park at 52nd Street.

Both detectives jumped out and ran to the car. The driver had his window down and immediately raised his hands when he saw the weapon in Nazareth's right hand. "Oh, God, please don't shoot!" he yelled in heavily accented English. As for the old woman in the back seat, she began to cry hysterically when she saw Gimble at the rear door pointing a gun at her.

It took nearly 10 minutes for the passenger to stop sobbing, and by then they had forfeited all hope of chasing down Resnick. The best Gimble could do was get out an alert out for a black livery car leaving Manhattan via the GWB, even though she realized there was no practical way to stop and search every black sedan. That simply wasn't going to happen. But she also hated the odds of finding Resnick someplace in Midtown since nearly 12,000 black limos work the streets of Manhattan. Finding a four-leaf clover in Central Park would be easier than stopping every black sedan with a male passenger in the back seat.

"We were so damn close," Nazareth grumbled. "I can't believe we lost him."

"Let's keep driving," Gimble argued. "We've got nothing to lose. Maybe he's still up ahead."

"We're not going to find him, Tara. Hell, we don't even know if that was Resnick's car in front of us. His might have been the one that turned off down around 16th Street."

Gimble was adamant. "As I said, we've got nothing to lose."

"All right. Let's do it." Once again they raced up the West Side Highway, which turned into the Henry Hudson Parkway at 72nd Street. Several times they pulled alongside black limos and checked out the back seats, but Resnick wasn't in any of them.

"That's it for me," Nazareth said as they neared 163rd Street. "I'm turning off before the bridge."

"No, Pete. Stay on the Henry Hudson until we get to Fort Tryon Park," Gimble insisted. "We can turn around there."

"What do you think's going to change between here and there?" he asked, mildly annoyed over her stubbornness.

"Do I ever trust your instincts, Pete?" she asked gently.

"Well," he replied sheepishly, "as a matter of fact you *always* trust my instincts. Okay, message received. We'll go up to Fort Tryon."

"Thank you. Hey, worst case we can walk around Fort Tryon for a few minutes and calm down, right?"

"You just want to see Fort Tryon."

"No, I want to catch Resnick. But if I can't, I'll settle for Fort Tryon."

"Fort Tryon it is."

"Or Resnick."

"Right. Or Resnick." He looked at his wife and shook his head. She was an incurable optimist.

Traffic turned sluggish as they neared the GWB and its confusing tangle of circular on and off ramps, but they soon had a clear road ahead of them. As they entered the bridge's shadow Gimble gestured furiously at the black sedan that had pulled from 181st Street onto Riverside Drive and was now merging onto the Henry Hudson. Nazareth was doing 63, but the limo was pulling away fast.

"I see him," he said. "Doing at least 75."

"You thinking what I'm thinking?"

"What? Oh, come on, Tara. No way that's Resnick," Nazareth laughed, "but I'm happy to write the guy up for doing 30 or 40 over the speed limit."

"That's definitely one of the three cars we were following back by Resnick's apartment building," she insisted.

"Looks like every other black car to me."

"No, the other two were Lincolns. The one that turned off down near 16th Street was a Mercedes with a small dent on the driver's door."

"And this one's a Mercedes with a small dent on the driver's door! Damn you're good, Tara."

"Why thank you, Pete. Now how about pulling him over?"

The Henry Hudson Parkway has enough bends in it to make anything above 50 MPH a challenge, so at 80 Nazareth felt as though he was about to go airborne. Yet as he rolled out of a long right curve alongside Fort Tryon Park he was shocked to find that the limo had disappeared.

"Where the hell did he go?" Nazareth yelled.

"He had to turn right, Pete. Hang a right! "

"Here?"

"Turn right!"

The tires squealed and the cruiser fishtailed as Nazareth took the Fort Tryon Place turnoff at 53, then powered up the winding drive toward the imposing stone walls surrounding what looked very much like a medieval European monastery. There in the parking lot overlooking the Hudson they found the black Mercedes sedan with its engine running and its left rear door open wide. The driver was slumped over the steering wheel, his back covered with blood.

The Wolf was loose at the Cloisters.

52.

Before exiting the limo Volkov had pressed the muzzle of his Glock against the driver's seat to muffle the sound and fired twice. Killing the frightened man wasn't something Volkov enjoyed doing, but the driver had sealed his own fate when he saw the flashing lights behind him on the Henry Hudson Parkway and told Volkov he was going to pull over. He changed his mind the moment he felt the gun at his temple and instead drove up the steep winding roadway to the Cloisters, a medieval art museum built from stone excavated from ancient French monasteries.

But the driver now represented an unacceptable risk. He would almost certainly cooperate with the police and tell them which way the Wolf had run, so the math was simple. At that particular moment a few extra seconds of escape time carried far more value than the driver's life.

"Thank you, my friend," Volkov said softly as he pulled the trigger. Then he sprang from the back seat, ran up a stone staircase toward the Cloisters' outer wall, and vanished into the tall shrubs that flanked the property. He moved swiftly among the heavy shadows, safe from the glare of the mid-afternoon sun, and in less than a minute had made his way to a black metal door at the building's western edge.

Several months earlier he had spent five hours at the Cloisters photographing the architecture, gardens, and Hudson River panorama, and on that day a member of the grounds crew had invited him to use this private back entrance. Almost completely hidden by surrounding foliage, the door was routinely kept unlocked throughout the day for use by the maintenance staff. Now Volkov cautiously pulled the door open, bolted it behind him, and stepped back into the Middle Ages.

Slanting shafts of sunlight from tall arched windows faintly illuminated the hallway as he passed silently under ancient vaulted ceilings. On his first visit to this place he had fondly contemplated what life must have been like for the monks who had roamed these stone corridors eleven centuries earlier, but on this day he was focused solely on eluding the two detectives who pursued him. He calculated that Nazareth and Gimble would expect him to run for the deep cover of the surrounding woods. But that wasn't his plan.

By doing the unexpected the Wolf would be quite safe within this shadowy inner sanctum from another age.

53.

"Why kill the driver?" Gimble asked sadly.

"So he couldn't tell us which way Resnick ran. This guy's a pro, Tara," Nazareth added, "and he's willing to kill anyone who represents a threat."

"You remember that, Pete. Don't try anything fancy with him."

"Not a chance. When in doubt, we shoot."

The detectives scanned the parking lot and the heavily wooded acreage adjacent to the Cloisters. With a two-minute head start Resnick could have run in virtually any direction, but Nazareth quickly narrowed down the possibilities.

"Okay, he wouldn't have run back toward us," he reasoned, "because he knew we'd be coming up the hill. And I doubt he jumped the parking lot wall because the slope down there is really steep. So I'd say he went down this road toward the highway, then turned off into the woods."

"Why not into the building?"

Nazareth gave that some thought. He eyed the road, then studied the hill that led up to the Cloisters' massive outer wall.

"Lots more places to hide outside," he nodded, "so that's where I'd expect him to be."

"But since he's a pro . . ."

"Yeah, in that case he'd most likely do the opposite of what we'd expect. You could be right, except I doubt they'd have an entrance back here."

"Stranger things have happened."

"I suppose. But he could also be hiding in those bushes up there waiting to pick us off."

"So we split up," Gimble said as she began jogging down the roadway, "and come at him from two directions."

Nazareth didn't like the idea, but since his wife had already set things in motion he began working his way up the slope alongside the building, carefully checking for movement in the bushes ahead. When he reached the wall he had a clear view to the right, where Gimble had just arrived at the top of the stairway Volkov had used a few minutes earlier. She waved for him to join her at the maintenance door she had discovered behind the thick vegetation. After reaching her he switched the gun to his left hand and quietly pulled on the door with his right. It didn't budge.

"The grass is worn down back here," he said, "so I'm guessing this door gets plenty of use."

"Agreed. Now all we need to know is whether Resnick is behind it."

"Only one way to find out. You stay here," he said, "and I'll run around to the main entrance and go inside."

"Put your phone on push-to-talk," she called after him, "and let me know what's happening."

"Will do." He keyed the phone as he ran, well aware that he'd make a great target if his quarry was hiding in the undergrowth. Nazareth had risked his life like this before, but something was radically different this time.

He and Gimble had their first child on the way.

54.

The Wolf prowled the shadows cast by 800-year-old marble columns as he made his way toward the main visitor area, following the voices of guests who traded grave comments on medieval art. And somewhere ahead of him came the echoed laughter of school children running wild in the courtyard garden. He was so intent on where he was going that he worried too little about where he had been.

"Stop where you are!" a uniformed security guard shouted from behind him. The guard had been making his rounds when he heard someone throw the bolt on the lower maintenance door and had hurried to find Volkov exiting the restricted area.

Up ahead an elderly couple, startled by the shouting, peered down the hallway in time to see Volkov turn and fire one round into the guard's right thigh. They clumsily grabbed each other and toppled to the floor as the Russian assassin charged past them and sprinted toward the Bonnefont Cloister at the building's southern end.

Volkov immediately understood he had blundered in shooting the security guard after mistaking him for a police officer. In his younger years, when his eyes and reflexes were flawless, he would never have pulled the trigger. Instead, he would have flattened the unarmed guard with one blow and gone quietly about his business. But by now nearly everyone in the Cloisters was alert to his presence, and he had no time to contemplate his next move. All he could do was run before being gunned down by two detectives who had somehow uncovered his true identity.

Being taken alive wasn't an option. The Wolf would either escape or die trying.

55.

Gimble heard the gunfire from her position outside the maintenance door, and she immediately hit the push-to-talk button on her cell phone. She caught Nazareth as he was barreling through the museum's main entrance with his badge in one hand and gun in the other.

"I'm on it, Tara. The shot came from your side of the building," he yelled. "Stay by the door in case he runs that way."

"Will do." She stood back from the door and prepared to take Resnick out if he came at her.

Nazareth quickly reached the elderly couple that had witnessed the shooting, and they both pointed frantically toward the Bonnefont Cloister. "That way!" the husband screamed. "He just shot a security guard."

"Get someone to help him," Nazareth shouted as he veered left and began sprinting down the cloister past a dozen or more visitors who called to him about a man with a gun. One of them nearly got knocked down when he stepped in the detective's way in order to video the action on his phone. Rather than flatten the guy Nazareth hurdled the low colonnade wall and landed inside the Bonnefont Cloister's large herb garden. When he found that he was alone he immediately crouched low and quickly looked in all directions, fearful that Resnick had trapped him out here in the open.

He called Gimble when he heard a low moan coming from a dense cover of shrubs just ahead of him. "I may have him," he whispered into the phone. "I'm in the garden at the opposite end of the building."

"Understood. I'll come around."

Nazareth held his pistol in a firm two-handed grip and slowly moved sideways toward the sound of an injured man. Had Resnick fallen? Suffered a heart attack? Or was he setting the detective up for a kill shot? Nazareth decided not to overthink the situation and sprang around the foliage ready to fire.

A groaned "Help me!" was all the middle-aged man on the ground could muster. He was bleeding heavily from inside his mouth after having caught the butt of the Wolf's gun on his right cheek. Only later would the guy feel lucky about not having been shot in the head. At the moment all he could focus on was the searing pain of his fractured jaw and broken teeth.

"Which way?" Nazareth asked urgently. The man pointed up at the wall but didn't speak. Nazareth moved to the wall and cautiously looked over. He hoped to see the killer lying on the ground with a broken leg after falling nearly two stories, but instinct told him that wasn't going to happen.

56.

The Wolf had trapped himself. After running along a cobblestoned corridor, knocking aside frightened visitors as he went, he found himself in the open-air medieval herb garden at the building's southernmost end. Now he had the museum behind him, the top of the outer wall in front, and the NYPD in pursuit.

He also had some unwelcome company in the garden. A portly man in a tan suit stood with his back to the far wall admiring the pink blossoms of late-blooming hollyhocks. He was perturbed by the Wolf's noisy entrance and couldn't resist saying so.

"Some of us come here to enjoy the quiet," he said peevishly before noticing the gun. He raised his hands as the Wolf swung the pistol but was powerless to stop the vicious blow. As the man lay stunned on the terrace the Wolf stepped onto his back as though he were a footstool and looked over the wall. He didn't like what he saw below, but he liked even less the prospect of being cornered in the garden. It was a fight-or-flight moment, and he chose to fly.

Vokov tucked the gun under his belt, placed his hands firmly atop the fortress wall, and swung both feet up and over. He hung there momentarily, his face pressed against the cold stone, wondering what he would do if he broke a leg when he landed. But he was out of options. He released his grip.

As he plummeted toward the ground he struggled to slow his descent by clawing at the rough-hewn stone blocks and succeeded only in tearing both palms open. Then as soon as his feet made contact with the hard soil he bent his knees and rolled backwards, reducing the shock of impact but at the same time sending himself somersaulting down the steep embankment. He didn't stop until he slammed into a small boulder and cracked two ribs on his right side.

This wasn't Volkov's first experience with intense pain, but on all the other occasions -- whether in Russia, Turkey, Bulgaria, or the U.S. -- he had been a young man. Now he felt he might pass out as he began limping toward the safety of Fort Tryon Park. But he refused to yield. All he had to do was make his way through those dense woods and reach the huge apartment complex alongside Broadway. Then he could vanish. He would enter one of the towers, get someone to open an apartment door, and hide out for as long as he needed to. It was a workable plan.

All it required was one open door and his Glock.

57.

Gimble had nearly reached the southern end of the Cloisters when Nazareth called her. He had caught a glimpse of Volkov entering the woods to the east and knew that his partner had the best chance of continuing the chase.

"He's heading east into the woods, Tara."

"I'm coming around the corner." She looked up and saw Nazareth pointing toward Volkov's last position.

"Angle to the right, and just keep your eye on him, Tara. *Do not* try to take him by yourself. I'll be a minute behind you."

"Got it."

Gimble headed into the trees while Nazareth raced back to the museum's entrance, then sprinted in his wife's direction. He was no longer a sub-4:00 miler, but he could still outrun most people on the planet. The problem now was knowing exactly which way to run.

"Talk to me, Tara," he called.

"I keep losing him behind the trees, but he's just ahead of me somewhere."

"Okay, stay behind him, Tara. I'll circle in from your left and outflank him."

"Understood. Be careful."

Despite the heavy foliage and fallen limbs it took Nazareth less than 30 seconds at top speed to reach the park's Broadway boundary.

"I'm near Broadway," he told her, "and I'm heading back up toward you."

"I lost him again."

"Fall back, Tara!" he screamed into the phone after spotting Volkov 50 yards ahead of him. The killer had concealed himself behind a wide oak trunk, gun ready, waiting for Gimble to come into view.

Gimble, meanwhile, had missed her husband's warning and was still on the move. "He's got to be just up ahead," she called.

"No!" When Nazareth saw Volkov step from behind the tree to line up his shot on Gimble he had no choice but to fire on the run. He aimed for the guy's legs and managed to place a single round just above the left knee. Volkov went down, spun around on his side, and immediately shifted into a prone firing position. He now had a clear shot at Nazareth's chest.

Before Volkov could squeeze the trigger Gimble launched herself toward him from behind and drove her right elbow into his back as she landed. The force of the blow fractured his left scapula and introduced him to a level of pain he had never known. She had her gun to his head before Nazareth arrived on the scene.

After a lifetime hunting, the Wolf had himself been hunted down.

58.

The detectives led Volkov in cuffs to a large open field where Gimble worked on his bleeding leg while Nazareth called for an ambulance. Fifteen minutes later an EMT had finished bandaging the leg wound, but Volkov refused to be lifted onto the stretcher. He hadn't said a word since being captured, and it was only the threat of being forcibly placed on the stretcher that got him to open his mouth.

"No one's carrying me," he snapped. "I'll walk. And you don't need to remind me of my Miranda rights because I already know them."

"Fine all the way around," Nazareth said. Volkov allowed the detectives to help him to his feet since his hands were cuffed behind him, and he maintained his steely composure despite the severe pain.

The facts were clear, but Gimble could still scarcely believe that America's most famous living photographer was a professional assassin. "None of this makes any sense to me, Mr. Resnick," she said softly. "I just don't understand."

He stared at her contemptuously. "I'm certain this is not the only thing you don't understand, Detective Gimble. But please don't look to me for answers. I'll tell you nothing. Not today, not ever. Now please take your hands off me and let me walk on my own."

Nazareth and Gimble removed their hands from Volkov's arms and allowed him to shuffle slowly toward the back of the ambulance. When he was a few feet away from them he looked back as though intending to say something after all. He moved his lips slightly, but the words never came.

A sniper round fired from the roof of a six-story building on Thayer Street, more than a quarter of a mile away, tore through his chest, killing him instantly.

59.

By 10:00 p.m. most of the uniformed officers had been pulled off the search after knocking on almost every apartment door within a half mile of the spot where the Wolf had been gunned down. Since the neighborhood was well accustomed to violent crime, no one paid a whole lot of attention to the sound of gunfire, even when it occurred in broad daylight. So the police interviews produced no results whatsoever.

The crime-scene investigators, meanwhile, had zero luck after scouring those rooftops that seemed to offer the likeliest vantage points for Volkov's murderer. Only a few of the buildings actually tried to keep residents from gaining roof access. The others had long ago stopped replacing the broken locks on a daily basis. In short, no one would have been particularly surprised to see someone walking around atop one of the apartment complexes. Beyond that, the police hadn't found a single piece of useful evidence. No shell casing, no footprints, no fibers, no nothing. Whoever had shot Volkov had known enough to clean up after himself.

At 11:15 Chief Crawford was still on the scene with his two detectives, fully prepared to keep the investigation moving, but Nazareth saw no point.

"I appreciate the support, chief," he said glumly, "but this is over. Unless a witness comes forward, we're finished."

"Can't disagree, Pete, but I'll hang in here as long as you want to."

"I know that, and I'm grateful. But this is a lost cause."

"What I'll never understand," Gimble added, "is how someone even found Resnick at the Cloisters. There's absolutely no way in hell that could have been planned. Resnick himself didn't know he'd be there until we got on his tail."

"Maybe, maybe not," the chief told her. "All you know for sure is that he was running. It's possible he meant to go to the Cloisters all along. If he was a Russian spy, a place like the Cloisters would have been a good place to meet an accomplice."

Nazareth briefly considered the idea, then shrugged. "That doesn't fit with the luggage in the trunk. I think he was headed out of town."

"But who else could have known he was at the Cloisters?" the chief asked.

"When I called for the ambulance I suppose someone could have picked up on it," Nazareth answered, "but I didn't mention Resnick's name. And, besides, in that amount of time no one would have been able to get Uptown, carry a gun to a rooftop, and shoot him. No way."

"Well, someone sure knew he was going to be here, Pete," the chief said as he walked toward his vehicle, "or this never could have happened. I say it was one of his Russian buddies who wanted him out of the way."

Gimble agreed with the chief. "Makes sense, Pete. Whatever Resnick knew -- and it must have been a lot -- was something the Russians didn't want us getting hold of."

But Nazareth heard nothing his wife had just said. He was thousands of miles away, deep in thought, trying to catch up with an elusive idea that kept skittering around inside his head. When he finally came back down to earth, he didn't look happy.

"What?" she asked him.

"No, nothing," he lied. "Just thinking."

She knew not to press the issue. From the tightness of his jaw she could tell that something had driven him to that dark, angry place he visited whenever the battle got especially ugly.

Nazareth had just declared war.

60.

On the drive home Nazareth refused to discuss business with Gimble. He was willing to talk about the upcoming weekend, the Mets, the weather, or Christmas. But each time his wife started in on the shooting he shook his head and waved her off. Eventually they both stopped talking completely.

Before heading to their apartment Nazareth swung by the 13th precinct on East 21st and asked Gimble to wait for him in the car.

"Ten minutes max, okay?"

"No problem," she said with a forced smile. "I'll be right here."

When he returned eight minutes later he carried a small vinyl case that he placed gently in the back seat. Before Gimble could say anything he once again shook his head and held his hand up. Whatever he had gotten at the precinct was going to remain a mystery.

Twelve minutes later they parked the cruiser in the apartment building's garage and began walking to the elevator. Nazareth took Gimble gently by the elbow, looked at her, and mouthed the words, "Turn your phone off now." By the time they stepped on the elevator they had both shut their phones down. Only then did he break silence.

"We've got a problem I need to check out," he told her. "When we get into the apartment start talking to me about having dinner with your parents on Sunday, okay?"

"So mysterious, Pete."

"Just a little bit longer, Tara. I'm either crazy, or I'm onto something."

They walked into the apartment slightly past midnight, and after kicking off her shoes and putting her gun on the kitchen island Gimble called over to Nazareth, who had already removed an electronic device of some sort from the carry case.

"Hey, Pete, how about visiting my parents on Sunday? We haven't been there for a while, and we don't have that many fall weekends left for a cookout."

"I was sort of hoping to chill, babe. Maybe watch some football and drink a couple of beers." He worked as he talked, moving around the entire apartment with the wireless electronic bug detector. Several times he stopped, marked a lamp or smoke alarm with a small piece of masking tape, then moved on.

"You can chill at my parents' house, can't you?"

"Yeah, but I don't have to drive to Brooklyn to do it."

"Pete," she whined playfully, "please. My mother has been asking when you and I will coming over for the last barbecue of the season."

"If we have to, fine, Tara. But I'd really rather hang out here."

"Thanks, Pete. I appreciate it."

"So that means it's already a done deal?" he laughed.

"Yep, done deal."

He had finished scanning the room, leaving five pieces of masking tape along the way: one in the kitchen, two in the living room, one in the master bedroom, and one in the spare bedroom where they maintained their own world-class gym. Gimble still wasn't sure what was going on until he mouthed, "The place is bugged. Say nothing."

He opened one of the kitchen cabinets, removed a large metal pitcher, and filled it with water. Then he visited each piece of masking tape and gently removed the listening devices that had been hidden throughout their apartment. Each device had been skillfully placed inside an object that virtually guaranteed all the couple's conversations would be captured. When he had removed the five devices, he returned to the kitchen and dropped them into the water pitcher. Then he walked toward the bedroom and motioned for Gimble to follow.

"What the hell's going on?" she asked as he closed the bedroom door behind them.

"Someone's been listening to everything we say here," he told her. "Ditto the cell phones, I'm sure. Ditto the police radio in the car."

"You can't be serious," she said angrily. "Who the hell would do that?"

"The same person who knew when you and I first talked about Resnick as a suspect," he told her. "The same person who knew when we began chasing Resnick outside his apartment building today. And the same person who knew when we got to the Cloisters."

"Who?" When she thought about someone listening in on their most intimate conversations she was in a mood to kill. "I'll go do the arrest myself right now."

"This is someone you can't arrest, Tara. And we'd never be able to prove it anyway."

"I give up."

"Think about it. Who always seems to know everything?"

When it finally hit her she felt mildly nauseous. "Dalton Stark?"

He nodded.

The sense of betrayal was overwhelming. She could handle murderers and rapists better than she could a friend who had stolen their trust.

"Pete, why would he do that?"

"Because he can, I suppose. And because for some reason he wanted Resnick out of the way."

"Enough to kill him? Come on, Pete. We're talking about a high-level government official murdering a private citizen."

"We can't prove that."

"Not right at this minute, but we'll prove it if we work on it."

"Highly doubtful. Stark could probably stop the investigation with a single phone call."

"So we do nothing?"

"No, we talk to him. Let him explain what the hell he's up to."

"And if he denies it, which is what I expect him to do?"

"Let's not go there until we've talked to him. I don't think he'll be surprised by the call."

"Seriously?"

"You and I are very good at what we do, Tara, and he knows it. My guess is he's expecting his phone to ring."

"Then let's ring it," she said angrily. "What the hell law gives him the right to bug our bedroom?"

"I assume Stark is somewhat above the law," Nazareth answered. "We'll have to settle this with him directly because I can't imagine any judge in the country knocking heads with the guy running the country's spy network."

"Fine. Let's settle it with him."

Nazareth speed-dialed Stark's number, put the call on speaker, and got an answer after one ring.

"You're probably not happy, Pete," Stark said coolly.

"I'm even less happy," Gimble snapped.

"Understood. I've been expecting your call since the apartment went silent a few minutes ago."

"You mean after we found all the goddamned bugs you stuck in here?" Gimble challenged.

"I could simply deny it, Tara, but I'll apologize instead. It was a national security matter, so I had no choice. And I promise you no one listened in on you and Pete unless you were talking about the assassinations."

"How the hell could you possibly do that without hearing everything else we said?" she demanded.

"With a device you'll never be able to buy at your local hardware store," he said. "Once we program the machine to recognize a number of keywords, it transcribes all related conversations. The system recognizes when the topic has shifted, then goes back and deletes any dialogue that's not relevant to our investigation."

"So if we talked about a Russian assassin," Nazareth said, "you got a printout of the conversation."

"Yes. But the device also learns as it goes and keeps building the list of keywords. In your case the words *Russian* and *assassin* soon led to *Alex Resnick,* and that triggered an immediate terror alert."

"Why would Resnick's name do that?" Gimble asked.

"Resnick was one of ours, Tara."

"What's that supposed to mean?"

"It means he was one of my most reliable operatives over the past seven years. He was a world traveler, had access to all the right people and places, and was extremely useful in moving information for me."

"He was a spy?"

"Depends on your definition, I guess. At any given time we have a thousand or more people just like Alex Resnick helping us gather intelligence," he explained. "Athletes, journalists, entertainers, professors, artists, business leaders, you name it. When we come across people who seem willing to help, we cultivate the relationship and gradually work them into the system. Because Resnick was very well placed and extremely capable, he played a role in a number of extremely sensitive situations."

"But he also played you," Nazareth offered, "by being a double agent."

"He definitely played us, yes. Three months ago we had a White House breach that cost the lives of three Secret Service agents and almost cost us the president. Someone had provided a local terrorist cell with extremely detailed information about the president's schedule as well as sensitive data about the building. We knew it had to be someone from inside, but we couldn't ID him."

"How could Resnick have been involved?" Gimble asked.

"He had done a photo essay on the first family a few weeks earlier. It's now obvious he succeeded in photographing things he shouldn't have been anywhere near."

Nazareth finally addressed the elephant in the room. "Why didn't you just arrest him, Dalton? When did we begin killing suspects instead of putting them on trial?"

"1947," Stark answered, "the year the CIA was created. Listen, guys, don't be naive. Resnick was not someone we could have put on trial. No way we could let that happen."

"Because he knew too much?" Gimble demanded. "Or because it would have made you look stupid?"

"Because he was a national security risk," Stark said flatly. "Now he's not. End of story."

"Not if Pete and I don't allow the story to end here," she added.

"Well, to begin with, this conversation never took place."

"Unless we just recorded it."

"Not possible, Tara. We're on a secure line that jams audio recording. So, as I've said, this conversation never took place. In addition, you and Pete can easily imagine the sort of damage you would do by going public with this."

"You mean the damage we'd do to your precious reputation," Gimble said sarcastically.

"No, I mean the damage you'd do to an important institution whose work keeps America safe from those who want to destroy us. I also suspect that making waves over this wouldn't help your careers a whole lot."

"Is that a threat?" Nazareth demanded.

"It's a statement of fact, Pete. If you accuse, I'll deny," he said simply. "And you'll lose. Here in Washington you've got no credibility whatsoever. I'm sorry to be blunt, but that's how it is. This is why you'd both be much better off accepting the reality of how things work in a dangerous world. I don't have the luxury of doing everything by the book. Neither do you, as a matter of fact.

You both have played fast and loose with the rules when it was necessary to get the job done."

"We've never killed someone who had a right to a fair trial," Gimble insisted.

"Well, neither have I," he taunted. "It turns out Alex Resnick, the famous photographer, was the victim of a random shooting, Tara. You've got a highly skilled sniper on the loose in Manhattan, and so far the NYPD doesn't know jack about his identity."

"No one's going to buy that, Dalton," Nazareth said, "and you know it."

"Keep an open mind, Pete. Gotta run right now, but I'll call back when I can." Then he was gone, leaving Nazareth and Gimble to consider their next move.

61.

The detectives were finishing breakfast when the story broke first on ABC TV's local news that morning and then got picked up by every other media outlet in the New York City area. All of the versions were substantially the same: the police commissioner had disclosed that two recent Manhattan slayings, once considered the work of a Russian assassin, were now being attributed to a crazed sniper. Having found no link between the two dead men, Sergey Gerasimov and Alex Resnick, the NYPD had concluded the gunman was choosing his victims at random. According to the commissioner, the investigation was in its early stages.

Nazareth and Gimble sat motionless on the couch as the story was broadcast into their living room. Only a few minutes earlier they had each gotten a text message from Stark: *ABC local TV, 6:00.* Now they confronted the sickening reality that the truth had been buried. For some reason the police commissioner had slammed the door shut on the facts, and the two young detectives were in no position to contradict him. Besides, who was going to believe that America's greatest living photographer had also been a Russian mole, a CIA spy, and an assassin? Right, no one. Stark had masterfully covered his tracks.

Gimble spoke first. "This scares me to death, Pete. A guy in Washington pulls the strings as though we're all mindless puppets, and there's nothing we can do about it. Stark had Resnick murdered, then got the police commissioner to look the other way. How can that possibly happen in America?"

"I'm surprised," Nazareth replied, shaking his head, "but I can't say I'm shocked. I'm sure Stark can bury almost anything as long as it's labeled *national security threat,* and he has the clout to label anything he wants."

"So what do we do?"

"We can fight a losing battle that probably gets us both fired, or we can walk away sadder and wiser." His wife frowned. "I don't like that answer either, Tara, believe me. But at the moment I think it's the right one."

She sat quietly for almost a full minute, then said, "I hate the answer, Pete, but I agree it seems like the right one. If Stark can get to the police commissioner, he can also probably get to the mayor and anyone else he wants."

Gimble's cell phone rang. She recognized the number and remembered that Stark had said he'd be calling back. "Stark," she said as she handed the phone to Nazareth.

He simply tossed it on the couch. "I'm going to work," he said with a weak smile.

Gimble nodded. "I guess I'll join you."

62.

Four nights later Dalton Stark sat alone in the private office of his luxury apartment across from the White House. The $15,000 ultra-secure satellite phone that he usually kept locked in a wall safe was on the desk in front of him. At precisely 1:00 a.m., or 8:00 a.m. in Moscow, he answered the call on the first ring.

"Good morning, Mr. President," he said in flawless Russian.

"Are you certain the assassin was this photographer Resnick?" came the response, also in crisp Russian.

"Absolutely. He had been operating here for many years, but he operates no more."

"What I find disturbing," said Russian President Ruslan Kotov, "is that you had used him as an American spy without ever seeing who or what he truly was."

Stark's stomach did a quick flip when he detected the displeasure in Kotov's voice. Yes, it had taken him much longer than expected to hunt down the renegade assassin, but in the end this mission had been successfully completed, had it not?

"He was very good at what he did, Mr. President."

"Better than you, perhaps."

"I am alive," Stark countered as sweat beaded on his forehead, "while he is dead."

Kotov's reply was overly long in coming. "Yes, I suppose that's true."

"Yes, sir, it is." Stark had expected this weekly phone call to result in praise for a job well done. Now his thoughts turned to South American cities where he might hide if Kotov turned on him. But how could that possibly happen? Surely Kotov realized he could never replace someone as well placed as America's top spy. Never again would Russia have an agent who wielded this much power. Impossible. He was untouchable.

"Good. Then we'll talk next week, same time."

"I'll be here, Mr. President."

Kotov clicked off without another word and contemplated the large, brooding winter landscape by Alexei Savrasov that hung on the wall to the right of his desk. Dalton Stark, he mused, had accomplished much since his Russian handler had proudly sent him to America as a young agent all those years ago. In fact, he may have accomplished too much, grown too fond of the taste of power. This sort of thing sometimes happened with high-level agents. Eventually they became threats to their masters and had to be dealt with.

This, Kotov concluded, would require some thought.

63.

Thirteen minutes after Kotov had ended the phone call a team of six FBI agents operating under a federal no-knock warrant used a steel battering ram to demolish the door to Dalton Stark's Washington apartment. Once Stark was on the floor, hands and feet cuffed, they scoured every square inch of the place. It took less than 10 minutes to find the wall safe, open it, and bag the satellite phone with its Moscow hotline.

Throughout the process Stark bellowed, "Do you have any idea who I am?" Finally agent Curtis Lafarge studied his prisoner's crimson face and calmly said, "We do, indeed, Mr. Stark." He then walked over to the floor lamp alongside the living room couch, unscrewed the finial atop the lampshade, and held it out for Stark to see. The finial held a listening device no bigger than a match head.

"One of five, Mr. Stark," Lafarge grinned. "Pete Nazareth sends his regards."

64.

"Short-sleeved or long-sleeved?" Nazareth called from the bedroom. Gimble was in the kitchen wrapping a couple of tuna salad sandwiches for the trip to Cape Cod. If they ate while driving they could reach their rental in Chatham by mid-afternoon, relax on the sand for a bit, and get to the Impudent Oyster for shrimp and scallops by 7:00.

"Bring both. It'll be in the upper seventies during the day and low fifties at night."

"Ah, you must be a detective."

"Just check your iPhone, Pete. The weather's always there."

"The phone is off, Tara. Maybe I'll look at it again in a few days."

They both knew he was incapable of going a few hours, much less a few days, without checking his phone. Escaping to Cape Cod for a week didn't mean they weren't on the job. They were NYPD detectives, after all, and they believed passionately in the rightness of what they did. So even though they had just scored the biggest win of their careers, they accepted the fact that their next case was never more than a phone call away.

The unmasking of Dalton Stark as a top-level Russian spy had not only sent shockwaves through the halls of government but had changed their lives as well. They had been invited to the White House, where the president awarded each of them the National Security Medal and urged them to accept senior intelligence positions in Washington. Although they had agreed to weigh the career shift, they had made it clear they were inclined to stick with their current jobs. They had also been promoted to detective first grade and were still hooked on the wild highs and lows of their work in Manhattan. Beyond that, they had their first baby on the way and wondered whether this was the right time to leave New York City and their families. Moving five hours away seemed like a gamble.

They had already taken the biggest gamble of their lives when they decided to go after Dalton Stark. After listening to him make light of Resnick's murder they had finally decided they wouldn't be able to live with themselves knowing that America's top spy was playing judge, jury, and executioner. They refused to accept that he was above the law, so they rolled the dice and took their story to the FBI's hard-edged deputy director, Gordon Bryson. Nazareth had spent some time with Bryson several years earlier at a counterintelligence training program in D.C. and believed the guy would at least hear them out.

Bryson did more than listen. At Nazareth's urging he got a warrant to conduct electronic surveillance of Stark's apartment, hoping to obtain evidence related to Alex Resnick's murder. For three days the detectives chewed their nails and waited for word that the FBI had overheard something useful. The longer they waited, the more they worried that Stark had infiltrated the FBI and sabotaged the investigation. Even worse, they feared Stark might end up pinning Resnick's murder on them somehow. When the call finally came and they learned that Stark was a Russian agent as well as the person who had ordered Resnick's murder, they felt the weight of the world lifting from their shoulders.

Another case closed. They had earned some time off.

The long drive to Chatham was more pleasant than they had expected. Traffic was light since kids were back in school and most families had already spent their vacation days. For folks like Nazareth and Gimble it was an ideal time to get away and relax before winter rolled back around.

After unpacking the car and slipping into their bathing suits they stepped onto the warm sand and breathed deeply of the salt air. Nazareth carried a Bud Light while Gimble sipped ice water with a twist of lime. They strolled along the water's edge for nearly a mile before their gentle conversation switched from seagulls and waves to unfinished business. It was Gimble who broke the ice.

"I'm shocked to hear myself saying this, Pete, but the president of the United States is waiting for our phone call." They both laughed over this absurd truth. The president was, in fact, expecting their call. He had asked them to come work in D.C., and they had promised him an answer.

"Yeah, it's kind of hard to believe he actually told us to call him directly. How often in your lifetime does that happen?"

"Basically never," she smiled. "But the reason he told us to call him directly is pretty obvious."

"Sure, he figures we won't be able to say no to him. I doubt he hears the word *no* very often."

"Okay, then," she snickered. "I'll just keep walking while you call him."

"Oh, no. Wait a second, Tara. This is one call I definitely don't make alone. We're partners, babe, so we both get on the phone."

"I'm afraid I'll cave, Pete. I'm not sure I can really turn down the president when he asks us to do something for the country."

"We're already doing something for the country," he pointed out. "What we do in New York City benefits America. Hey, we don't need to be in Washington to have an impact."

"But you can't deny that taking down Stark had a much more immediate impact on the country than solving the next Manhattan homicide."

He shrugged, not quite sure he agreed with her. "It's a lot to consider, Tara. Why don't we just hang out on the beach for a few days before calling him?"

She nodded and took his hand as they walked back to the cozy weathered cottage with the pale blue shutters. The sun was getting lower in the sky, and the chilly wind off the Atlantic made them glad to be indoors. Maybe they'd use that stone fireplace after all.

Later that night, long after their fine dinners and some window shopping along Main Street, they settled next to each other in bed and turned on the eleven o'clock news. The lead story left them speechless.

"Former U.S. spy chief Dalton Stark, the man suspected of being a Russian agent for more than 30 years, has escaped from the Central Detention Facility in Washington where he was awaiting trial on espionage charges. A source close to the investigation says that a five-state manhunt involving the FBI and local police is now underway Here with more on that story is correspondent..."

They had heard enough. Gimble clicked the remote and studied the quiet fury in her husband's face. She had seen his eyes like this before, so no words were necessary.

Tomorrow, she knew, they would be calling the president.

CPSIA information can be obtained
at www.ICGtesting.com
Printed in the USA
BVOW03s2337171116

468259BV00001B/3/P